UNEXPECTED EDEN

RHENNA MORGAN

Paradise, love and power...and a prophecy with a price.

Most people believe Eden no longer exists. Lexi Merrill's about to learn they're wrong. A hard-working bartender with a self-sufficient backbone and a wary nature, she knows pickup lines like a second language.
So, when Eryx Shantos barges into her world with too-smooth words and a body to back it up, she locks up her libido and vows to keep her distance.

Eryx has other ideas. As king of the Myren race, Eryx is duty-bound to enforce the laws preventing exposure of their existence to humans. Yet The Fates have led him through his dreams to Lexi, a temptation he doesn't want to resist. The question—is she Myren, or human, which makes her forbidden fruit?

When Eryx's nemesis tags Lexi as his next target, Eryx insists on taking her home where he can keep her safe. Lexi had no idea "home" would mean the one-and-only land of creation…or that she'd trigger a prophecy that could doom her newfound race.

Previously released by Kensington's Lyrical Press in December, 2014.

Electronic ISBN: 978-1-945361-04-3

Print ISBN: 978-1-945361-06-7

For Abegayle and Addison.

*I'll never fit the soccer mom mold, but I'll help you chase your
dreams the same way you've helped me chase mine*

*S*low breaths in, slow breaths out. All Lexi had to do was focus on the thump of Rihanna's latest hit, keep the drinks flowing, and stick to her half of the bar. The mother lode of testosterone on Jerry's side couldn't sit there all night. Could he?

"Don't suppose you've noticed, but there's a scrumptious not-from-around-here type giving you the eyeball." Mindy grinned and handed over the latest round of drink orders.

White t-shirt, killer muscles, and dark chocolate hair halfway down his back? Yeah, she'd noticed. Repeatedly. And every time she went for a visual refill, his silver gaze shocked nerve endings she'd long thought dead.

"Drop it, Mindy. Guys like that are an occupational hazard and you know it."

"Honey, that man is way past hazard. More like Chernobyl." She leaned into the trendy concrete countertop. The modern pendant lights spotlighted her platinum hair and ample cleavage. One thing about Mindy—she knew how to work her assets. "I'll bet the fallout's worth it."

"It's packed tonight. You gonna get those drinks out and stash a few tips, or waste 'em on eye candy?"

Mindy's dreamy smile melted and she pulled the loaded cocktail tray close. "All work and no play, huh?" She shook her head and turned for the crowd. "Have fun with that."

Well, hell. Another social interaction down the toilet. At twenty-five- years-old, she ought to be able to handle a little female bonding in the form of man-ogling. Especially when four of those years had been spent tending bar. But damn it, some things weren't meant for discussion. Her overactive man-jitters being one of them.

Crouching to snag a fresh bottle of vodka beneath the counter, she peeked behind her.

Lips guaranteed to make a girl forget her name curled into a sly smile.

Busted.

She spun away too fast and scraped her forehead against the rough edge of the bar. "Son of a fucking, no good piece of shit." Head down, she counted to three and fought the need to check for witnesses, thankful the music was loud enough to cover her curse. The graceless gawker routine wasn't normally her deal, but for the last thirty minutes she'd come up woefully short in the finesse department—and it was all the dark-haired man's fault.

New bottle ready for action, she faced two middle-aged men dressed like frat boys and settled into her pour-and-bill groove. The routine was a comfort, a stabilizing rhythm to counterbalance the ever-present gaze heavy on her back.

"Hey, Lex." Jerry smacked her shoulder and motioned behind him, never breaking stride as he headed for the register. "Tall, dark and handsome wants to see you."

She wouldn't look. Not again. The giggling trio of barely legal blondes fighting their way into ordering range wasn't nearly as nice on the eyes, but at least they kept her anchored. "Since when did you take up matchmaking?"

"Since the guy offered me a Benjamin to make sure it was you who took care of him."

What?

She spun.

The stranger met her surprised stare head on, his smirk a potent mix of humble and confident. "Sold me down the river, did you?"

"Damn right." Jerry winked, shoved a stack of wrinkled bills into the register, and swaggered toward the waiting blondes without so much as a wish for good luck.

Lexi huffed and took an order from the none-too-shabby twenty-something guy right in front of her. Mystery man could cool his jets for a minute or two. Besides, if his banter matched his looks, she'd need every second she could get to batten down the hatches.

She filled orders with slow deliberation and an extra bit of bravado, grabbing snippets of recon where she could.

A vicious looking man sat next to her dark-haired hunk. Lazy raven waves fell to a hard jawline, a tightly trimmed goatee making his harsh face a downright menace. Entirely the wrong selection for wingman material.

Out of customers and bar space, she faced both men and wiped down the counter. "What can I get you?" The catchall phrase came out shakier than she wanted. She tried to cover it with an intensive, yet completely unnecessary study of the bottles stocked below the counter.

"You disliked my tactic." God help her, the man had a voice to match his face. An easy glide that left a slow burn in its wake. Kind of like fifty- year-old Scotch. "I admit it's not my style, but I was desperate."

Not exactly the approach she'd expected from a hottie,

but it did help ease her tension. "There's not a thing desperate about you and we both know it."

He answered with a megawatt smile that damn near knocked her off her feet. Utterly relaxed, he rested muscled forearms on the bar and raised an eyebrow. "Have dinner with me."

She shouldn't be able to hear him in such a crush, let alone register a physical impact, but she processed both loud and clear. "I don't even know you."

He offered his hand. Long, strong fingers stretched out, showing calluses along his palm. "Eryx Shantos."

Wingman stared straight ahead, his aqua eyes cold enough to freeze a soul.

"Lexi Merrill." As their palms met, a rush fired up her arm and down her spine, and she shook as though she'd cozied up to a blow dryer in a bathtub. She ripped her hand away and rubbed the tingling center up and down her jean-clad hip.

Eryx didn't so much as blink, his sword-colored gaze glinting with dare and determination.

Maybe fatigue was taking a toll on her imagination. Or the flu. Or a desperate need to get laid. Gripping the bar for support, she took an order from a cute little brunette trying to avoid a middle-aged, bald guy's come-on.

Except for a slow pull off his beer, Wingman stayed stock-still. His angry expression screamed, *Stay the fuck back.*

"Now you know me," Eryx said. "Have dinner with me."

"I have to work."

"Then lunch."

"I work then, too." A lame excuse, but true. Two jobs and part-time college didn't leave a lot of room for being social. Not that socializing ever managed to work in her favor.

"Breakfast, then."

A half-hearted laugh slipped out before she could stop it. "You're persistent, I'll give you that."

"You have nooo idea." Wingman tipped his longneck for another drink, fingers loose around the dark glass despite his tight voice.

Eryx shot him a nasty glare.

"Your friend doesn't talk much." Lexi grabbed a few empties and dunked them in a tub of soapy water.

"His name's Ludan. And he may not be able to talk at all by the time the night's over. Depends on if he manages to keep his tongue intact."

"Yo! Need a few Bud Lights." Two college-age men in need of manners shoved their way to Ludan's free side.

Ludan straightened and pushed the men back a handful of steps with nothing more than a glare.

No way was she dealing with the fallout from a brawl, even if the young punks could use the lesson. "Stand down and kill the scary badass routine."

Ludan faced her, his eyes a shade closer to white than blue. It took a tense breath or two, but the muscles beneath his black t-shirt relaxed and he smirked. He eased down on his barstool and snagged his beer. "Your woman's got bite, Eryx."

She snatched a pair of Buds from the cooler and popped the tops off. "I'm not his woman."

"Not yet." Eryx's calm retort landed between them—part taunt, part promise. The sheer resoluteness in his expression sent a rush she didn't dare analyze clear to her toes.

Better to get down to business and add some distance before she did something she'd regret. "Tell me what you want to drink. I gotta get back to work."

"I've already told you want I want."

Lexi planted a hand on her hip and thanked God he

couldn't see her pounding heart. "A tall order that's not on the menu."

Eryx nodded, a slow, sultry move that intimated a whole lot more than simple agreement. "Some things are worth waiting for."

A blast of déjà vu hit and left her stunned. A hot gush of frustration shoved in behind it and spun her back toward her half of the bar. With a thump on Jerry's arm, she motioned toward Eryx. "He's all yours. I want the sane side back."

She worked her portion of the crowd with single-minded enthusiasm. *Worth waiting for.* It was just a line. Guys like Eryx were landmines waiting for a trigger.

In front of her, a couple nuzzled nose to nose, an out-of-place intimacy amid the harsh lights from the dance floor. Her heart stuttered. Was she bypassing something good? Maybe she should circle back. See if he needed another—

He was gone, his wingman with him. A gaggle of women, one with a naughty tiara and bachelorette sash wrapped around her, crowded between the leather and chrome barstools.

The tiny thread of hope she'd refused to acknowledge snapped in half. She snatched a bag of ice from the back cooler and shook it over the longnecks along the front bin of the bar. She knew better than to wish for things like love. Hell, she hadn't even done a double take on a guy in more years than she could count. She could get a massage from a team of Chippendales and she probably wouldn't get excited. What made her think she'd ever find anyone worth laying her heart on the line?

She turned for the rear register and shoved her disappointment deep. Better to study that topic later—say in about five years. She'd finish out the night, prep for tomorrow like she always did, and be glad she'd avoided the drama.

Pinpricks raced down her spine and warmth surrounded her. Not the slick and humid dance floor variety, but comforting, infused with leather and sandalwood. Out of place. Delicious.

Ordinary patrons reflected in the wide mirror before her, faces bright with the glaze of alcohol. Nothing stood out. No danger.

But she could have sworn warm, rough fingertips grazed her cheek.

PERCHED on the high retaining wall at the end of the parking lot, Eryx glared at the streetlight overhead. One flick of his wrist and he could fry the whole damned contraption with an electric pulse. Better on his patience for sure, but not so great for his plans. Smart women like Lexi weren't usually keen on dark parking lots at two-thirty in the morning.

Tapping his boot heels against the wall, Ludan cracked his knuckles and scanned their surroundings for the fiftieth time. As Eryx's somo, Ludan looked out for his wellbeing, but the nasty bastard sometimes took the job too deep into mother hen territory. "We need to go back to Eden. Recharge for a few days and then come make a play for your woman. If the Rebellion catches us here with our energy this low—"

"The rumors are just that. Rumors." Eryx shifted on the cold concrete, anything to get the blood flow back into his too-stationary ass. "The Rebellion hasn't launched an attack worth merit in over seventy years. I bet I couldn't find five people who've seen Maxis in more than that. I'm not cranking my men into a tizzy over hypotheticals."

"And the ellan?" Ludan's cool gaze slid to Eryx. "You gonna keep ignoring them too? The old coots are chomping at the bit to know what's got you so tied up in the human realm."

"Only half of them are old coots. The rest are as young and eager to modernize our race as we are." If you could call one hundred and fifty-two years old *young*. From the human perspective, it probably seemed closer to eternity.

Ludan looked away and gripped the ledge. Better than throwing a punch—which would probably be his preference.

Hard to blame the guy. Ten years helping Eryx look for the woman who visited his dreams every night would send most people running. Ludan? Loyal to the core and still right here with him. But that didn't mean he'd give up on his argument. Ten more seconds tops before he chimed in again.

Ten.

Nine.

Eight.

Se—

"You're the malran. You call the shots." Ludan crossed his arms. "But even without the Rebellion threat, you're risking your throne and a death sentence."

And there it was. The lecture he'd had coming since he finally tracked a clue from his dreams to Lexi's workplace. Humans were a no-no. Do business with them? Walk freely in their realm? Tangle in a bout of good, hot, sweaty sex? All fair game. Fill them in on the Myren race or interfere in human destiny? That shit earned you the axe, a mandate passed down by The Great One himself when he'd created Eryx's people.

"We've been here too long," Ludan said. "Both our powers are damned near gone. Any attack outside of one-to-one and we're screwed."

The service door *kachunked* open.

Eryx shoved off the ledge.

"Sorry, man." The bartender he'd bribed for Lexi's attention earlier ambled toward the mid-size pickup on Eryx's left with a sympathetic shake of his head. "You've got it bad."

Eryx leaned against the brick wall, crossed his arms, and notched one boot over his ankle. "You telling me she's not worth the trouble?"

The man's keys jangled against the quiet night and a perky chirp mixed with a flash of headlights. He shrugged and tugged open the driver's door. "Hard to say. Never met a man who made it through the gauntlet." He tossed his black duffel bag across to the passenger's side, shot a man-to-man nod at Ludan then smirked at Eryx. "Good luck."

"Fan-fucking-tastic. Your dream woman's the hard-to-get type." As the truck pulled away, Ludan leapt to the asphalt and planted his hands on his hips. "We're never getting home."

Crickets and the drone of cars on the interstate filled the silence. "Would you go back if you were me?"

It was an underhanded question. Ludan knew the toll Lexi's dream visits took on his ability to reason. How he woke strung out with need, zeroed in on the single purpose of finding his mate. "If you were this close, would you risk losing her?"

Ludan didn't exactly hang his head in defeat, but he sure studied the asphalt hard. "No." He turned and stuffed his hands in his pockets. "Better not to fuck with The Fates."

The door rattled and eased open.

His skin buzzing, Eryx pushed to full height.

Ludan sidled further away and switched to telepathy. *"You sure you wanna do this? You can't be sure she's Myren."*

"I'll figure it out. The pictures in her mind were definitely of Eden."

Under the unforgiving street lamps, Lexi's tan skin glowed. Soft-black hair brushed her shoulders and her hips swayed, slow with an unpretentious sexuality. A distracted frown tugged her lips, her face downcast. She looked up and froze, bits of gravel crunching beneath her fancy shoes. "You gotta be kidding me."

"I told you I was willing to wait." He tried for a light-hearted tone, but it was no easy task. A decade of tracking one irresistible woman did crazy things to a man's insides.

She zigzagged a look between Eryx near her red Jeep Wrangler and Ludan a stone's throw away then glanced at the closed door behind her. She adjusted the purse strap at her shoulder and narrowed her blue-gray eyes. "You're one step past stalker."

He held up his hands. "I swear it's not like that. I really do want to take you to breakfast." So he'd gone a little further with his scan of her memories when they'd shaken hands than he should have. She always caught an after-work breakfast with a man who looked to be in his mid to late fifties, and she drove the Wrangler parked behind him.

"It's nearly three AM."

"And we're all hungry. Perfect timing." He lowered his hands and hoped Ludan wasn't sporting his perma-scowl. Non-threatening wasn't his strong suit.

"Smart girls don't go to breakfast with strangers." She nodded toward her Jeep. "Let alone get near a vehicle with unknown men nearby."

"Your bartender pal clued me in." Hopefully, she'd buy the lie, not that it felt good on his tongue. "And you could always call a friend to join us. Public place, your own car." He paused to let the idea sink in. "What's there to lose?"

A breeze ruffled her loose hair. Her face slackened and a flutter of energy drifted across the parking lot, barely perceptible.

Ludan perked up.

It was Lexi. It had to be. Humans couldn't generate such a ripple—at least not any he'd ever met.

She tugged her purse to her chest and rooted around inside. "Waffle House. A few miles down the road." She fisted a wad of keys and dropped the purse back to her hip. "I meet a friend there after work. A cop, just to be clear. So don't get any ideas."

Satisfaction fired hot in his veins, the fact some strange older man would be along for the ride a paltry detail. He closed the distance, slow and steady, and traced the angle of her cheekbone.

Her eyes widened.

The Fates were never wrong. They might be coy with their reasons and damned vague in their instructions, but there was one thing he was sure of. They'd led him to his mate.

CHAPTER 2

Maxis Steysis cinched his victim's wrists with a rope. With practiced efficiency, he secured the unconscious man's legs in the optimum position, immobile and dangling off the edge of the rudimentary cot. "Slave!"

Damned zeolite. The mineral coated every inch of the tiny basement cell, its power blocking his Myren gifts and clawing at his very soul. He'd deal with it though, as he had countless times before. Power always came with a price, and Paul Renner had a power worth suffering for.

A rhythmic clang of metal resonated in the hallway. Gaze rooted to the floor, Brenna shuffled in with her basins.

He pointed to the corner near Paul's feet. "In your place."

In the candlelight, her ivory gown looked more like linen than the rough fabric it really was, and she quivered so violently even the dark braids at either side of her head shook.

Nabbing her at the malleable age of eight had been a stroke of genius. His first slaves had been too old, keeling over about the time they got good at their new lot in life. But this one—this one he'd sculpted to fit his needs and still had plenty of years left to burn. It was a tradeoff. Humans might be easy to control, but turnover was a bitch.

Maxis stuffed a hand towel into his prisoner's slack jaw, and backhanded him across the cheek.

Still chloroform-groggy, the man blinked and shook his head. He rolled to face Maxis and jerked against the restraints, his shout muffled by the cloth in his mouth.

Maxis drew his dagger and the cold *zring* of metal on metal sliced through the room. He motioned with the blade toward the large metal basins. "Put them in place."

Brenna jerked forward nearly fumbling the bowls to the stone floor.

Maxis tapped the flat of his weapon against his thigh. One would think after the number of times he'd done this, she'd be less skittish. Then again, she was human. They always cowered in the end, covering their asses even if it meant leaving someone else to suffer. Even a grief- stricken nine-year-old boy.

The memory brushed cold and hollow across his soul. The human boy he'd thought was his friend, trembling behind a wall of teenagers just as Brenna trembled now, while a bunch of human teens beat him until he'd had no fight left. He could have tolerated the fists, but the damning truths they'd mocked him with rattled his heart even now.

No human would ever hold such power over him again.

Eyes averted and fists clenched at her sides, Brenna shuffled back into her corner.

Paul's struggles slowed, but his gaze bounced from wall to wall, his shallow breaths loud in the tiny space.

"It's zeolite," Maxis told him. "Your family won't reach you here. Or anyone else."

No doubt he'd still try, but his mind would only slam against the non- responsive crystal. Mental connections were natural for Myren family and mates, a telepathic link as instinctive as an animal's need for air.

"I met your brother several weeks ago." Maxis shifted and the candlelight spilled across the man's drawn face. "A dull man, really. Can't handle his liquor. Gets quite chatty when he's been drinking."

Paul stilled but for the rapid rise and fall of his chest.

"He told me about the unfortunate incident from your childhood. The one where you used your link to mentally shred your sister's mind to bits."

Maxis hunched closer to the man and the sweet scent of terror tickled his nose. "Frankly, I think it's a waste you never used the gift again." He leaned in and whispered, "I assure you, I won't make the same mistake."

Shaking his head, Paul tried to speak around the fabric, and a bead of sweat slipped down one temple.

Maxis hesitated. Maybe he should let the poor bastard have a word or two before he met his maker. He gripped a corner of the cloth. "No shouting. Understood?"

The man nodded.

Pulling the gag free, Maxis stood and cross his arms. "Speak."

"I don't know what you're talking about." Paul's voice cracked. "I think you've got me confused—"

"I'm not confused." Maxis shoved the man's linen pant legs to his knees. "I scanned your memories while you were out to make sure what your brother said was true. You can kill anyone you share a link with by destroying their mind at any distance. It's quite a unique gift, and I want it."

"You're crazy." Paul tugged at the ropes. "You can't do that. Only the malran can take someone's powers."

"He's the only one who can naturally." He lifted his dagger and twisted it, the blade flickering in the candlelight. "I found a way around it. Took me years and several wasted bodies, but I got there."

The muscles along Paul's neck and shoulders tightened as he strained against the ropes.

"Our powers stem from the brain, but getting past the natural defenses our bodies create is impossible under normal circumstances. There's a moment though, just before a person passes to nirana, when the mind lets go, leaving the door wide open for an opportunist such as myself." He clamped the man's leg above the ankle and sliced Paul's dorsalis pedis artery.

The man's scream ricocheted off the walls.

Maxis quickly stuffed the gag back in place. The cater-wauling raked at his nerves and the last thing he needed was to screw this up. A power like this wouldn't come again for a very long while and it was the last he needed to fill his arsenal. For now.

He sliced through the same artery on the man's other leg.

Rich blood spilled into the basins. The man's skin grew paler and his eyelids fluttered.

Maxis felt for a pulse. Weak, almost ready.

With a quick slash of his blade, the ropes fell free. He scooped the unconscious man from the cot and dashed to the adjacent room. His powers surged back to life once past the zeolite-ridden threshold, and his skin tingled with the bite of fine electrical sparks.

He tossed Paul on the bed, gripped both sides of his head, and pushed his spirit deep into Paul's mind. He sucked every gift the man possessed into his own body. There wasn't time to be choosy. Better to swipe and run with it all than risk being buried in his psyche when he died.

Maxis' vision faltered. He couldn't breathe beyond the pain, the onslaught of the man's skills reverberating against every nerve.

The man's death-chilled face slipped from his fingers, and the lifeless body thudded on the thin mattress.

Heavy footsteps pounded down the wooden steps into the basement. Maxis struggled to regain focus.

"Sir." His spy's clipped baritone cut through the room.

The muscles along Maxis' shoulders eased. He adjusted his long coat and turned. "You'd better have a damned fine reason for not trailing the malran as ordered."

"You told me to contact you if the malran showed any unusual behavior, and I couldn't reach you via link." The man glanced at the lifeless heap on the cot behind Maxis and swallowed. "He's made an…unusual…contact with a human."

"Unusual how?"

His lackey flushed and shifted, uncomfortable. "As in, romantically."

Interesting. Unlike some freer-thinking Myrens, Eryx normally kept his distance from humans outside of business. The ellan had been grumbling for years of Eryx's disassociation from council matters. If the human in question had anything to do with Eryx's absence, it might be worth some research.

"Not exactly a world class exposé, but something to investigate." Maxis snatched a cloth from Brenna and swiped the traces of blood from his blade and fingers. "Give me his coordinates and I'll follow up myself."

HEADLIGHTS SWEPT across the dash as Lexi pulled her Jeep into the Waffle House parking lot. Aside from Ian's baseline brown sedan and the black and chrome Hummer settling into the slot behind her, the place was empty. The pimped-out black and chrome behemoth didn't seem like Eryx's style, but then, what did she know? A handshake and a parking lot conversation didn't exactly make her his new BFF.

She killed the ignition and sucked in a fortifying breath. Why had she invited Eryx? Ian was bound to launch an inquisition the minute they sat down. Add her wonky response to Eryx's presence and she'd be as fidgety as a ripe teenager on prom night before her first cup of coffee was done.

The memory of Eryx's fingertips against her cheekbone flared and a shiver snaked its way deep into her belly. Just like the phantom stroke she'd felt in the bar, his touch had been gentle, yet firm, a rasp against her skin. It seemed…familiar.

The door opened and Lexi flinched, smacking her knuckles against the steering wheel. "Jesus!" She snatched her purse from the passenger seat to cover her fluster and hopped to the ground with a glare. "You scared me."

Eryx shut the door and smiled. "You looked like you were about to run. I figured I'd better take action before you could."

She aimed a pointed look at the Hummer then turned for the door. "Flashy."

"Not my style." Eryx's palm settled at the base of her spine, a comfortable weight that slowed her steps. "Ludan wanted leg room, so we took Ramsay's."

"Ramsay?" She reached for the door handle, but Eryx caught her wrist before she could connect and tugged her hand away, the heat of his chest tight against her back. Warm breath brushed her neck, a hint of mint mixing with the crisp spring night.

"My twin." He released her, stepped away, and opened the door. "You'll like him."

God had made not one, but two of these delicious males? She strode into the restaurant with as much ambivalence as she could muster. "You're assuming I'll know you past breakfast."

Ian stood, his take-no-shit expression trained on Eryx.

On, the bright side, he didn't seem surprised by the additional guests, which meant he'd listened to his voice mail for once. The downside? He didn't look too thrilled about playing Tonto.

Well, too bad. She needed an opinion unbiased by her undernourished sex drive and Ian was her only real friend to turn to. He'd get over it. Eventually.

"Ian, this is Eryx and..." Lexi leaned back and looked for Wingman, only to find him headed toward the barstools at the counter. "Ludan?"

"He's not much on social." Eryx reached past Lexi and offered his hand to Ian. "Eryx Shantos."

"Ian Smith." The man-to-man bit kicked in quick. A firm handshake. Pointed stares.

The whole thing made Lexi want to squirm. "You two going to duke it out or are we going to have breakfast?"

Ian broke the manly death clutch first, gaze still glued to Eryx with an unconvincing smile. "It's a guy thing. We can't help it."

Guy thing, her ass. Ian had shot past helpful friend and darted right into nosy father figure.

He stepped back and motioned Lexi toward his side of the booth. Lexi started forward, but Eryx snagged her wrist. "Sit with me?"

Simple, humble words, spoken low and with such sincerity that an unaccustomed pleasure fanned from head to toe. "I..."

Hazel eyes steady, Ian waited to take her lead. Whatever his thoughts on the situation, he made it clear the decision was hers.

Eryx's touch drifted across her pulse.

Every nerve ending hummed. "Sure." The word croaked from her tight throat and she slid across the yellow booth. At this point, her recourse seemed limited to hiding under the table or straddling Eryx with a demand he placate her hormonal version of Girls Gone Wild.

Denise sidled up to the table, tight black curls pulled into the same high ponytail she wore every night. Her makeup had worn off hours ago, likely in the middle of the post bar-hopper crush. "You having the usual?"

Lexi nodded and straightened the unused menus stashed behind the napkin holder.

Flipping to a fresh page on her note pad, the woman noshed out a few snaps from her bubble gum and focused on Eryx. "You?"

"I'll have the same."

Lexi craned her neck for eye contact. Damn but he was tall, which kinda sucked. Glaring up at a guy never held the same punch. "You don't even know what 'the usual' is."

"I don't care what it is." Eryx's response was more volume conscious than her snarky quip, but it still carried. He slid his hand across the worn wood-patterned Formica and settled it over her white-knuckled fist. "I'm here for you."

The smacking bubble gum stopped.

Lexi's gut did a dive and barrel roll combo.

Ian pointed at the cup he'd been nursing when they arrived. "Just the coffee for me. I can't stay long."

Lexi glared at Ian. She could almost picture the cartoon bubble above his head: *You made your bed now lie in it.*

"So, tell me about yourself, Eryx." Ian glanced at Eryx's hand on hers. "Where are you from?"

"I have a place here in Tulsa."

Denise set two new cups of coffee on the table and Eryx asked for her pen. She dug into her stained brown apron and handed one over before hustling toward Ludan.

Ian plowed ahead with his questions. "And what do you do?"

"Geological work." Eryx pulled out his wallet, snatched a business card, and scribbled on the back. "Lexi mentioned you're in law enforcement."

"Retired, actually. I do private investigations now."

Eryx sat the pen aside. "My company does exploration for natural gas and minerals." He slid the expensive card stock across the table with a look of unrepentant confidence. "If you want background, that should be enough to get you started. Ludan's info is there, too."

Ian reclined against the booth and crossed his arms. "And will I find anything to be concerned about?"

Eryx lifted his coffee mug and took a leisurely sip, never breaking eye contact. "Not a thing."

Lexi didn't breathe. Hell, she was afraid to move. Part of her wanted to hug her friend, and another, more primitive part of her thought it might be wise to head on home. This much male posturing had to have dangerous side effects.

Ian relaxed, focused on her, and stuffed the business card in his pocket. "You give any thought to what we talked about yesterday?"

Lexi did a mental three-point turn. "I'm sorry, what?"

"Your jobs and school." Ian leaned into the tabletop with one elbow and snatched her chin between his thumb and finger. "Those dark spots under your eyes aren't going to go away if you keep this pace."

Eryx leaned into the table and studied her face.

"I'm fine." She shoved Ian's hand away and scooted closer to the inner booth wall to put more distance between her and Eryx. "I'll quit the bar routine as soon as your caseload's full. You can't afford me full-time yet."

"It's not just fatigue, Lexi, and you know it."

An awkward silence settled between them. It was too bad

his wife and unborn child had become an unsolved missing persons case. He had the daddy thing down pat.

He scrutinized Eryx then grinned at her. "I say you go with this one." It was said almost under his breath, but not nearly quiet enough for Eryx to miss. He fished out a few dollar bills and slid from the booth. "I hope you two don't mind if I call it a night?"

Eryx stood as Ian did.

Lexi panicked. Her social life preserver was a mere handful of steps from the front door. "Do you—"

Ian crowded into Eryx's personal space. "I can only think of a few instances where breaking the law would be justifiable." He held his hand out to Eryx. "Hurting Lexi would be one of them."

Eryx clasped Ian's hand. "Understood."

Heat flooded Lexi's face. She massaged her temples and locked her gaze on the syrup bottle. She'd thought Ian would help her get a feel for Eryx, not throw her under the proverbial bus.

Plastic and steel groaned as Eryx settled beside her. "There's nothing wrong with someone looking out for you."

"That was embarrassing." She didn't even try to cover her petulant tone. Why bother?

He cupped the back of her neck and the warmth filtered down her spine. "Not how you'd thought breakfast would go?"

"Not in the slightest." Her husky reply wasn't appropriate for a rundown Waffle House.

"What was he telling you to go with?"

"Nothing."

The quiet chatter of the cook and waitress at the other end of the room filled the silence between them.

Eryx's free hand settled on her forearm. "Give me something, Lexi. Let me know you." His warm voice matched his touch. "Just open the door a crack."

Shit. No blatant come-ons or carnal angles to get her naked. This guy went for depth. Real conversation. Her instincts screamed to let him in, to ease her grip on distrust.

The heat of his palm spread to create a type of emotional blanket. It felt good. Right. Damn near necessary.

"Ian thinks I need to get out more. Be with people." She grumbled the confession. "I don't..." The right words wouldn't come. "I don't fit. Ian's one of the few people I click with. Everyone else either confounds me or lodges a knife in my back." Not that she was bitter, or anything.

His steel-gray gaze met hers, steady and unblinking. "Maybe you're in the wrong place."

Lexi's senses prickled, ready for action. Not so much from what he'd said so much as how he'd said it. Temptation with a trace of caution.

Eryx shifted in the booth and eyeballed Ludan at the bar. His lips tightened and his eyes narrowed.

Ludan frowned and refocused on his coffee.

With a slow inhalation, Eryx cupped her jaw. "What kind of woman are you? If you see a challenge, do you take it? Or do you sit at the side of the rapids and watch while others race by?"

An odd question. Deep. Or could just be a sneaky way of asking, *"Your place or mine?"*

"It depends," she said.

Eryx kept his silence, no movement but for the gentle tightening of his fingers against her skin.

"I crave the rapids, but if my intuition warns me against it, I'll sit them out." There. Truth and a warning all at once.

He traced her lower lip with his thumb. "I understand instinct." His gaze dropped to her mouth. "I'm going with mine."

He lowered his head.

A kiss. Dear God, he was going to kiss her. Here. With everyone watching.

Her lips tingled and parted, very much on board. Her heart pounded, frantic with indecision and panic. She should push away. Keep her distance.

His lips brushed hers and flutters rippled through her belly. A shaky exhalation slipped past her suddenly ravenous mouth, mingling with his warm breath. Sensual. Intimate despite the clothes between them.

Eryx rested his forehead against hers and sucked in a heavy breath. "I think you don't fit in because you're in the wrong place."

What? He wanted to talk *now*? It was all she could do to breathe and feel at the same time. "You mean the wrong job?"

"No, I mean the wrong place." His voice grew stronger. Firm. Determined. "You're not among the people you were born to be with."

The tiny flame of hope in her heart sputtered, and a chill settled in her chest. She pushed away, desire dropping to something short of disgust. The good-looking ones always ended up a few notches shy of sane. "You know, I think I'm going to head home. Can you let me out?"

Eryx held her in place. "A white sand beach wrapped in black rock walls. You've dreamt of the place." His thick voice, little more than a whisper, dripped with urgency.

The picture he painted pulled an instant image from her recurring dreams, but she smacked it down. "Yeah, I'm pretty sure that's Hawaii, right? I'd love to go there. Now let me out."

"The sky holds a constant rainbow. Everywhere you look the colors shift, some more prominent from different angles."

Lexi's heart catapulted back to where his lips had sent it minutes before. She swallowed to hide her surprise.

"White barked trees with dark veins. Deep evergreen leaves shaped like feathers hang loose toward the ground. The tips are indigo blue."

Denise clunked plates on the table.

He couldn't know about those images. No one knew about her dreams. Not even Ian. "Why are you telling me this?"

Eryx held her gaze, his lips pressed tight for so long she thought he wouldn't answer. "Because I searched your memories. And the places you see in your dreams? That's where I'm from. Where I think you're from."

The white noise turned deafening. "I think you're one of our lost."

Not the smoothest delivery Eryx had ever given. If he was smart he'd cheat and read Lexi's emotions. As a male Shantos he carried the sum of all Myren gifts—a helluva perk right about now if he'd lower his standards to do it.

She paled and tucked her arms in tight.

Fuck it.

He opened his senses. Panic, sharp and hot, flared across his chest.

Lexi's panic.

"Let me out." Lexi dragged her purse out and shoved his shoulder. "I need air, let me out."

He slid from the booth.

Lexi darted toward the door.

"Handle the tab," he said to Ludan, still perched on a barstool with coffee in hand. *"And keep the waitress busy."* The last thing he needed right now were interruptions and her frown said she was on the verge of intervention.

He barreled through the doors and snatched Lexi's arm as she swung her car door wide. "Lexi, wait."

She jerked away and her purse thunked against the Jeep. "Leave me alone." Her voice trembled.

With a quick swipe, he cinched his arm around her waist and steered her to the rear of her car. "Lexi, breathe. Just breathe." He pressed her against the Jeep, his thighs on either side of hers yet still far enough away she had space. He cupped her face, tight so she couldn't evade. "I'm not crazy. I swear it. Hear me out."

"I've heard you out." She batted at his hands, face flushed. "You're nuts."

"You said you used your instincts. Use them now. Dig deep and tell me what you feel." It was a gamble. With her this keyed up, the tactic could backfire, but it was a damn sight better than letting her run and hide now that he'd opened a vault he couldn't reseal.

Huffing, she pressed her palms against the Jeep. Her eyes softened, and energy rippled across his shoulders.

"Your friend said you're tired." Hopefully the tie to someone she trusted would make her listen.

She relaxed a fraction.

"If I'm right, it's with good reason. You need Eden's energy to thrive." "Eden?" Her voice quivered and her gaze darted around the parking lot, but she grasped his wrist. Not like she meant to shove him away, but more like she hung on for dear life.

"Eden. Where I'm from. Where I think you're from."

Inside, the waitress gestured enthusiastically, her smile bright. Whatever Ludan had said or done was working.

He cupped Lexi's neck. "Reach out. Use your senses and feel me. I know this is fast and I swear I'll explain everything if you promise not to run."

A semi roared past on the highway, and crickets' chirping filled the void as the truck lumbered away.

An intimate stroke of energy coiled around him. She was only gauging his intent, feeling him out as he'd asked, but damn.

He groaned and pulled her tight against him, hands buried her silky hair. "Praise The Great One, that feels good." Her lips were so close. Full and slightly parted. A natural, dusky rose. He pressed his hips forward and her softness yielded to his.

Lexi gasped. "What feels good? What are you doing?" Breathy. A little shaken, but right there with him. She hummed beneath him, and her blue- gray eyes darkened.

"Your energy." He traced her jawline with his lips and cupped her ass, imagining the action without the barrier of her jeans. "It's strong enough I can feel it."

He had to be careful. One slip of his own energy and he'd trigger her awakening if she was Myren, but damned if he could navigate reason beyond that. Not with her husky voice and the soft press of her breasts against him.

"Stop." She shoved his chest and tried to wriggle away.

He froze. Stop meant stop in his book, but the energy coming off her didn't match her command. Gripping her shoulders, he eased back only enough to make eye contact. No way was he letting her run from what burned between them.

"Energy? Really?" Her voice had an arctic bite. "Christ, I'm stupid. I've heard a million come-ons, but making up some bullshit place called Eden and saying you feel my energy? You expect me to buy that bit?"

Eryx got up nose to nose, her breath so warm and sweet he thought about carting her home, the tenets of his race be damned. "It's not a come- on and you know it. You felt it."

Something burned in her gaze. Pain? Fear?

He sampled her emotions and nearly buckled beneath the

intensity. The acrid taste of hurt, but underneath it was a burning pulse. Need. Pure and simple. He locked his arms around her, one hand fisted in her hair. "Where I come from, a man doesn't play games. Partners honor what they feel and act on what they need." He brushed his lips against hers and reveled in her subtle tremor. "You touched me in a way you can't yet comprehend, and I responded. You responded. It's natural and there's not a damned thing dishonest about it."

He trailed his tongue across her lower lip. Bubble gum. Not overpowering, but enough to test his control. To drag him deeper. "Are you going to listen to your past? Or the part of you that knows this is right?"

Her fingers dug into his shoulders.

He braced for her to push him away. "It's all you, Lexi. Your choice. I won't ask for more than you're willing to give, but honesty is non-negotiable. Step away if you can't face it, but don't lay the faults of other men at my feet as an excuse."

She blinked and her eyes sharpened, all the softness in her face replaced with acute awareness. "I didn't mean it like that."

"Yes you did." He pressed his hands against the Jeep's rear window, caging her. "I don't blame you for it. It's how sexuality works here. But it's not that way in Eden, and won't be that way between us. Ever." He inched closer, desperate for her touch. "Now, are you going to take what you need, or leave us both miserable?"

She licked her lip, innocent and seductive in one swipe. "You're different."

"More than you know. And I'll show you, but you could put me out of my fucking misery with a taste of those sweet lips before I do."

She leaned in.

Her lips met his and a carnal one-two punch ripped reality out from underneath him. The slick heat of her mouth. Her needy little moans. The sensual flex of her hips against his. The waiting and searching to find her was worth it. Every damned second of it.

He skimmed her waist, her jeans rough beneath his fingers. The edge of her tank teased his knuckles as he caressed underneath. Just one touch of skin. That's all he needed.

Wind gusted leaves across the asphalt.

Warning tingles flared across Eryx's neck. With Myren speed, he swept Lexi into the shadows of the restaurant, shielding her from the hidden presence he sensed as he sent a mental summons to Ludan.

A tall male with long dark hair shimmered into view. Dressed in a loose black shirt and leather pants, he looked like a pirate cliché. He crossed his arms, his teeth bared in an insincere smile. "I'm surprised to find our malran passing the night in the arms of a human woman. She must be special for you to lose those ridiculous braids you normally wear. They're for your people, right? A sign of your devotion?"

Maxis Steysis. Praise the Great One. His family's nemesis looked a whole lot different now than he had seventy years ago. He'd been a lanky bookworm, but the years had hardened him, both in physique and expression. His pale green eyes were unmistakable.

Maxis leaned out, craning his neck to catch a better glimpse of Lexi. "I hear the ellan are concerned with your lack of attention to Myren proceedings. Perhaps this woman explains your distraction of late?"

A well-placed taunt considering any involvement with a human would send his council into all kinds panicked inquiries. Not that he was stupid enough to react.

Lexi shifted behind Eryx.

He reached back and gripped her waist. Not much in the way of warnings, but the best he could do without a link.

She murmured something, but stilled.

He'd have time to worry about whatever was rattling around in her head later. Right now, he needed to keep her safe. "Why are you here, Maxis?"

"Ah, so you do remember me?" Maxis grinned, a pompous lopsided affair. "Maybe it's happy coincidence?"

"Coincidence has never factored between our families." Eryx kept his fingers lax, though the urge to cast a fat stream of fire squarely into Maxis' chest tickled his palms. "Going head to head with me doesn't say much for your judgment."

Maxis shrugged. "I'm not too worried. You wouldn't reveal your nature to a human. That would break your precious laws."

Lexi twitched and her hand fisted in his t-shirt at the small of his back.

Maxis straightened, shoulders back and arms down, but slightly away from his sides. "I, on the other hand, don't give a shit what humans think." Eryx braced himself, weight on the balls of his feet and ready to move. Maxis aimed his palm at Eryx and an angry arc of electricity shot out. *"Ludan, now!"* Eryx swept Lexi into an airborne spin and the salvo pierced deep in his shoulder. He backhanded a fireball.

The volley grazed Maxis' side.

Ludan crashed into Maxis' other side, plowing him into a nearby retaining wall.

"Ludan, he's got—"

Ludan's arms convulsed with a layer of crackling blue and red electricity and he lost his grip on Maxis.

Maxis darted to the sky and his image shimmered into nothingness.

Ludan snarled and held his charred hands in front of him. "I'm going to kill that son of a bitch." He crouched to give chase.

"Stand down." Eryx checked the parking lot for witnesses and lowered his voice. "I need you here."

Lexi tried to escape his arms, but Eryx held firm.

Ludan stalked closer. "Are we past hypotheticals now?" His voice shook with rage. "Maxis' family line doesn't carry offensive skills and he threw some nasty volts. I'd say that's cause for concern."

"Later, Ludan." He jerked his head toward Lexi.

Lexi slammed both palms into Eryx's shoulders and fired a cursing barrage to make even Ludan blush. "Let. Me. Go."

Eryx winced and tugged her tighter, angling his shoulder to ease the pain.

Lexi hesitated and torque to see his shoulder. "You're hurt."

"I'm fine. My sister will fix it."

"Is she a doctor? We need a doctor. My Jeep's right there, we'll just—"

"Lexi."

She stilled, her breath coming fast and heavy.

He cupped her face and scrambled for something to say. Anything to reach through her panic and confusion. "I'm different, remember? I'll be fine and I still plan to answer your questions, but I need to make you safe first. Let me take you home."

Poised to run, she stared him down with wide eyes, her face flushed.

Eryx prayed, both to The Great One and The Fates who had led him to this moment. He'd do what he needed to keep her safe no matter how she answered, but he'd rather not do it with her kicking and screaming.

She nodded. Not much, but enough to let him suck in a decent breath.

"You sure about this, Eryx?" Ludan's quiet question lumbered heavy between them. Considering the consequences Eryx would face if Lexi wasn't Myren, the weight was appropriate.

"I'm damn sure not leaving her here." Eryx spun her facing Ludan and locked his arms around her waist. "Call it, Ludan."

CHAPTER 4

*L*exi swayed and gripped Eryx's forearm at her waist. The stuff she'd seen wasn't possible. Was it? Her heart pounded so hard it hurt. Early morning Waffle House diners trickled into the restaurant, but not one looked toward her. "Why don't they see us?"

"Because we're shielded," Eryx answered. "Ludan, call the damned portal. I'll cover the mask."

Mask? Portal? Not good. Or safe. Or sane. Spots crept at the edges of her vision and her throat tightened. She should pull her head out of her ass and run, but something kept her rooted in place. A whisper of change. The tipping point in her life she'd craved.

"She's not ready for this." Ludan raised his hand, fingers tilted upward, palm toward the darkest corner of the parking lot. Charred flesh covered his muscled arms, blending with the stark black of his T-shirt.

Lexi tried to take a step back, but barely budged with Eryx plastered behind her. "What's going on?"

"Just watch. Ludan's wrong. You'll handle it fine." His

comforting words didn't help much, not with the way he scanned the skies.

The space where Ludan aimed shifted and blurred. Shadow blossomed into a pale gray sphere. It swirled in the center and thickened until a cave- like entrance formed. Smoky wisps floated near the bottom and the edges sparkled.

Ludan lowered his hand and faced her. His blue eyes beamed brighter, the whites around the irises glowing. Creepy. Yet somehow expected?

"Time to go, Lexi." Eryx said.

She craned to see his face. "What is that thing?"

"The gateway home. To Eden."

Like that made a cave popping up out of nowhere a perfectly reasonable occurrence. Desperate for a full breath, and some distance, she pried his arm from her waist and twisted free.

Eryx winced.

Damn it. She hadn't meant to hurt him. Maybe she should push the hospital idea again. "That man was after you, not me."

His gaze swept the space behind her then lasered onto her. An honest-to-God cage couldn't have held her more firmly. "The man you saw? His name is Maxis. About five minutes ago you jumped to the top of his most wanted list because you're a means to get to me."

"But—"

"You said you wanted answers. They're right in front of you." His tone hardened, lines deepening at the corners of his mouth. "Choose."

A slow burn of defiance simmered in her gut. Ultimatums weren't her strong suit. Never had been. "And if I don't go?"

"Then I stay here with you. I won't leave you alone."

"Bullshit." Ludan snarled across the distance. "You're

already too weak. The strike on your shoulder proves it. He'd have never hit you if you weren't drained."

And he'd done it protecting her. The last thing she wanted to do was make matters worse. "What's he talking about?"

"He needs to go home." Ludan fisted his hands at his sides and shifted unsteadily. "He's been here too long, looking for you. Now that Maxis knows you're valuable, Eryx won't leave you. That puts him—"

"Leave it," Eryx said.

"Like hell." Breath labored, Ludan prowled forward. "We can't keep this up. Both of us are lights out in minutes if we stay." He glared accusingly at her. "Show your mettle, woman, and choose."

She staggered back. Christ, she couldn't even process. Maybe they'd knocked her out in the parking lot when she'd left work and this was all in her head.

"You know this is right." Eryx said, his voice low, only for her. He cupped the back of her neck. "Trust me."

Warm fingers. Confident. His whole presence drowning out reality. He'd nailed the images from her dreams, a freaky feat for sure, but not something to discount. While it scared her seven ways to silly to admit, part of her had come to life the moment she'd seen him. Stretched and blossomed in a burst of color. What would it feel like to curl against him and laze beneath more of his touch? If it was a dream, then what was the harm?

This is your chance. What you've been waiting for.

"I'll go." Even as the words slipped free, she couldn't believe she'd said it.

"'Bout fucking time," Ludan said from behind them.

Eryx swept her into his arms and strode into the mist.

The soft, cool cloud enfolded them, and her stomach

lurched. Maybe this wasn't a good idea. She jackknifed in Eryx's arms.

He grunted and shifted her farther from his injured shoulder, but kept stalking forward.

"I can walk." Or run the other direction if he'd give her the chance.

He kissed her temple and his warm breath eased along her chilled skin. "Better if I do the walking. Just don't wiggle. Focus on the quiet."

Her muscles coiled, ready to jump into action. Void of sound, the portal packed a strange Zen quality. Nowhere near the spinning Sci-Fi vortex she'd expected. No black hole to suck them up and spit them out.

Ahead a pale ball of light flickered, growing larger, bold but without the violent glare. Her skin tingled and the hair along her arms floated to attention. She held her breath, squeezed her eyes shut, and braced for impact.

Warmth, easy on her skin. A few bird chirps. The light, crisp scent of spring—flowers, maybe a recent rain?

She cracked one eye open.

Holy crap. She wasn't dead or delirious. They'd really taken her somewhere else. Someplace straight out of fantasy. "It's so…bright."

Eryx eased her to her feet and chuckled. "Colorful. More vivid than Evad."

Vivid was an understatement. A spectacular sunrise full of pinks and corals stretched the horizon, and vibrant thick grass shimmered as far as she could see. She crouched and ran her fingers over the damp surface. Little silver veins ran through the center and edges of each blade, the texture like moss. "The same, but different."

"Pretty much sums it up." Eryx guided her up. "How do you feel?"

Was that a trick question? "Alice in Wonderland comes to mind."

Ludan snickered behind her.

"I meant physically." Eryx said with a grin. "Notice anything different?" She flexed and clenched her hands, studying her palms as she took internal stock. "Kind of like after a few energy drinks, but without the shakes."

Eryx's grin morphed to a smile as bright as the sunrise behind him. "Told you," he said to Ludan.

"Could be adrenaline."

The sky's holographic weave of rainbows stretched without a single cloud, a deeper color than what she'd seen in her dreams. If those parts of her dreams were true, would the rest be too?

A cozy cottage made of dark gray stones and a black slate roof sat in the distance, nestled at the base of a giant black mountain. Trees with mahogany trunks and pale pink leaves lined the slopes. "I know that place."

The steady rumble of Eryx and Ludan's voices silenced.

"You know what place?" Ludan glared and stalked toward her. She pointed at the horizon. "The house—"

Ludan snatched her outstretched hand and the same rush she'd felt in the bar fired up her arm. A blur and a whip of wind, and her hand was free, the tingles gone.

"You. Will. Not. Touch. Her." Eyes bright as a supernova and face a livid red, Eryx gripped his friend in a vicious headlock.

Ludan's gaze stayed locked on Lexi's, his mouth crooked in an awkward grin. "Spitfire." The word croaked out, probably the best he could do with Eryx's thick forearm at his throat.

Eryx freed him with a shove. "Stay the fuck out of my—"

"Easy." Ludan held up both hands and jerked his head toward Lexi.

The two stared each other down.

Eryx dipped his chin, nostrils flared.

Ludan frowned. The same odd, silent exchange she'd seen between them at breakfast.

Lexi inched forward and glared at Ludan. "What did you do?"

"He didn't believe you." Eryx slid behind her, and curled one hand around her throat. A possessive, Neanderthal move that sent pleasure spinning through her veins. "He scanned your memories."

"You can do that?" Her past wasn't exactly a place she wanted people trouncing around unattended. "Why?"

Ludan screwed his lips up in a shit-eating smile and crossed his arms.

Eryx's hand flexed, not threatening so much as claiming. "He can and he did, mostly to protect his father. Only six people alive in this world who know where Graylin lives and you're not one of them. He wanted to see what you saw—not that it excuses his actions."

Lexi fought to untangle her thoughts, the action nearly impossible with Eryx so close. Her skin hummed beneath his touch. "I saw it in my dreams. It's not like I get a choice in what shows up."

Ludan stood rooted in place with a smug expression.

"And why are you looking at me like that? Less than five minutes ago you were ready to rip my head off."

Ludan stared back, silent. One breath. Two. Uncurling his arms, he sauntered close enough to draw a growl from Eryx. "That was before I saw your past." His ice blue eyes drew her in, almost hypnotic. "Where you've been takes courage. I respect warriors."

Her heart seized. How far back had he gone? How much had he seen?

"One of Ludan's special gifts is the ability to consume a

person's memories rather quickly." Eryx tucked her into the crook of his arm. "He won't make such a presumption with you again."

Wind rushed overhead, whipping Lexi's hair away from her face. A man dropped from the air, and landed with a resounding boom.

"What the hell?" She tried to breathe, her lungs suddenly two sizes too small to do a decent job.

"Easy." Eryx's thumb skated across her inner wrist, calming. "It's just like in your dreams. No different."

The men surrounded her, all three poised and ready to leap into action. Holy crap. The new guy was Eryx's twin. Or a futuristic version from some other reality. Silver mesh tanks and black leather pants and boots weren't standard issue back home.

"We clear?" Eryx asked his twin.

The new arrival sized her up, a slow glide from head to toe. His gray eyes twinkled and a dimple punctuated his sly grin.

Gazing at Lexi, the twin nodded. Wicked vibes poured off him—the bad boy type that snagged women three states away with little more than a wink. "Not that you gave me much notice to scan the place, but yeah, the grounds are free."

He sauntered forward, hair loose to his shoulders, and offered his hand. "I'm the better brother, Ramsay."

Oh, yeah. Definitely a player, this one.

Lexi gripped his hand and turned it for a more businesses-like shake. "Not sure I'm buying the better part. I'm Lexi Merrill."

Ramsay's eyes twinkled with a naughty glint. "My brother's a lucky bastard."

"Only if I can keep her alive long enough to gloat. If you're done playing Romeo we need to get her settled and engage the scout teams. I want Maxis Steysis. Now."

Ludan perked up and took a few steps closer. "Finally."

"The quarans are on their way to the training center." Ramsay gestured toward Eryx's injury. "Galena's en route to take care of you two. She shouldn't be another five or ten minutes."

Eryx kept scanning the perimeter despite Ramsay's claim the area was free from any intruders. "Anything suspicious reported while we were gone?"

Ramsay's eyes dimmed and his mouth pressed to a hard line. "We lost a warrior. Doesn't seem related, though. Died in pursuit of a criminal fleeing to Evad. We've tried to notify the baineann, but she's gone missing. Witnesses say they saw her leave her house in tears."

"Keep looking. I want to meet her as soon as she's found." Face grim, Eryx settled a hand at Lexi's lower back. He nudged her toward the cottage and glanced at Ludan. "You sure Graylin's alright with this?"

"You kidding? Pops is all over this."

Light. Almost happy. Granted, she'd only known Ludan a handful of hours, but she doubted he pulled the levity card often.

Something had happened during their brief contact. Some connection born of experience that made her less frightened of his hard appearance and more determined to protect his soul.

A thought sparked and she pulled Eryx to a stop. "How do these people know we're coming? We just left. You didn't..." Lexi gestured to their pockets. "You didn't call or anything."

Ramsay guffawed, and the sound bounced off the mountain beyond. "Got a long day ahead of you, brother."

Eryx tugged her back into motion and gave Ramsay a brusque look. "So do you. I want squads working around the clock until we can get Maxis contained." They stepped onto the cobblestone path leading to the front door of the cottage, and Eryx steered Lexi in front of him. The door opened before they reached it, though no one stood beside it.

Lexi opened her mouth.

"I opened it." The tension hadn't left his face, but a grin slipped into place. "More questions, I know. You'll get your answers as soon as we've got a plan in place to find Maxis."

He guided her into a large, open room decorated in shades of gold and yellow. A well-worn desk sat nestled in a corner, equally used leather-bound books stacked to one side. Thick cushions, soft fabrics, fancy patterns. Nothing low-end about this place.

The men huddled barely two strides into the room, strategizing with rapid-fire words.

She meandered through the homey space, a perfect book getaway on a rainy day. Plants with long-bladed evergreen leaves spilled from their containers to end in white, bell-shaped bulbs.

An old painting hung above the fireplace. Set against an ivory backdrop, two hands were clasped together so the fore-arms faced the viewer—one masculine, one feminine. A Pegasus covered the female's skin, an impressive steed rearing back on its hind legs as it pawed the air with wings spread up and wide. An intricately detailed sword wrapped in long strands of ivy covered the man's.

A tingle of awareness stirred. Had she seen it before? It seemed familiar, but she couldn't seem to find a specific memory.

"It depicts an old prophecy." A man with wavy, thick gray hair to the nape of his neck approached her, hands folded formally at his waist.

His clothes were odd—a tank and loose-fitting, gray silk pants with a long-sleeved, loose overcoat that hung to his shins. Kind of like a new age Hugh Hefner.

He stared at the painting. "Legend says when two Myrens mate and produce the marks shown there, it will spark the beginning of a new era in Eden."

"That's a rather non-committal prophecy." The words slipped through uncensored before she could stop herself.

"You mean, is it an era of promise, or an era of decline?" He smirked, more playful than catty.

Lexi kept her silence. For all she knew, this dude was the high potentate of this beautiful place. He sure talked like someone official. She'd bet last week's paycheck he was related to Ludan though. The height, build, and eyes were too close not to share DNA.

"Many people have pondered that over the years," he said. "Some are the very epitome of gloom and doom. I choose to anticipate a change for the better." He held out his hand, his smile a dead-ringer for Ludan's. "My name is Graylin Forte. I'm Ludan's father."

Lexi shook his hand. Dad was definitely more easy-going than the kid. "Lexi. Lexi Merrill."

Graylin's eyes sparkled, mischief crinkling the corners. "I know who you are. Eryx has been looking for you for years."

CHAPTER 5

*E*ryx bailed on Ludan and Ramsay and their plans to find Maxis, and bee-lined across the room to make sure his meddling mentor shut the hell up.

"You're the second person to say he's been looking for me." Lexi shot a sidelong scowl at Eryx and crossed her arms.

"I told you I'd answer your questions and I will." What he wanted was to touch her. To stroke the back of her neck and kiss the tension right out of her. The PDA wouldn't phase anyone else in the room, but he doubted Lexi was ready for a dunk in Myren culture.

"Ludan told you about her?" he asked Graylin.

Graylin frowned. "I served your father for the better part of my life with the same devotion as my son now serves you. Did you think I wouldn't give my support? Your secret is safe with me."

Lexi perked up. "Secret?"

Eryx palmed her neck before he could check the action, the simple contact grounding him in a way he wasn't sure he'd ever understand. "Secret makes it sound like something I'm ashamed of. Necessarily covert is more accurate."

Lexi leaned into his touch and her eyes softened. So natural. Like they'd been together for years instead of hours.

The front door swooshed open and his sister strode through the door. Her waist-length auburn hair was tangled from flight, and her black tunic and leggings smudged with garden dirt. In less time than it took most people to state their name she scanned him then Ludan. "Ramsay said you're hurt, but I don't see any blood." She focused on Ludan's hands and grinned. "A little on the crispy side though. Who'd you piss off?"

"Had a little run-in with Maxis," Eryx said.

Lexi stepped away. "His shoulder's hurt."

Galena glided across the room, checked Eryx's shoulder for all of three seconds, and shrugged. "He'll keep." She zeroed in on Lexi and pulled her into a quick, tight hug. "You must be Lexi. I'm Eryx's sister, Galena. Let's get the brutes healed and we'll chat. I'm sure you've got lots of questions and men always take forever with answers."

Lexi had barely returned the embrace when Galena stepped back and motioned toward the kitchen. "Eryx, you're up first."

"No, heal Ludan." Things were too far out of control. Maxis on the loose and his long-stifled desire for Lexi wouldn't change overnight, but he could damn sure put a lid on his meddling friends and family and see to Lexi's needs. "If anyone's answering Lexi's questions, it's me."

He steered Lexi toward the hallway, striding past Ramsay still stationed near the entrance. "I want a search status every two hours."

Ramsay opened his mouth, took one look at Eryx, and snapped it shut. With a nod and an unrepentant wink at Lexi, he shot out the open door.

They rounded the corner to the kitchen, the scent of fresh brewed coffee filling the cozy space. Eryx pulled out a chair at the far side of the maple-wood table and motioned Lexi to sit. "Graylin, I hate to ask on short notice, but Lexi hasn't eaten. If you can get her something to tide her over, I'll ask Orla to come and handle the rest of the cooking while we're here."

Lexi slid into her chair. The morning sun angled through the picture window behind her, the blue undertones of her dark hair glinting as she scanned every window and exit. "I'm not hungry."

Graylin pulled out two large platters. "Nonsense. You'll need your strength if you're to be awakened. That requires both food and rest."

"Awakened?"

Well, that was one way to get her mind off escape. Eryx glowered at Graylin, pulled a chair close to Lexi's, and pointed at the one in front of Galena. "Get your ass in the chair," he said to Ludan. "I want you healed and ready in case we get any more surprises."

Nostrils flared and shoulders pulled back, Ludan pushed away from the stone island. "As you wish." He plopped in place and the chair groaned beneath his weight. "Malran."

"What's a malran?"

Interfering jackass. "A loose interpretation would be leader," Eryx answered before Ludan could do any more damage.

The room went uncomfortably silent, both Galena and Graylin sporting baffled expressions. Eryx settled his arm along the back of Lexi's chair.

Ludan arched an eyebrow. *"You're not going to tell her?"*

"Not yet. And I'd appreciated it if you and your father stayed the hell out of my personal life."

Lexi's lips were drawn tight, fists clenched atop the scarred, honey-stained tabletop. All things considered, she'd been a hell of a trooper. Sharing his day job on top of every-thing else didn't seem like an intelligent next step.

Galena clasped Ludan's burned hands, and Ludan averted his face with a growl. "Hold still, Ludan."

"What's she doing?" Lexi whispered the question, a bit of her tension easing.

Eryx leaned close to her ear, and lowered his voice—not that his sister needed such a courtesy. With Galena's skill she could heal a near fatal wound in the middle of a riot. "She's an empath. She'll take his wounds into her body and then heal herself from the inside out."

Lexi edged forward another inch or two. "Does it hurt?"

Eryx followed Lexi's gaze, focused on how Ludan refused to watch. "No. Not for him anyway. Galena will feel what he feels, but to a lesser degree. He just hates to watch her take the wound. We all do."

For the next few seconds, Lexi's scrutiny fell to Galena.

The burns along Ludan's arms faded and reappeared on Galena's sun-kissed forearms without so much as a whimper passing his sister's lips.

Lexi sat back, a mix of respect and awe on her face. "That's amazing."

Graylin set two platters of food before them as Ludan shoved to his feet.

Galena laughed and picked a ripe, pink berry off one of the plates. "I'm fine, Ludan. Really." She popped the fruit between her lips and motioned for Eryx. "Come on, Eryx. Let's get you done."

Eryx shook his head and nudged the platter of fruits and cheeses closer to Lexi. "Rest for a minute. We'll let Lexi have a go with her questions."

Head cocked, Lexi stared at her plate. Cheese that was really blue and kelly green fruits weren't everyday fare in Evad.

The room grew silent.

She looked up and blinked. "Let her heal your shoulder. I can wait."

Not the most convincing statement he'd ever heard, but given the night she'd had, he didn't blame her. "I'm fine. Galena can use the time to rest and you deserve answers. Where do you want to start?"

Lexi nudged a slice of cheese along the side of her plate. "You called this place Eden. As in *the* Eden?"

Considering Maxis' attack, it was the last place he'd expected her to start, but a logical choice all the same. "We're Myren, a race that's existed for over six thousand years. The Great One—God, in your definition—created both humans and Myrens here, in Eden."

Lexi splayed her hands flat on the table, fingertips white against the wood.

"Humans came first, then Myrens a bit later," he said. "While we're similar at our core, our race has greater abilities. Think of us as version two with major upgrades."

"So, why aren't humans still here?"

Eryx accepted a glass of strasse from Graylin, the potent burn of the clear liquor something he could use right about now. He passed a cup of black coffee to Lexi. "When you put two similar races together and one is more powerful, what do you suppose would happen?"

Lexi lifted the cup to her lips and blew across the surface. Bits of steam danced at the rim. "That depends." She rested her elbows on the table, mug nestled between her hands. "What does more powerful mean? Flying?"

He shook his head. "Flying is just a matter of using our minds in conjunction with the energy around us. It's a fairly unobtrusive gift. The ones with the potential to cause problems are those tied to the elements— fire, water, earth, wind, and storm. Every Myren is born with one or two of them."

She took an absent sip of her drink then pulled back with a jerk.

Eryx slid the sweet cream closer to Lexi. "A little stronger than what you're used to?"

She added enough her cup almost overflowed. "That stuff makes espresso taste like hot chocolate." She stirred and took a tentative taste. "I thought there were only four elements."

"Not for us. You'd know the element of storm as lightning or electricity, but we can manipulate it the same as other elements."

She traced the table's wood pattern. "Myrens tried to hurt the humans didn't they?"

"The Great One separated us, creating Evad—what we call the human realm—for them and leaving Eden for us. Evad has only the amount of energy needed for humans. It's why we can't stay there long. We get weak. Over time we end up at the same level as humans."

"An equalizer for a Myren who stays too long." She rolled her lips together as if mulling over the concept. "But if you can go back and forth between the two places, what's to keep Myrens from bringing humans here? Your power doesn't drain here, right?"

Pride flared white-hot in Eryx's chest. With her quick wit and common sense she'd make a perfect malress. "Our laws and warriors keep things in check. We're held to two sacred tenets. One forbids divulging our race to humans. The other bans any interference with human destiny."

"And the penalty?"

"Death."

Silence settled around them. Galena toyed with her food, and Ludan and Graylin stood motionless.

"That's why looking for me was a secret." Lexi's slate-blue gaze locked onto his, daring him to say otherwise. "You're not sure I'm Myren. I could be human and if anyone finds out, you're toast."

"It's possible you're human, but I doubt it. My dreams have been too pointed. For you to be anything other than Myren makes no sense."

"Dreams?" Her single-word question paired with an expression Eryx couldn't quite catalog. Curiosity for sure, but wary too.

"Yes. For about ten years now. They helped me find you."

Nibbling her lower lip, she gazed at the tabletop. Distant.

Not a good sign. When sharp women like Lexi went silent it usually went hand in hand with plotting, bad assumptions, or both. He had enough obstacles to jump where she was concerned without her spry mind adding more to the equation.

"Eryx, why don't you let me take care of your shoulder and give Lexi a minute." Galena stood behind the chair Ludan had vacated. "Lose the shirt, please."

Maybe Galena was right. Maybe Lexi was just overrun with information instead of plotting her escape.

He stood and stripped off his ruined shirt, wincing when a piece of burned-in fabric ripped his flesh.

Lexi snapped to, assessed what was going on, and shifted to sit in front of him. "We can talk if you want." She shrugged awkwardly. "You know, keep your mind off of it."

It took two, maybe three beats before he realized his mouth hung slightly open. She wasn't plotting to run. Or if she had been, she wasn't now. This woman, this brave, stubborn female who'd been carted off to a realm she'd never known existed, with a man she barely knew, was looking out for him. He cleared his throat. "What else do you want to know?"

Her attention drifted to Galena. "What are the other differences between us?"

Galena probed the burnt skin at his shoulder, and he sucked in air. "We're faster and stronger than humans, can move objects with telekinesis, and can communicate telepathically with those we're linked to."

Her gaze brightened and she sat an inch or two taller. "That's how you talked to Graylin and Ramsay before we got here."

"Exactly. Families are born with telepathic links between them. Think of it as a being able to pick up the phone and call or find your immediate family without needing the phone."

"But it's only between families?"

"To start with." He covered her hand. "But we can form links with others if we choose." One touch and his thoughts went screaming into dangerous territory. "Mates always form a link."

She shivered and yanked her hand out from under his. No matter how agitated she might be over her circumstances, her body answered to his in the most primitive of ways.

"All done." Galena tapped his healed shoulder and stepped away with a huff. "If you boys could stay out of trouble, I'd appreciate it." She frowned at Ramsay. "And do me a favor. Try not to make the next call sound like an emergency if there's no gushing blood or internal injuries. You know I always think the worst."

Drying his hands with a worn hand towel, Graylin stepped away from the counter where he'd been putting away utensils. "Eryx, why don't you take Lexi to your room." He nodded toward the windows and the rapidly rising sun. "It's darker below ground and she could probably use the rest."

The mere thought of Lexi anywhere near a bed sent a fresh charge of heated thoughts through his head.

"Don't get any bright ideas." Smirking, Galena lifted a vibrant yellow mug from a hook below the cabinet and poured herself coffee. "If Lexi's Myren, you could trigger her awakening, so keep your hot and heavy to a minimum."

Lexi stood, grabbed her mug, and stared out at the lake beyond the windows. Her elbows were tucked close against her sides, her back ramrod straight. "You didn't cover the awakening thing."

"We can talk about that after you've had a chance to rest." He cupped her shoulders and pulled her back against his chest. "A few hours couldn't hurt and you've already got a lot to process."

Lexi nodded, a tiny movement that didn't match her vibrant personality.

"I appreciate you letting us stay," he said to Graylin. "I'll get Orla to come help out while we're here."

Graylin waved his thanks off and headed toward his bedroom at the other side of the cottage. "Have her contact me if she needs anything. I'll make a run into town for supplies."

Galena held her mug to one side and half-hugged Eryx before pulling Lexi into another. "Eryx's right," she said to Lexi. "Rest before you bite off anymore information. You're safe here and have plenty of time to catch up on what you need to know."

She stepped away and gave Ludan a saucy pat on the shoulder. "I'm off to get cleaned up, but I'll be back later."

A straight shot of strasse fisted in one hand, Ludan situated himself in a kitchen chair. "I've got things here. Go." He lifted his chin toward the rear staircase and pushed the chair back on its rear legs. "Your woman looks like she's about to fall over."

Time alone. With Lexi. In a bed. More than enough reasons to bail. Besides, he'd need every second to strengthen their connection. Because there was still one frightening answer he'd yet to give her. One that might well send her running back to Evad.

~

LEXI HAD NEVER DONE MUCH in the way of drugs growing up, but damned if this didn't feel like the downswing of a week-long bender of something highly illegal. Eryx was touching her. Again. His hot palm at the base of her spine, he steered her through a shadowed hallway adorned with museum-quality knives and swords.

Her body was juiced—either from the coffee or Eden's extra energy. Ever since he'd lost his shirt in the kitchen, she'd had a hard time keeping her fingers to herself. If a man was going to put such fine muscles on display, a woman should at least get a chance to exercise a little tactile appreciation.

Eryx took one step down a sparkling onyx staircase and held out his hand.

The space below wasn't pitch black, but frighteningly close. "We're going underground?"

Candles set in wall-mounted sconces flickered to life and she jerked back.

Eryx chuckled, a slow delicious rumble that rippled across every nerve ending. "I'll always see to your needs, Lexi." The silver of his eyes darkened to a stormy gray. "All of them."

Her stomach flip-flopped and her thighs clenched. Never in her life had she been on the receiving end of such a look. Carnal promise without a lick of guile or pretense.

Where I come from a man doesn't play games. Partners honor what they feel and act on what they need.

Maybe what he'd said in the parking lot truly hadn't been

a line. The idea thrilled and terrified her all at once. She slid her hand in his, and his heat enveloped her. Candlelight shimmered off the glittery rock walls. "Don't you have electricity?"

"We don't need it. Our gifts cover what we need, and most of our people want to keep things as The Great One made them." At the bottom, Eryx motioned her forward. A giant set of arched mahogany doors sat at the end of a short hallway with two open rooms on either side. "That's not to say we don't do commerce with humans if there's something we need. Ramsay would go nuts if he had to do without a regular fix of technology and modern music. The first thing he does on a trip to Evad is power up his iPhone."

The double doors opened wide and she jumped, crashing into Eryx's unyielding form behind her. A draft of air rushed from the room, cool against her keyed up body. "That's going to take some getting used to."

"You'll get there." Eryx nudged her forward—another one of those subtle touches he couldn't seem to stop. Not that she was complaining. "No one expects you to adapt overnight." He strode past her to another, smaller set of double doors already open. "The bathroom is in here if you want to wash up. I'll see if I've got something you can sleep in."

Unlike the hallway's candlelight, the room had a soft pink glow. Lexi wandered toward the center of the big room and studied the floodlight-sized holes in the ceiling.

Well, I'll be damned. Myrens might not have electricity, but they had their own version of skylights to handle underground lighting. Handy. Especially since she couldn't pull off the fire tricks Eryx and his family could.

"This is the best I can do for now." Eryx strode toward the gargantuan bed situated against the far wall, a charcoal silk robe gripped loosely in one hand. "I've asked Orla to bring you some things until we can get yours from home." He tossed the robe on the matching comforter with its sapphire trim and braced one hand on one of the massive carved bedposts. "You all right?"

An image of her and Eryx, a tangle of limbs and heat on the silk sheets, flashed in her mind. The muscles low in her belly contracted and a flutter rippled at her core.

She needed to focus. Maybe get her head out of the soft porn business for a few minutes. "Yes, I..." She looked at the bed again and searched for the right words.

Eryx closed the distance and hugged her close.

His warmth seeped into her agitated muscles. Without the shirt, his scent was stronger, the sandalwood more prominent than the leather, but one hundred percent male.

She inhaled deep. Everything about him fit. Left her feeling comforted the same as when she'd woken from every dream. Was he the presence she'd felt there? Was she even ready to share such a detail with Eryx?

He cupped her cheeks and tilted her face, his lips so close she nearly moaned. "Do you want me to go?"

Go? No, not nearly the action she wanted. Not with his mouth a breath away. "I'm overwhelmed."

A muscle ticked in his cheek, and he scanned her face before focusing on her lips. "That makes two of us." Hot breath fanned her skin just before his mouth touched hers.

Sweet bliss. She fell into it without another thought. Whether her common sense was simply too fatigued to argue, or destiny had pulled rank, she didn't care. She craved him and was done with resisting.

He fisted one hand in her hair and slid the other down her spine, pressing her hips flush against his. Slanting his head, he deepened the kiss, his tongue slick against hers, his erection an insistent pressure at her belly. He groaned into her mouth and rolled his shoulders.

Shit! She tried to push away, deep crescents marking his

shoulders where her nails had been.

Eryx jerked her back in place. "No." He grinned, nipped her lower lip, and then licked it with a wicked swipe. "I like it." He skated his lips against hers, a wet silky glide that urged her lips to part. "Put them back." The growl behind his words…God, she loved that. Wanted more of it. Preferably louder while that sweet hardness shafted in out of her.

He crushed his mouth against hers and lifted her up, urging her legs around his waist.

She gave him what he wanted, latching her nails deep in his back and hanging on for dear life as he made for the bed.

A soft *swoosh* billowed around her. The soft mattress at her back, his hard body a delicious weight at her front, and those relentless lips….yeah, sleep was so not a priority right now.

An embarrassing whimper slipped past her lips as he drew away from the kiss, her hips lifting reflexively to make up for the loss.

"Easy." His grated whisper stirred the fine hairs around her face, tickling her cheekbones. His hot gaze trailed a slow, ravenous path from her neck to her breasts.

She sucked in a ragged breath. "What's wrong?" His hesitation whipped at her heart. No man held back when a willing woman and a bed were in the same room. Especially when said woman was already stretched out and panting to rival a triathlete. She planted her palms in the mattress to push away.

"Oh, no you don't." Eryx captured her wrists, pinned them on either side of her head, and nestled his lips below her ear. Warm breath fluttered against her skin. "You're perfect. Too perfect."

The scrape of teeth against her skin. It wasn't nearly enough. She wanted more, arched her neck to give him better access. To feel his bite and the slide of his tongue.

"I have to be careful with you, Lexi. More careful than I want to be." He punctuated the statement with the hot press of his lips at the curve of her neck.

She shuddered beneath him, pressing her breasts against his naked chest in a bid for attention.

Eryx trailed a path of kisses and licks along the neckline of her tank, his hips rocking into hers in a decadent rhythm. He savored the skin above the valley of her breasts and pressed a long kiss there before lifting his gaze. "We have to stop." He clenched his jaw, his eyes scrunching closed. "Praise the Great One, I want to take care of you, but we can't do this. I could hurt you."

Snaps of blue-white electricity arched above them.

Eryx pushed away before she could protest, and landed a good four feet from the bed, his breath as labored as her own. He jerked his chin toward the robe tossed in a pile at the foot of the bed. "Put that on and get some rest. I'll have Orla wake you in a little while."

"Aren't you tired?" God. What a lame question. Could she be any more bubble-headed?

His mouth crooked in a tortured smile. "Sleep won't come easy for me at the moment. I'll be fine. Ludan and I will be upstairs if you need anything." He angled for the door.

The unfamiliarity of the room, the weight of everything she'd seen, the denied passion—it all coalesced at once. "Wait."

Eryx looked up, his hand on the doorknob, and jaw locked tight. "Would you mind...."? Christ, she was screwing this up. And, gauging from the expression on his face, torturing him in the process.

The silk robe lay at the foot of the bed. To hell with that. "I'll sleep in what I've got on and keep my distance, but I'd like it if you stayed."

CHAPTER 6

$\mathcal{M}$axis pushed his unfinished breakfast away and sipped his coffee.

Skittish, Brenna kept her back to him at the sideboard whenever possible, her gait more delicate than normal.

Understandable. His early morning visit to her chamber had been harsher than he'd intended. A little stress relief for his lapse in judgment with Eryx in the way of Brenna's not so willing body.

His coffee cup clinked against its saucer. "Did you feed my guest?"

Brenna flinched. Hands gripped tight in front of her, she turned and bobbed her head, eyes averted.

"Good," he said.

A deep purple bruise stretched from her temple to her tightly clenched mouth. One strong wind and the tears would come again.

"Never underestimate a human," his grandmother had said. *"They're primitive beings and require a steady hand to keep them in line."*

Good advice he'd do well to remember. Humans couldn't

be trusted, especially the ones with soulful brown eyes. "Clean this up then head to your rooms. You've got one day's rest then you're back to your chores. Understood?"

Brenna nodded and set about gathering the used dishes, plates clattering beneath her jerky movements. With an impressive stack cradled against her chest, she turned for the door.

He lowered his voice, barely above a whisper, but thick with warning. "You wouldn't try to escape me would you, Brenna?"

She stopped and shook her head. A fork teetered, nearly tumbling from the pile.

"And what would happen if you tried?"

"I'd be lucky if I made it to another estate." Empty gaze locked on the wall behind him, she gave her deadpan recitation. "If I did, another Myren would kill me because humans are forbidden here."

Not an entirely true statement. Forbidden true, but unlikely another Myren would kill her. More like shuttle her off to one of the malran's do-good warriors. Definitely not a detail he planned to share with Brenna. "And if they don't?"

She paled and the dishes wobbled and clattered. "You'll find me and kill me yourself."

"Well done." He dipped his chin and lifted his coffee cup. "You're dismissed."

He sipped the dark brew and stared at the empty doorway. Too much wistfulness in her tone. Best to watch her for a few days and make sure she didn't do something stupid. Breaking in a new house slave was the last thing he needed. He'd do well to remember that the next time his temper got out of hand.

With a quick swipe, he wiped a trail of moisture from the corner of one eye. Blasted fucking sun. His sensitivity to light grew more pronounced as the color of his irises faded.

They'd once been as green as his grandmother's. Evanora's emerald gaze was purported as the first thing to capture the malran's attention two generations ago.

For all the good it had done her. Instead of ending up malress of the Myren race, she'd wound up pregnant, only to have Eryx's grandfather abandon her in favor of a commoner.

He stood and marched toward the guest wing. The thick crimson rugs muffled his heavy strides and the dark stained walls lent a welcome refuge for his vengeful thoughts. Evanora would have her revenge. It was only a matter of time before a Steysis sat on the throne and humans served the Myren race as they were meant. If he played his cards right, the grieving baineann stowed in his guest room might be the trump card he needed in his overall strategy.

Hysterical females were the last thing he'd willingly saddle himself with, but the one he'd found yesterday, prone and sobbing near his army's training ground, had been too good to pass up.

Well, the golden torc around her neck had been too good to pass up. A warrior's torc—presented to each warrior's baineann to denote her station. Between her tears and the faded bonding mark along her forearm, it didn't take a genius to deduce her mate had very recently died—most likely "on the job." And didn't that leave an ideal opportunity to leverage?

One more possible inroad to the Shantos camp.

He paused and stretched his senses out around the property, a smooth- surfaced net gauging for any unwarranted ping of energy. Brenna in the kitchen and his guest above, as he'd expected. Few Myrens knew of his home, let alone visited, but interruptions wouldn't serve his task.

Waiting outside the closed door, Maxis strained his ears for any whisper of movement.

Nothing.

He rapped on the door and stood back.

The gentle swoosh of fabric sounded, followed by soft footsteps.

The handle turned and Phybe's timid face peeked between the tiny opening, her weak smile belying her red-rimmed eyes. "Wesley."

Maxis stifled a harrumph. Barely. After seventy years hiding his identity from the bulk of Myren civilization one would think he'd choose his aliases with more care. "I hope you're feeling more yourself this morning?"

She pulled one pale pink lip between her perfect teeth and fidgeted with the doorknob. Her appearance matched her demeanor—pale, light brown eyes and unremarkable, straw-blond hair. The type of woman one might appreciate given enough time, but never one to call direct attention. Perfect for his purpose.

He nudged the door wider and let himself in. A flick of energy spread the curtains open wide, letting in the unmerciful sun. "I wanted to give you more time to sleep, but we need to get you back to your family. I'm sure by now they've noted you've gone missing."

Too much longer and they'd follow her link to his doorstep.

He strode to the small sitting area situated near the fireplace. Fruits and pastries covered the table, not a single piece touched. "I really wished you eaten."

She stayed grounded near the doorway, one hand against her stomach. Her pale blue cotton gown accented her fragileness. "My stomach can't abide the thought of food."

"Please." He motioned at the table and pulled a chair out for her. "Won't you at least have a zurun before I see you home? It would do my worried heart good."

The flowery words nearly made him retch, but they

worked. Joining him at the table, she peeled a bit of the baked confection between her dainty fingers.

He situated himself in the chair opposite her. "I can't have one of our fine warrior's baineanns going about uncared for, now can I?"

A shiver rippled through her tiny frame.

He let her stoke on her loss for a moment, counting each bite that passed her lips. "Would you care to talk about it?"

"There's not much to talk about." She took another bite. "He chased one of our criminals to Evad. Said humans were at risk because the man was violent. That's all I know. He'd barely been gone ten minutes before I felt a violent pain in my chest. The pain they tell you you'll fill when your mate dies—it's so much worse. I couldn't breathe or think. I just…ran."

She shoved away from the ivory plate.

He stood and held out his hand. "Have you contacted anyone in your family? Anyone at all to let them know you're safe?"

Phybe shook her head and stared at her food. "No. It's selfish of me, I know. I just can't…" She swallowed, ignoring the hand he offered, and clenched her fists in her lap. "I should have contacted his family, but I couldn't bring myself to do it. Not yet."

Maxis *tsked* in the most solicitous tone he could manage, cupped her shoulder, and urged her to her feet. "It's all right, my dear. You'll see. Your fireann's fellow warriors and their lovely wives will support you. I understand the malran is very supportive of those who suffer the loss of one serving our race."

Her lips pressed together in a shaky line and her eyes clamped shut. "It's customary for a baineann to present herself to the malran if her mate dies in service. I never thought I would be one to practice the observance."

Maxis pulled her close for a conciliatory hug, putting as much warmth behind the gesture as he could feign. "I'm sure the malran will be most sympathetic to your situation. Give him a chance to make things right."

Phybe pulled away, her face flushed, gaze darting in every direction but the one where Maxis stood.

"Let's get you home before your family can hear of what's happened from someone else. I'll see you there myself." Another hour in the infernal sun flying to Havilah and back was the last thing his tortured eyes needed, but losing the chance to get Phybe in the malran's good graces would be worse. If the malran's men hadn't yet come looking for the woman, they soon would. Maxis wanted her waiting and ready.

The trip went off with little conversation, only the barest essentials to gain direction to her home along the way. They flew through the air, their bodies at a respectable distance but for a mild line of cool weather. Maxis hovered close, sheltering Phybe from the brunt of the unexpected chill.

They touched down on the outskirts of an isolated village reserved for warrior families. The small, pleasant homes were a colorful hodgepodge of adobe walls and slate roofs, deep green plants dotting the scenery with their vibrant rainbow blooms.

"I'm afraid it's best I remain here, my dear." Maxis took her hand and laid a chaste kiss to her knuckles. "I wouldn't want any of your peers to get the wrong idea—you being seen with a strange man and all."

Phybe remained silent, her free hand toying at the torc around her neck.

"May I ask you one last question?" he said.

She gave a small nod and folded her hands demurely in front of her. "You do have friends to lean on here, don't you?

Someone you can talk to? I hate the idea of leaving you here alone at a time like this."

Her gaze dropped to her lap. "I suppose so."

Ah. Finally. He'd been prodding and hinting since he'd found her to no effect when all he'd to do was ask. "Perhaps you need a friend outside your current circle. I would be honored to offer you my link. You could call on me whenever you needed someone to talk to."

He paused, letting her adjust to the idea along with its implications. Linking with a Myren outside of family or mates wasn't taken lightly as it allowed two people not only to communicate telepathically, but also to locate each other. Other than the link a warrior made with his strategos upon his oath of fealty, such connections were rare due to the risks involved. It wasn't the type of act anyone knew how to take back.

Maxis set his face into a mask of sincerity and politeness and waited. Wariness sparked in Phybe's gaze. Had he misjudged the situation?

A trembling smile lit her face. "Yes, Wesley, I will link with you."

His inner predator purred with triumph. He'd won. He reached for her tiny hand. Slowly, so as not to startle her, he sent tendrils of his energy through their joined palms.

Her tentative response tickled through his skin, a delicate thread of pale pink in his mind's eye.

Latching onto it quickly before she could summon it back, he wove it firmly within his own. If the link provided him precious knowledge from within the Shantos camp, his gamble would be worth it. Particularly if he could use Phybe to prove Eryx had brought his delicious human into Eden.

He laid another, more reverent kiss atop her hand, the warmth of his success putting an extra bit of sincerity in the act. "I'm honored by your trust." He released her, reached around her to a shoulder-high bush, and plucked a flower about the size of her ear. The petals were the coral of an Eden sunrise, the flower's center a deep indigo with tiny white dots.

Phybe cocked her head and glanced between the bush and the flower in his hand.

"My grandmother once told me the krocious flower symbolizes a steadfast heart." He tucked the blossom between her blonde hair and temple so it rested in the ridge above her ear. "I'll be that for you, Phybe. You are not alone."

A tear slipped free and her lips quivered. "Thank you. Your comfort means more than I can ever repay."

Maxis tucked a strand of hair behind her other ear and smiled in what he hoped was something remotely sweet. "I'm sure someday I'll have to rely on you for some kindness. I only hope the malran shows a decent amount of contrition for the loss of one of our own, especially one lost trying to protect those vile humans."

Phybe shuddered and glanced toward the row of homes in the distance. He caressed her shoulder and turned her toward home. "Go. Contact your family. Let them know you're safe and then go see the malran. I'll come to check on you in a day or two. Would you like that?"

She nodded and trudged toward the village, disappearing into a villa with sunny yellow walls.

A chipper color, perfect for his mood. He'd had a very fortunate morning. And Phybe would definitely repay him.

Sooner than she could anticipate.

THE SOFT SNICK of a door latch nudged Lexi from sleep. Silk sheets caressed her cheek, and gray stone lined the walls. Not her apartment.

The previous night's events dominoed into place as she eased back the bed covers. Her heart slugged along at an unwilling pace and her thoughts staggered in a haphazard pattern. Where was Eryx?

Her gaze connected with a dark wooden trunk and she jolted upright. Not just any trunk, but an ancient piece of artwork with wrought iron handles and hinges—one that floated in the air, waist-high near the bathroom doors.

A full-figured woman who looked to be in her late fifties or early sixties poked her head around the still drifting box, and Lexi yipped.

"I waited until I thought you'd had enough of a nap before I brought your things." The woman lowered her hands as though she were motioning a church choir to sit.

The trunk dropped to the floor with a muted *thunk*.

"So much easier to handle these things on my own than wait on those boys to see to them for me." She dusted her hands, planted them on her hips, and hustled forward. "Now then. I'm Orla Weathers."

Cinderella's fairy godmother, cornflower blue gown and twinkling eyes included—except this version had silver hair to her hips, proudly displayed her curves, and didn't carry a wand. Kind of a fairy godmother gone flower child.

Orla plopped on the edge of the bed and pulled Lexi into a motherly hug. "I knew my Eryx was up to something. Had to be with him in Evad all the time, but the boy refused to talk." She edged back, but kept a hold on Lexi's shoulders. "Doesn't matter. He's found you now and that's what counts."

Try as she might, Lexi couldn't get any traction for her thoughts. A decent cup of coffee would fix it. Or at this point, maybe a case of Red Bull.

Orla's happy expression faded. "I'm so sorry." She stood and put a good three feet between them, twisting her fingers.

"I've completely startled you. And after the night you've had—"

"Wait." Lexi scissored her legs, not an easy feat with her jeans still on even if the sheets were slicker than sin. "Maybe we could try again?" She stepped forward and offered her hand. "I'm Lexi."

Orla took one glance at Lexi's outstretched hand and beamed, hustling forward. "Oh, sweetheart. I'm not shaking hands with the woman who's got my boy's heart. You're family now."

Strong arms wrapped around her once more, but nothing gripped her as tightly as Orla's words.

Family.

A steady warmth spread through Lexi's chest and her throat tightened. Maybe Orla had misunderstood her involvement with Eryx. Or had a penchant for drama and romance novels. "You're Eryx's mother?"

Orla pulled away, a wistful smile on her slips. "No, Eryx's parents passed to nirana many years ago. I'm the lucky woman who's seen to him and his team of hooligans since he came squalling into this world." She tapped the edge of the bed and bustled away. "You have a seat and I'll get these things unpacked for you." The woman might be past middle age, but she hustled with the energy of a two-year old. "If you want I can help you get a bath drawn before Eryx gets back. The tub in there looks decadent. Not surprising given Graylin's eye for fine things."

Lexi halfway listened while Orla pulled outfit after outfit from the case, none of which looked like anything from home. There were at least three simple gowns similar to Orla's, a stack of leggings and tanks like the ones Galena had worn—all silks or cottons in bold, jewel colors. Right behind those came four pairs of lovely leather sandals with sparkling beads woven into the design.

Orla chattered about Graylin and Ludan, how she'd been surprised to learn of the cottage, and that she had plans to lecture her boys about keeping secrets.

It was hard to follow the finer conversation details and catalog the trunk's contents at the same time. "Is all of that for me?"

Orla looked up, whatever she'd been talking about screeching to a halt. "I'm sorry." Lexi tugged at the hem of her tank top. "That's just a lot of clothes for a few days."

"A few days?" A wide-eyed blinky blink, but otherwise Orla stayed frozen in place.

"Well, I figured Eryx would bring me some things from home. Or I'd go myself and get some." Or would she be going back? Could she? And what about Ian? *Shit!* She looked around the room for her purse or phone. Ian had probably left a hundred voice mails by now.

Orla waved nonchalantly and grabbed another armful. "Oh, I've got those right here." Sure enough, she straightened with a pile full of Lexi's folded jeans and t-shirts. She winked, shuffled to the dresser, and tucked Lexi's clothes from home in the top drawer. "I thought you might like to give the Myren clothes a try. Evad fashions have their time and place, but Eden's fabrics feel so much softer."

"How did Eryx get my clothes? He doesn't even know where I live. And where is he anyway?"

Orla barely spared a backward glance. "From your memories I suppose."

Lexi stomped to the trunk and peered inside. "I don't appreciate people rooting around in my head." Two pairs of capris, a stack of shorts, not one set of pajamas or under-wear. Yep. She and Eryx were gonna have words.

"I'm sure he didn't mean any disrespect. It's just his way." Orla pried the handful from Lexi's clenched fingers and neatly tucked each piece into the next drawer. "A person in his position can't help but make snap decisions. Taking care of people is what he does."

"What is his position?" Finally, someone she could get to talk. "He said it was a leader or something?'

Orla slowed, twisted slightly and met Lexi's stare. "He's our malran." "Yes, I know, but—"

"I see you've met Orla." Eryx's deep voice cut through the room.

Orla and Lexi jumped at the same time, though Orla looked a bit guilty. Decked out in a fresh pair of jeans and a perfectly fitted gray t-shirt, he filled the doorway. He glowered at Orla and jerked his head toward the hallway behind him. "We'll be up in a bit. I need some time with Lexi." Imperial with a touch of pleasant.

To her credit, Orla looked undaunted, glaring at him with an equal amount of bite. The two scowled at each other silently for a minute.

Oh, yeah. Telepathy.

"It's not nice to talk behind people's backs." Lexi stalked into the bathroom and slammed the doors shut behind her the old-fashioned way. Hopefully, plumbing worked the same here as it did at home. Having to go back out and ask for help after such a dramatic exit wouldn't leave much of a lasting impression.

Give or take a few odd levers, the concept was universal. Still, she took her time nosing through the Grecian-themed room complete with floor- to-ceiling columns and twining ivy around a monster claw-foot tub. Eryx deserved to wait. She'd damn sure done her share of it lately. Now that she'd had a few hours to sleep, she felt a whole lot less inclined to let Eryx dole out bits of information as he saw fit.

After she'd doused her face and rinsed her mouth, she pushed the double doors wide and froze. Eryx lay on his side atop the now-made bed propped on one elbow. A veritable lion sunning himself on a hot rock.

"I don't like you getting in my head." There. Better to get right to business and make sure Eryx knew his boundaries. His slow, seductive grin unwound a good portion of her anger, which only made her want to throw something on principle.

"I don't see why not." His gaze raked her head to toe and he blatantly stroked the growing bulge behind his jeans. "You certainly get in mine. And under my skin."

Crude. And erotic as hell. Her mouth went dry and her skin prickled for touch. An invisible hand curled around her waist and tugged her forward until she tumbled onto the bed.

Before she could right herself, Eryx had her tucked beneath him, his hard length pressed against her thigh. "I won't take your memories again. Not unless you allow it." His lips brushed her forehead. "It's actually considered quite rude to do without permission, but I needed something to go on before I approached you."

God, if she could just think for a second. Maybe two. But his body... her wits couldn't rub two thoughts together. "Ludan didn't seem to have any qualms."

"Ludan *is* rude."

A laugh bubbled up from her belly. So light and unexpected. Free like when she was around Ian. "Point taken."

He ran his thumb across her lip, his gaze following the action. Hungry. Focused.

If she didn't start talking, she'd get zero answers. She brushed his hand away and tried to scoot out from under him. "We need to talk."

He hauled her back in place, captured one of her hands, and pulled it to his lips. With a playful nip at her knuckles, he smiled a smile to melt chocolate. "I've spent years trying to find you." He nuzzled the sweet spot behind one ear, and lowered his voice to a husky rasp. "My family's busy doing other things, and your sweet body's under me. The least you can do is let me touch while you interrogate."

Shockwaves rattled her and her eyelids fluttered shut. He'd known her less than a day and he'd already found one of her top three magic spots. "I can't think when you touch."

"Good." He dragged his lips along her jawline. "I'd rather you feel anyway."

Her body thrummed, very much on board with his plans. "No." How she pushed the refusal past her lips was hard to figure.

Eryx stopped cold, the languorous burn in his eyes banked by shrewd observation.

He'd been so playful. So light. "I'm sorry, I just want more answers." She tried again to push away, but he only pressed his weight more firmly against her.

With a grip on her chin, he steered her face to meet his. "No sorry. Not ever. No means no." He brushed her hair away from her face. "I told you we don't play games here. I meant it. When something bothers you, you tell me. When you want something…" The heat from seconds before crept back into his steel gaze. "You tell me that, too."

Oh, God. Didn't that leave an open playground for her eager mind?

Before she could realign her thoughts, he rolled to his back, taking her with him, and cradled against his chest. "Now," he said on an accepting exhale. "Ask your questions."

Crap. So many. There were always the basics. "Tell me why you think I'm Myren. I can't do any of the things you can do."

"None of us can until we're awakened." So matter-of-fact, like he wasn't rearranging her entire world while he drew lazy circles down her spine. "We're born with the same abilities as humans, but around eighteen to twenty-one we undergo an awakening ritual. The parents choose the age based on the maturity of the child."

She propped her arms on his chest to better see his face. "Why wouldn't you be born with your gifts?"

He grinned and stroked her shoulder. "I'd call it The Great One's safety precaution. You don't want a bunch of kids flying around with fire and lightning at their fingertips."

Well, at least he wasn't too far ahead of her on the learning scale. He couldn't be more than his late twenties, early thirties tops. "So you've only had your powers a few years. Right?"

Eryx's eyes crinkled deep at the edges and his laughter rumbled to touch places she'd never admit. "More like one hundred and thirty-four. I was awakened at eighteen, which makes me one hundred and fifty-two years young. By your standards, I'm in my early thirties. We live four to five hundred years, barring unfortunate events."

Well, didn't that put a new spin on things? "Kind of takes dating an older man to a new level." She traced the line of his sternum, the cotton of his t-shirt softer than silk. "How does it happen? The awakening?"

The lightness in his expression evaporated. Wherever the explanation was headed didn't look promising. "The ritual is private, only immediate family." His gaze grew distant. "The day before the event is a big celebration, as are the two to five days after."

"Why the gap? Why not celebrate right after?"

The smile came back and his laughter shook the bed. "Because no one's in any shape to celebrate until a few days after. The parents are wiped and the kid is amped out. It's like chugging espresso every half hour, every day for a week. No one feels up to a party."

"And you think I haven't been awakened?"

Eryx nodded.

"You said you think I'm one of your lost?"

Another nod, this one slower. "Some Myrens, for a host of reasons, choose to leave Eden and live out their days in Evad. We don't forbid it, so long as they keep the knowledge of our race from humans." He paused a moment and a tickle fluttered along her shoulders—not the good kind. "I saw your history in foster homes. We'll never know why your family left, but it certainly makes your Myren heritage plausible."

All the answers made sense. So why did she feel like she wasn't getting the Full Monty on information. "So what is it you're not telling me?"

Eryx tucked a strand of hair behind her ear. "I searched for you for a long time." So cautious, careful. "I woke up every morning raw from dreams as real as this moment. Now that you're here, I'm not in any hurry to give you a reason to run."

Shit.

Okay, so not great news.

Still, better to know than not.

She hoped.

Eryx sighed. "If you're Myren and you undergo the awakening, you'll have all the basic gifts known to our race plus one or two unique to you."

"And if I'm human?"

His jawline tensed. He sucked in a deep breath and held it for a handful of seconds. "You'll die."

CHAPTER 7

Eryx dropped from the sky and shook the entire manse with his landing. He stormed the castle entry, his gut a churning mess of irritation and grief. He'd wanted the dead warrior's baineann found, to know she was safe and to offer his condolences, but the timing was shit. Leaving Lexi still shell-shocked from the info bomb he'd dropped was hands down one of the hardest things he'd ever done.

Ludan landed and held Eryx back by the elbow. "She'll be fine. She's a fighter. Trust me."

"You think reminding me you know more about my woman's past than I do is a smart move right now?" The threat ripped past his throat, part whisper, part growl.

Ludan had the decency to flinch as he released Eryx's arm. "I wasn't thinking." An apology of sorts. Or as close to one as the Forte men ever gave.

It didn't kill his agitation with the world at large altogether, but it did ease the throttle. "If she runs—"

"She won't. She's not the type to panic." The sheer defiance of Ludan's jaw left Eryx more than a little edgy.

"Something tells me whatever you saw in her head, I

never want to know."

"Wouldn't be anything you could do about it now even if you did."

The cryptic comments weren't helping, a part of his subconscious plotting to rip the arms off whoever had hurt Lexi in her past.

One of the giant doors *kachunked* open and Galena stuck her head out. "Would you two hurry up? I can't keep these two apart much longer and Phybe doesn't deserve that bitch's interference."

Eryx downshifted. "Two? And who's Phybe?"

"Who's the bitch?" was Ludan's follow up.

Galena held the door open and did a mock sweep of her hand for them to enter. "Phybe is the mate of the warrior who died. She's in the parlor off the kitchen. It was the only place safe to store her until you got here."

Eryx started forward, Galena's rigid stance making his steps a tad more hesitant than normal. "And?"

"And your ex is in the formal receiving room."

Ludan ground to a halt at the same time as Eryx.

"Oh, hell no." Ludan spun toward the gardens fronting the castle with a backward wave. "Let me know when you're done."

"Some somo you are."

Ludan paused. "From Maxis and any other fire-breathing demon, sure. With that viper?" He shook his head and resumed course. "You're on your own."

Eryx looked back to Galena, still holding the door wide.

"Hey, we warned you," she said with a wise-ass shrug.

They had, but he hadn't listened. Serena Dorez had seemed like the perfect diversion over twenty years ago, a way to ease the loneliness of his never ending obligations. In the end, she wanted one thing and one thing only—his mark. She'd take out an infant if it stood between her and her goals.

"Don't call her my ex." Eryx headed for the parlor.

Galena lowered her voice and fell in behind him. "I'm going with you. Someone needs to protect that poor baineann if things go south. If Serena interrupts, you can throw yourself on the fire-breathing dragon and save us."

Sick as it sounded, a confrontation with Serena would be a damned fine outlet for the swirling pit of fire in his stomach. He hadn't had time for his daily natxu, let alone a healthy spar with Ludan. Maybe it was time Serena got a taste of her own medicine.

By the time they reached Phybe, his heart had settled into a more reasonable rhythm. The baineann stood when they entered and dropped to her knees in the most formal of greetings. "Malran."

"I think ceremony is the last thing required today." Eryx guided her to her feet. "If anyone should kneel, it's me."

Phybe's lower lip trembled, the pale pink color making her seem even more fragile. The skin around her eyes was puffy, and her pale skin splotchy at her cheeks.

His throat tightened and his eyes stung. Of all his duties, this act cut the worst, even beyond sending men into battle.

"Have you contacted your mate's family, Phybe?" Ever the gracious hostess, Galena swept forward and led Phybe to a nearby chair.

Phybe bobbed her head, wispy locks of blonde hair framing her face. "His mother is all he had left, but I contacted her this morning." She peeked at Eryx beneath her lashes then ducked her head. "I understand your men were searching for me. I shouldn't have run as I did. I'm sorry."

Galena perched on the arm of Phybe's chair and rubbed slow circles between Phybe's shoulder blades. "No one blames you for your actions. Losing the connection to your mate is said to be excruciating. I can't imagine I'd do anything different."

Eryx crouched in front of Phybe and grasped her cold hands. "I'm not angry, Phybe. None of us are. We take care of our own, and you are most definitely ours."

Phybe's shoulders shook and an indelicate sniffle echoed through the room.

"Do you have family or friends from your homeland?" Galena paused, waiting for her to look up. "Perhaps you could invite them for a visit. Someone to keep you company for a few days?"

Phybe shook her head and met Galena's gaze. "It's just my mother and father and they're older. Upsetting their routine would be too much for them."

"Well, then you can come and spend some time with me. Do you garden?"

Galena was good. Always had been in these types of situations. Her easy demeanor always pulled out the best in people, even the most challenging of personalities.

Unbidden, the thought of how Lexi might handle such duties rushed to mind.

"I'm afraid I don't know much about plants." For the first time, Phybe's lips lifted in a tremulous smile, her face wet with tears. "Those I have at home tend to run on the brown side."

"Well, then I have plenty for you to practice with and learn. I'll make sure to come by for you in the next few days and we'll get you indoctrinated."

"I'm sure the other warriors' wives will spend time with you the next few days as well," Eryx said.

Phybe went rigid.

Eryx sampled her emotions, careful to hide any stir of energy to give his actions away. A veil of shimmering gray hovered around her shoulders. Anxiety. Maybe fear. "Phybe, are you having problems with the women? If it's more comfortable, we can bring you here."

"No." Phybe sniffed and wiped her checks with one of her clenched fists. "Really, I'll be fine. I actually made a new friend today." She hiccupped and batted away another tear. "Last night, actually. He found me and brought me home."

She opened her hand and showed a tiny krocious flower mangled in her palm. "He gave me this." A ragged sound jangled past her throat. "I probably should have cared for it better."

Eryx picked the damaged bloom from her palm and twirled it. "It's perfect. Just like you." He tucked it behind her ear and tapped her chin. "I'm glad he found you and brought you home."

Phybe gave him a shaky smile. "I think my friend was wrong about you."

An odd statement. Eryx might have made some edgy decisions since he'd taken the throne, but most people approved of the changes.

Phybe smoothed out the fabric along her blue dress. "He thinks it's a shame my fireann died keeping humans safe from a Myren. But I think you're right to protect them."

Eryx sat back on his heels. It was true not every Myren loved humans, but most viewed them as equals.

"Oh, there you are." A dramatic voice rang through the tiny room.

Eryx and Galena groaned.

With a pointed look at Galena, Eryx stood and faced the worst decision of his life. "Serena."

Unquestionably beautiful. An angel's face with Satan's heart. She strode forward and her formal green gown billowed out behind her, a ridiculous adherence to the oldest of traditions. "I can't believe you didn't come to see me as soon as you arrived."

"I thought Galena told you to wait in the receiving room." Eryx positioned himself to block Phybe from Serena's view.

The bitch wouldn't recognize a fragile moment if she saw one.

"The receiving room is where unknowns wait for you, Eryx." She placed her palms against his chest and exhaled with a throaty purr. "I'm hardly unknown."

Eryx set her away. "Galena, would you see Phybe home? I need to handle this."

The two hurried from the room without a backward glance.

A glow tinted Serena's cheeks. "I'm glad you're home."

Praise The Great One, she was full of herself. He'd been gentle with her for years, opting for a soft end to their short relationship to avoid any bratty outbursts—not to mention keeping her highly affluent and politically minded family at bay. Now he had to think of Lexi. The last thing he needed was Serena trotting around the castle wreaking havoc.

He snatched her elbow and spun her around. Her gasp cracked through the room.

"It's time you and I had a candid chat." He pulled her into the kitchen and two of Orla's cooks scampered out of his path.

Serena tried to subtly tug herself free without tripping in her attempts to match his long strides. She lowered her voice. "Praise the Great One, Eryx. What's gotten into you? You're making a scene in front of the help."

Eryx kept moving through the long dining room. "The help. That's rich."

Now free of an audience, she leaned against his momentum and jerked harder. "Let me go."

He clamped tighter and plowed ahead.

"Damn you. Let. Me. Go." Serena's wild shriek rebounded off the stone walls.

The foyer in sight, he flung the main doors wide with a

burst of energy and spun Serena to face him. "I need for you to fully grasp what I'm about to say once and for all."

"I will *not*." The late afternoon sun spilled through the doors to surround her in a majestic halo. "You'll apologize for your treatment of me, particularly in front of servants, before we have any conversations." He grabbed both her shoulders and poured every ounce of frustration and anger from the last few days into his glare. "We. Are. Done. There is no us. There never really was and there most certainly will not be in the future."

Serena flinched and then froze.

Shit. Maybe that had been too much, but damn it he was tired of tiptoeing around the topic. "I've tried to be decent and let you down easy, but you've refused to listen. From now on you will exercise the decorum appropriate to one of my acquaintance and nothing more."

Beneath his grip, she tensed, and a mottled redness crept along her neck to her temples.

No remorse. Directness was his best bet with Serena if he wanted this done once and for all. "Are we clear?"

She edged closer, fearless as a cobra. "You dare to talk to me that way? Treat me this way in front of subordinates? I waited for you. Made myself a laughingstock. And you think you can speak to me like this?"

She eased back and straightened, a demented gleam settling in her otherwise pretty gaze. "I'll find a way to make you pay for what you've done to me. One way or another, you'll hurt as you've hurt me." With the regal bearing of a long-standing queen, she glided out the door.

Yeah, definitely right to be direct. The woman was insane. Pretty, but a nut job all the same.

He set out in search of Ludan. Full disclosure with Lexi and a three-man security detail might not be a bad idea for the foreseeable future.

CHAPTER 8

A hint of sun bled through the bedroom skylights to lift away night's shadows. Funny how Lexi's heart felt the same way. The last twenty-four hours had been a roller coaster of discovery and emotion, but she'd never been more alive. Like the first twenty-five years of her life were insignificant.

She nestled closer to Eryx and savored the quiet morning. His unique sandalwood and leather scent wrapped around her. Eryx seemed to think of everything. Even going so far as to take her to visit Ian the day before on the pretense of planning for an impromptu getaway to explain her absence. It was kind of nice having someone look out for her. Anticipating her needs before they even crossed her mind.

No matter how she might want to stick her head in the sand, she couldn't ignore the niggling thought in her head anymore. He had to be the presence from her dreams. She'd never seen a face, but she always woke with the same feeling she had right now. Content. Protected. He'd said dreams were what led him to her, so it only made sense her dreams would reciprocate.

"I can't read your thoughts, but I like where your emotions are headed." Eryx's husky voice teetered on decadent. He shifted until he lay half on, half off her, lips skating down her neck.

Hold up. She wiggled and shoved at his chest until she could see his face. "You can read my emotions?"

Eryx hung his head and sighed, not that he let her gain much distance. "Yes, I can read them." He leveraged himself so he rested on his elbows at either side of her head and his hair fell around them in a dark curtain. "It's one of my gifts. I turn it off and on at will, though when I'm asleep it's not so simple."

He studied her, breath slow and steady. "Things are different here, Lexi. You'll have to learn to accept new truths. New ideas. Who I am."

Yeah, but apparently on his schedule.

"Still doling out information as you see fit?" She tried to shove out from beneath him, done with the powerless chokehold he held on her.

"Stop it." Eryx held her in place, the lines of his face sharper than she'd ever seen them. "You're not the only one with fears. Not the only one afraid of how they'll be judged. You think it's easy for me? For any of us knowing how much or how little we should share without pushing too far?"

Lexi closed her eyes and swallowed around a swell of remorse. He'd been good to her. They all had. And here she was acting like a shrew. "You're right."

His triceps flexed beneath her palms. So strong. Solid. Like Eryx.

Everything she'd always wanted. "I keep waiting for everything to get ripped away. To find out what the catch in all this is."

Eryx dragged his thumb along her jawbone. "No catch.

Just the life you were meant to have. Assuming you choose to accept it."

There it was. The question dancing in her head with the grace of an elephant. Death was a heck of a lot more than an inconvenient side effect if Eryx was wrong and she wasn't Myren. The need to squirm and pace writhed beneath her skin. Room to move while her brain jackhammered at the consequences of her decision.

"You said Myrens can't divulge their existence to humans. Does that mean I can't have contact with Ian anymore?" It was the one consideration preventing her decision. The one, aside from death, with any potential to make her walk.

"You can't break the laws, Lexi. I've already pretzeled them bringing you here without proof. You can still be around him, but you can never tell him who or what we are."

She traced the curve of his shoulder. "But I can visit him."

Eryx nodded. "You'll have to be careful though. You'll move differently afterward. Contain more power. And you'll never be able to stay for longer than a few weeks. The environment drains you. It's why you felt so fatigued."

Lines of worry marked his brow. He commanded the people around him, whether he realized it or not, and had serious control issues, but she'd yet to sense even a flicker of true deceit in his soul. Her heart kicked up a notch. *Tell him.* "I want the ritual."

Eryx froze. "You're sure?" He held her tight, cradled between the steel beams of his arms.

The pounding in her chest strengthened and a swell of emotion pooled at the hollow of her throat. "I'm sure."

He exhaled, slow and ragged, one corner of his mouth lifted in an unsteady grin. "I'll ask Orla to arrange the celebration. Give you a few days to get—"

"No." She wriggled up a bit, needing a more confident angle to make her case. "I want it now. Today."

"Lexi, there's no rush."

"I talked to Graylin while you were gone yesterday."

Eryx stilled, his head tilted to one side.

"According to him, it's better for me to hurry."

No physical flames ignited, but Eryx's anger licked hot along her skin. "Graylin needs to mind his own business."

"But it's true, right? The longer I'm human, the longer you're exposed and I'm more vulnerable. Is that wrong?"

Eryx's jawbone looked as though it might snap at any moment, his muscles ripcord tight. "No, he's not wrong."

"Is there any reason not to do it today?" He shook his head.

"Then this is what I want."

The tumult in his gaze would have flattened her had she not already been horizontal, eyes flooded with both hope and terror.

He lowered his head and brushed a reverent kiss across her lips. "Your wish. My command."

ERYX SKIPPED another pebble across the lake's surface, tiny ripples echoing out from the twenty or so others he'd thrown before it. Still a lot more peaceful than the chaos rattling around in his head.

A perfect Eden day. Sunshine, spring weather, an easy lakeside picnic...ideal for Lexi's celebration day.

He should be excited.

Still doling out information as you see fit?

Lexi's comment still stung. He could only imagine the words she'd sling at him when the day was over—assuming she lived that long.

"Stop fidgeting, Eryx." Orla's snap matched her towel's sharp pop as she shooed an eager fly from the food.

Ramsay, Graylin and Ludan stood beneath the frius tree's tall branches, their voices void of the strain clogging his own throat.

"It's perfectly normal for a woman to take her time getting ready." Orla smoothed an unseen wrinkle along the vibrant blue linen tablecloth. "Especially when her man leaves her a beautiful gift."

A deep sapphire gown accented by a platinum belt encrusted with diamonds, and cuffs to match. Bold, like the woman. Damned if he didn't have the drive of a horny teen backed up with the lust of a seasoned warrior. He should be patient. More balanced.

A cool spring breeze floated across the water's surface and brushed his face, but did zero to sooth his need to pace. "What the hell's taking them so long? I sent Galena in there to help, not add hours to the process."

"Perhaps Galena's adding to her Myren education. We've already established Lexi knows nothing of mating, let alone that you want her for your own." Orla tossed a hand towel on the chair he'd vacated and planted her fists on her hips. "From the sounds of things, she doesn't even know you're the malran."

"She knows." A petulant answer, but he was past the point of caring.

"But does she know what a malran is?" Orla tottered closer, insistent.

The smooth surface of the lake barely rippled. Too bad his patience didn't match. "In a manner of speaking."

"Whose manner, may I ask?"

Something snapped. One second the lake filled his vision, the next he towered over the woman who'd all but raised him. "I told her I was our leader. We'd only just met and she knew nothing of our race. Should I have explained I was her equivalent of a king right off the bat?" He threw his hands up. "Oh wait, you'd have me also tell her I want her as my baineann right after I'd carried her through a portal and thrown fire from my palm!"

He faced the lake and fought to calm his raging breath. Heavy gazes burned into his back, the peace of the spring silence awkward. He'd never advanced on Orla like that before. Ever.

"Forgive me." Orla's voice floated to him, consoling. "I was only thinking of Lexi. I didn't consider the obstacles in your path."

A sharp ache pulsed at his jawline, his teeth clenched tight enough to smooth his molars. Shame hung heavy around his neck. "I should apologize to you."

Closing the short distance between them, he pulled Orla to his chest and kissed the top of her gray head. If he couldn't keep his emotions in check, he'd never make it through the night. Not with the deception ahead.

A throaty chuckle rumbled from Ramsay's direction. The grin on his twin's face grew to a full-on smile as he crossed his arms. "You're a lucky man." He jerked his head toward the garden gate. "Prepare to walk the gauntlet, brother."

Sweet Great One on High.

Lexi strolled along the winding path, Galena beside her. The flowers, the waving grass, the muted stones on the home behind her—all background details to her focal point. Midnight-colored hair, loose about her shoulders. Tanned skin wrapped in a body-hugging blue gown. Pride tried to get him to shut his slack jaw, but the rest of him was too shell- shocked to care.

The perfect malress.

Primal instinct pounded at him.

Take.

Protect.

Indulge.

No. Not yet. She needed him to guide and teach her. Not sling her over his shoulder and stomp off to some hidden cave.

Rounding the last curve on the path, Lexi met his rapt stare. A blush stole across her face and her fingers fluttered at her sides.

Eryx pushed open the garden gate, his movements harsh and embarrassingly gawky.

Galena slid past them, eyes diverted with a know-it-all smirk.

He cupped Lexi's elbow, drew her closer, and slid his hand until he'd circled her wrist. It seemed so small and vulnerable, the flutter of her pulse frantic beneath his thumb. He kissed the delicate spot. "I've seen many beautiful things, but nothing moves me like you, Alexis." He pulled her close, the sweet scents of rosemary and mint clinging to her skin. No matter what it took, he wouldn't give up. She was his mate…whether she realized it yet or not.

CHAPTER 9

*E*ryx caressed Lexi's back, and a heightened, sensual awareness washed across her in a white-hot mass. He didn't seem to give a fig for their audience. The more he touched her, the less she did either. Could he tell Galena had talked her into wearing nothing underneath?

"Your gifts are beautiful. Thank you." Her lips trembled as she spoke, her voice whispering a need that didn't match her proper words.

Eryx shifted and the silk of her gown teased her thighs and stomach. "I like you in Myren clothes." His guttural words stroked her in all the right places. A wicked smile crept into place, and he tickled the hollow at her throat with rough fingers. "I like what's missing underneath even better."

"Praise the Great One, Eryx. Stop pawing her so we can eat." Ramsay's lighthearted comment cut through the sexual haze.

Orla chirped orders to the men, and Galena guided Lexi to the head of a large table beneath a mammoth shade tree.

Feathery sea foam leaves danced above her. The tree's branches spanned the width of a small home and bathed their party in nap-worthy shade. At its furthest reach, over the edge of the still lake, one lone branch dipped to kiss the water's surface. Ironic how similar her life had become. Drawn to something so much bigger, dipping in one tiny toe but ready to go under.

Voices chattered. Random personalities perfectly interwoven as a group. She'd never believed such bonds existed. Those were fantasies. Created in books and on the big screen. God knew she'd never experienced it in any of the homes she'd lived in. But this? They quipped and laughed with each other with a familial trust she couldn't quite grasp.

"You're a part of it now, you know." Graylin leaned forward and the wooden chair groaned beneath him. His expression matched the one Ian often sported—sage, know-it-all, and fatherly. "They're giving you space and time to adjust to their antics, but they're your family now."

Lexi's heart lurched at the thought. A family of her own. People to banter with. People to love and watch out for who would do the same for her.

No. It wasn't possible. They'd only just met her.

"Don't try to make sense of it," Graylin said. "Some things just are. You accept them, give thanks, and go on."

Lexi fidgeted. "You make it sound simple."

A smile flickered on his face. "Most things are simple until our minds complicate them. Your mind, in particular, appears to be a trouble maker."

An indelicate sound lurched from Lexi—somewhere between a cough and a hiccup. She waited for her brain to serve some witty retort, but nothing came.

Galena swatted Ramsay's hand away from a large bowl, while Eryx and Orla prepped two large platters of meat.

Maybe Graylin was right. Maybe it was as simple as jumping in. To let the current sweep her into the fray. Lexi cleared her throat. "Was your celebration like this, Eryx?"

The chatter paused.

Stares bounced back and forth between everyone. And holy shit, was that a blush on Eryx's cheeks?

He finished carving the slab of meat in front of him. "No, it was bigger. But then my parents had time to plan. Dad loved a good celebration."

"Celebration my ass." Ludan stacked a pile of dishes at the end of the table, the plates clinking. "It was a damned national holiday. For both of them."

Wow. That big of a deal? "You both went through it at the same time? I thought it was hard on the parents?"

"It is and it was." Eryx tossed an annoyed look in Ludan's direction. "Our parents were wiped for days which left the two of us plenty of time to explore our gifts while they recovered."

Orla lightly cuffed the back of Eryx's head. "You may have left your parents alone but you were holy terrors for me. I'll swear I bandaged you boys for two days straight with your aerial antics."

Lexi giggled as she tried to imagine either Eryx or Ramsay doing anything graceless. Somehow the image wouldn't compute. "Were either of you scared?"

"I was scared shitless," Ramsay said with a grin. "Eryx was too, even though he pretended not to be."

Eryx laughed and threw the hand towel he'd been using at his brother's head. "Try to keep my image intact for my woman."

His woman. The words sent a loop-de-loop thrill through her belly. So possessive and dominant, which should have rubbed her the wrong way, but did exactly the opposite.

Eryx's seductive gaze settled on her, and pleasant ripples fanned out across her skin.

"Ah, yes. Your manly image. Let's see…" Ramsay coughed dramatically and placed a theatric hand at his chest. "He's the soul of bravery, wisdom and discipline. Women flock to him and he has no equal in the sensual arts." Ramsay picked up whatever bizarre entree he'd been working on and placed it in the center of the table with a raised eyebrow. "That work better for you?"

Ludan rolled his eyes. "I think the short version is 'Well hung and loaded.'"

More laughter and commentary bubbled up, not a bit of it as interesting as watching Eryx move. Innocent actions, handing out drinks to his family and helping Orla when needed. Simple. And here she was with her brain on vacation and her hormones on overdrive.

Flock to him in droves indeed. The idea of another woman approaching him, let alone touching him, sent her nails digging deep into her palms. She'd likely be arrested in under a week for murder.

Eryx dragged her to her feet and hugged her tight. He nuzzled her ear. "Let go, Lexi. Whatever's in your head right now, you've got nothing to fear. Not from me."

In slow degrees, her pulse slowed and her skin cooled. Eryx pressed a cool, watermelon colored drink into her hand and lifted his own. "A toast to Alexis. May her journey tonight be swift and the gifts she receives suitable for her new life in Eden."

Cheers rang out and each member added their own best wishes. Food was passed around the table and drinks refilled at a steady rate. With each drink, Graylin, Ramsay, and Orla grew more animated, though it seemed a bit bass-ackward they got the spiked drinks and she went cold turkey.

Orla brought out a tray of miniature-looking mudslides, and Eryx pulled Lexi from her chair, settling her on his lap so she reclined against his shoulder.

He traced the outline of her face, the care and sincerity written on his face so overpowering her lungs refused to work. "I need you to trust me tonight, Alexis. Completely. Can you do that?"

Her throat tightened. This wasn't a matter of sharing an intimate secret or guarding a respectable sum of cash. This was her life. Staring into his eyes, she reached for her inner compass. Listened for the quiet voice that had always guided her.

A calm strength bloomed inside her chest. Love. So faint. Easy to discredit as wishful thinking. Definitely too soon. Better to set the concept aside. "I trust you," she said instead. "I know you'll take care of me."

Eryx pressed his lips against hers, a simple, reverent kiss. His hand tangled in her hair and he rested his forehead against hers as his eyelids slid shut. "May the Great One make your journey a fast and easy one," he whispered. "I need you here with me."

Lexi hugged him, something about his demeanor pricking at her instincts. "I'll be fine. This is right, I know it is." She sifted through his thick hair and the memory of him looking down on her this morning leapt to mind.

His chest expanded and collapsed on steady breaths. He met her steady gaze, nodded, and handed her one of Orla's chocolaty concoctions. His smile lacked its usual fullness. "Then you'd best have your dessert so we can get on with things."

Condensation coated the glass and a cool bead slipped over her fingers. What was she missing?

He nudged the drink toward her lips. "You're thinking too hard. Enjoy." She tilted the glass for a sip and moaned. Sweetness to rival Godiva's milk chocolate with a delicate bit of mint. A pleasant distraction of the highest order. And there was booze in it. Definitely a plus on the stress management side.

She took another drink. Then another. When she sat the

glass down, more than half was gone. "That's good, Orla. What kind of liquor is it?"

Galena's gaze darted to Eryx then back to Lexi. "It isn't alcohol."

Seven desserts on the table. One empty and the rest untouched. Her facial muscles loosened, skin slackening as though it might slip right from her skeleton.

"It's a Myren sedative." Eryx's voice was warm and soft at her ear. "It's better this way. Less apprehension for you." His fingers at her hip tightened. "You said you'd trust me."

Her brain wouldn't work—not like normal. Closer to day-old oatmeal and a fine strainer; shit was going nowhere fast. Fury prickled through her bloodstream, but it couldn't compete with the thick lethargy. Her eyelids lowered even as her heart screamed in betrayal. "You lied to me."

A PACK of Harleys rumbled down the street as a pair of chatty joggers nearly crowded Maxis off the sidewalk. He hated Evad. Even the less populated cities like Tulsa were loud and polluted compared to the natural beauty of Eden. And the technology, nothing more than novelties. Poorly designed toys to distract humans from their empty existence. He'd lost count of the gadgets he'd destroyed, his Myren energy melting the guts with little more than a push and a swipe.

The antiquated apartment building on his side of the street was straight out of the fifties with its generic red brick and crackling white paint trim. Wrought iron bars over the windows didn't say much for the place.

The park across the street was more updated, as was the trendy restaurant perched over the Arkansas River on massive steel beams. Zigzagging between them were more joggers clad in outfits to rival a neon rainbow.

Better to get on with his mission and leave the chaos behind. Mere supposition that Eryx had taken his new toy to Eden wouldn't suffice with the ellan. He'd need proof.

Eryx had stumbled beautifully sending one of his minions to retrieve Lexi's belongings—nearly hand delivering her home address to his contact within the Shantos camp. The odds he'd find any evidence in her lodgings were slim, but it was a fine place to start.

He yanked open the weathered screen door and pushed wide the glass- paned door behind it. Dank, stale air filled the shadowed stairwell. Four apartment doors marked each corner, with a sea of industrial gray tile to connect them.

Maxis strode to a set of mailboxes set into the center wall. Eight uniform slots in tarnished brass noted tenants in unmatched labels.

Alexis Merrill.

A heady buzz skimmed beneath his flesh, but he tamped it down. Excitement had already led him to one misstep with Eryx. He couldn't afford another.

A quick check of the numbers on the doors—one through four. He needed number eight. The top floor for the malran's new toy. How sweet.

Three steps from the top, a door opened, the brass eight catching on sunlight from the interior. A middle-aged man in a blue button down and faded jeans stood at the threshold, a stack of mail in his hands.

Maxis slowed his steps and scanned the three remaining apartments for activity. One with an animal, two others vacant. With a curt nod, Maxis angled toward the one next to Lexi's and made a show of digging in the front pocket of his jeans.

The man pulled Lexi's door shut and shot her deadbolt into place with a flick of his wrist.

Maxis feigned a worried glance at the man then pretended to shove his non-existent keys back into his pocket. "I don't think we've met." He held out his hand. "Are you a friend of Alexis?"

The man considered Maxis' outstretched hand for an uncomfortable string of seconds. A none-too-subtle warning. He accepted Maxis' palm. "Ian Smith." His gaze slid to the door behind Maxis. "Lexi didn't tell me she had a new neighbor."

Maxis scanned Ian's mind. A retired cop turned investigator. Ian's memories were full of little else, at least in recent years.

Ian tugged at his hand.

"Forgive me." Maxis let go and sidestepped toward the door he'd pretended to be his own. "I've only met Lexi once since I moved in, but she seemed a nice girl. One can't be too cautious when looking out for a young woman."

Ian scrutinized Maxis from head to toe. A shrewd old man with a penchant for details.

A complication he could do without. If Maxis was smart, he'd eliminate the threat. Make the man a missing person before he could mention meeting Maxis to Lexi. Then again, good outlets for info were hard to come by.

"I apologize for holding you up." Maxis turned for the door he'd indicated as his and mentally flicked the lock. He opened the door only enough to slide through then closed it behind him with an unhurried *kachunk*.

He stepped deeper into the vacant apartment and waited. Ten seconds. Twenty. Thirty.

Praise the Great One, would the man ever leave? Footsteps sounded on the wooden stairs.

Finally.

Maxis drew in a steady breath, tracking Ian's energy out into the parking lot. He peeked between the bedroom's dusty blinds. Lexi's friend tossed the mail into the passenger's seat and folded himself into a pathetic sedan.

Maxis tapped his lips. A woman across the street pushed a too-chubby toddler in a swing. A duck trailed two laughing young boys with a sackful of bread.

Ian's memories hadn't given him any proof, but had shown Eryx and Lexi together the day before, announcing an unexpected trip out of town.

He closed the blinds and left the musty apartment. He'd search Lexi's apartment next. If that didn't work, he could always pay Phybe a visit and see how her presentation with the malran went. Maybe the trip they'd mentioned was to Eden. If so, all he'd need was one confirmed sighting and he'd have everything he needed to put Eryx's downfall into play.

exi basked in a deep, dreamless sleep. Something pricked her consciousness. Something important. It wiggled along her senses with a fine static electricity, silent and mysterious. Like the dreams she'd had as a kid where she wanted to wake up—needed to badly—but couldn't lift her eyelids no matter how she tried.

Delicious heat settled along her side and the clawing need to surface subsided. Her spirit curled into the unseen haven and nestled into the dark restful place where worries and fears didn't exist.

A voice reached to her, faint, far away. "Stay strong for me."

The musky, worn scent of leather and spice tickled her nose. Odd. She'd never been able to smell in her dreams before.

A velvet touch skated along her temple and a whisper tickled her ear. "I love you." The words barely registered. Had she heard them right? Oh, wait. This was a dream. No one had ever said those words to her. She was just—

Nnnnguuuaaaah! Lexi arched against a violent, blistering pain in her chest. A scream gathered in her throat and lodged tight, her airway barricaded by pure agony.

Not a dream. A nightmare. She tried to move, to run, but her arms and legs wouldn't cooperate. Her lungs hitched—two gasps in, five huffs out. The space where her heart was supposed to be hummed with a nerve-numbing current that radiated everywhere.

A presence flittered in her mind and a sizzle zapped along her synapses. "Who's there?" Her grated question echoed against a mist of nothingness. Maybe she was hallucinating. The last thing she remembered was Eryx and—

The drink. Eryx had drugged her. Her stomach lurched and a wail ripped past her throat. She hadn't thought the pain could get worse, but she was wrong. Eryx's betrayal clawed her from the inside out and mingled with the H-bomb mushrooming in her chest.

Light flickered in the soupy fog of her nightmare. She shuddered hard enough to rattle her teeth and darkness crept along the edges of her mental vision. A string of enraged shouts registered somewhere in the distance, the words too vague to process.

She needed relief. For someone to lift the five-hundred-pound branding iron from her chest and let her roll over and die.

Sparkling white exploded in her mind's eye and shoved at the darkness. Galena strode through the mist, her sunshine-colored dress billowing out behind her, her face schooled for battle.

Lexi curled her dream self into a ball. Each thrum of her pulse ricocheted until she thought she might shatter. She couldn't keep going. Didn't want to.

Cool fingers wrapped around her huddled shoulders and her pain shifted. Lexi froze. One minute she'd been on fire, unable to process beyond the pain. The next, she was centered and wrapped in feminine arms. She shifted for a better look.

"Don't move." Galena huffed as though she'd run a marathon. "We've had to fight for hours to reach you. If I lose contact with you everything you were feeling will come back."

Moving. Pain. Bad. Got it.

"Fire." The one word nearly killed her. The torture hadn't ceased after all. Was merely held at bay by Galena's touch.

Galena stroked Lexi's trembling arms, her body not exactly spooned against Lexi's back, but close enough to comfort. "It's your awakening." The dream landscape changed and a bit of the tension in Lexi's belly uncoiled. Above them stretched an endless black velvet sky dotted with silver and diamond stars. "I've got control now." Galena's voice eased, her words a steady croon. "Relax and let me help you. This is normal. I promise."

Her awakening. Memories dive-bombed her with the same intensity as the burn still spreading through her despite Galena's efforts. This was it. She was in it.

And Eryx had tricked her. Fury jumped on top of the pain, demanding retribution.

"You've got to relax, Lexi. We've been at this for over four hours and your body can't take much more. Eryx is so worried he's a mad man."

"Drugged me." Lexi coughed the accusation and breathed through the vicious stings beneath her skin.

"Of course he drugged you. It's custom. No one walks into their own awakening." A fatigued chuckled rumbled in Galena's chest. "Well, except Eryx and Ramsay. But they're idiots."

A bit of Lexi's self-righteousness anger swapped seats with the bite of embarrassment. "Custom?"

"Mmm hmm." Galena stroked her forehead, an absent yet caring touch.

Lexi moaned. This is what it would have been like if she'd had a sister.

Or a mother.

Anyone.

"It's better for the person being awakened to be relaxed so the anchor can slip more easily into their mind. Even with the sedative, you fought my entry."

"I was pissed."

"So I learned." Galena tucked a strand of hair behind Lexi's ear. "You've really got some trust issues, girlfriend."

Quiet from her peanut-gallery brain. Hard to argue with facts. "I'm dreaming?"

"Sort of. More of a drug induced hypnosis, for all the good it did us." Her lilting voice settled into Lexi's burning pores. "You're going to be fine now. Think of things you find pleasing and let go."

"Eryx?" She croaked the question.

Galena laughed, but it was a weary one. "Are you saying you find him pleasing, or asking about him?"

"Okay?"

Galena sighed, so much unspoken emotion behind the sound. Frustration. Anger. Fatigue. "He's exhausted, but he'll be fine. He won't let anyone else funnel energy to us, so Ludan and Ramsay are feeding him. Stubborn man. Now relax and stop worrying. His ego is big enough."

Her smoldering soul sighed with relief. "How much more?" The way her voice cracked she wasn't sure Galena understood the question.

"You've been at it a long time—longer than anyone anticipated." Galena's usually smooth tone had its own grit.

Lexi dragged her eyes open through sheer will. Galena's pale face hovered over her, lines bracketing her mouth. "Hurting you."

"I'll live." Her face dipped closer, eyes narrowed. "And I expect you to as well. If not for yourself, then for my brother."

HEAVY CLOUDS HUNG above Maxis as he flew toward the furthest reaches of Asshur. Dark rough rock stretched as far as the eye could see, hiding the isolated stronghold he'd been building for the last fifty years.

He rounded the last of the craggy mountains, and a heavy clasp of pride gripped his heart. Absolutely nothing to boast about—which was precisely the point. No one would easily find this garrison.

Landing in a well-hidden cranny, Maxis stretched his senses a good hundred yards. The subtle energy of those who waited inside pinged against the smooth-as-glass surface, but otherwise the area was desolate.

He ducked behind a jutting wall of rock. Darkness. A sweet relief to the stabbing sun, broken only by distantly spaced sconces with low, simmering coals farther down the tunnels. Were it up to him he'd have forgone any light. His sun-beleaguered vision navigated the darkest environs with perfect clarity, but his guests and guards weren't blessed with such skills.

A draft caressed his neck and the pungent scent of dirt filled his lungs. Each footstep landed with a punctuated clip against the black path. Gaining ammunition to use against Eryx and his throne was one thing, but his real plans lay minutes ahead. The big picture strategy to advance the Lomos Rebellion and ensure his place as ruler.

The thought wrenched his gut tight. Everything his grandmother had fought for, so close. His father had proven a failure, for the rebellion and his only son. More abusive and coddled than respected leader. His mother hadn't offered much more, abandoning him when he was barely nine and choosing an unborn child sired by a human over him. But Evanora... she'd been steadfast. The one person he'd been able to count on. Would she be proud? Respect the actions he was about to take?

He rounded the final bend. His colleagues sat comfortably around the fire pit, female slaves at their feet in simple, white cotton gowns. A common sight among his people if his plans came to fruition.

"Good of you to meet me, gentlemen." Refreshments lined the buffet behind them, an elegant display of cheeses and bite-sized meats barely touched. "I trust you've found your accommodations satisfactory?"

Grunts of agreement rumbled through the dome carved room as Maxis circled the arched row of elegantly carved chairs. He greeted his first guest, scanning the man's recent memories. "She didn't see to your needs, Thyrus?"

The slave ducked her head another inch.

Thyrus' chest puffed up and his multiple chins wobbled with an off- handed shake of his head. "No, but then I didn't push the ma—"

Maxis struck, coiling his fingers around the woman's neck in a brutal grip.

Her scream pierced the room and streaks of blue-white electricity sparked from her convulsing body. The veins at her temples strained, fingers clawing against his grip. A choked gasp. Dazed eyes.

Done. He released his grip.

The woman slumped to the floor in a boneless heap. The pristine white of her gown stood out against her red, blistered skin and a tinge of burnt hair tainted the air.

"I was very specific about your instructions." He kept his voice low and even, barely loud enough to carry over the crackling fire behind them. "Find your place. Now."

The woman pushed on trembling arms to her knees and her curly chestnut hair spilled over, hiding her face. Tears dropped to the cold, stone floor.

Maxis faced his remaining guests. "Reese. Cutter."

Cutter was an unremarkable man. Moderately built with lackluster brown hair and an average appearance.

Reese was the opposite. An imposing force with a warrior's build, and hair like a lion's mane, he glared at Maxis with nothing short of condemnation. "Was that necessary?"

Maxis shrugged and circled away from the men. "It's efficient." He sprawled in the throne-styled chair opposite his guests. "While you may not yet be fully on board with the ideals of the Rebellion, I expect you'll hold your counsel until you hear what I have to say. Agreed?"

Reese tossed a food scrap into the pit. "You didn't leave me much of a choice." The leather of his fitted coat groaned as he reclined into his seat. Of the three, Reese presented the greatest challenge, the one least inclined to submit.

The one Maxis wanted—damn near needed—in his camp.

Maxis crossed a leg over one knee. "The Rebellion's lost too much ground since Evanora's demise, thanks largely to my late father's poor leadership. I'm prepared to fix that. To take the steps necessary to forward our principles among our people."

"Or you could let the Rebellion die." Reese stared at Maxis from across the room, his expression as deadpan as his statement. "It's an antiquated belief at best."

"A statement I'd expect from a man who trained to serve the malran." Maxis steepled his fingers, warming from the buzz of adrenaline. "One would think with the way he turned you away you'd have a bit more incentive to see someone else on the throne. Someone who appreciates your skills."

Reese scowled.

"I'll get back to that." Maxis focused on Thyrus. "We need to expand our audience. Find an ally within the ellan."

Thyrus sat a little taller and fiddled with the expensive rope belted around his burgundy solicitor robe.

"I'm sure you've heard the grumblings from council members of late," Maxis said. "I've personally witnessed the malran spending an inordinate amount of time in Evad. Both our government and our citizens are questioning why. We'd be fools not to leverage the situation and find an ellan eager to align with us."

The three men exchanged furtive glances. Cutter shifted in his seat, his gown similar to Thyrus', but pale green and several notches down in quality. "You realize we risk our identities with such an approach. We could be charged with treason."

Maxis smiled to cover his irritation. "That's why we find the *right* ellan. One discontent with the malran and his behavior of late."

Cutter drummed his fingers on his thigh.

Thyrus shrugged and snagged a slice of cheese off the plate on his side table. "Reasonable. Tricky, but reasonable."

Reese sat silent and unmoving, his broad shoulders making the two men at his sides look infinitesimal.

Maxis stood and paced before the fire, hands clasped behind his back. "Not as tricky as you might think. Especially if we find one with a valuable secret to ensure our own are kept." He halted directly in front of Reese. "You're familiar with this practice, aren't you Reese? You, of all people, know the value of keeping certain secrets buried."

Reese glared hot as the fire pit at Maxis and fingered the hilt of the dagger anchored at his hip.

"You're the key to the second step in my plan," Maxis said. "With you as our strategos, we can build an army. A fully trained contingent that will force the malran and the ellan to respect our beliefs." He lowered his voice, taunting. "I've got the land to train them. All we need now is you." Unmoving, Reese held Maxis' gaze. He'd been rejected as a warrior for the malran, deemed unworthy to serve for the secret he refused to share with Ramsay at his swearing in. A secret Maxis had used to bring Reese here today. A secret powerful enough to build a partnership.

"This is your chance to use your skills. To show what you're capable of." Maxis held out his hand. "All I ask in return is a link so show your support. Are you with us?" He let the unspoken, *Or do I share what you fear most with anyone who'll listen,* hover in the air.

Reese's pupils dilated and a flush tinted his cheeks. He took a good long look at the exit then focused on Maxis. "Agreed." The terse acceptance barely made it past his rigid lips, but he clasped Maxis' hand nonetheless and speared his link into Maxis' palm.

Pain. Sharp to his shoulder. Maxis welcomed it, a secret shadow in his soul settling on a sigh as he wrapped his own spirit around Reese's energy and forged the connection.

He pounded Reese on the shoulder, a weight he hadn't realized he'd carried now lifted from his chest. "That leaves us one last item to cover, gentlemen." Maxis ambled in Cutter's direction and stopped near his kneeling slave. He fingered a lock of her hair. "You've enjoyed the use of her?"

Maxis didn't need to scan Cutter's thoughts to know how thoroughly he'd used her. Cutter had his own secrets. An impulse to force himself on women, the screams of his victims driving Cutter's pleasure to euphoric heights—and a few unfortunate, aristocratic deaths. Luckily, Maxis had been there to lend the eager fool a hand.

Cutter's gaze darted to the woman then to Maxis before giving a hypnotic nod.

Crouching next to the woman, Maxis tucked the strand of hair behind her ear and absently stroked her head. "She's yours. Consider it a gift of friendship as we begin our endeavor together."

Cutter's moderate frame expanded. "Th-That's more than generous of you, Maxis. You've clearly invested much time in her training. Are you sure?"

"What are friends for?" He returned to his throne, his steps lighter than they'd been in years. "In fact, I propose we capture, train and distribute slaves to strategic points. How best to convey our point than with a good dose of reality?"

"Not so sure you'd find common folks eager to take on slaves." Thyrus absently petted the head of the slave at his side. "Too much risk if the malran finds out."

"You think the good people of Asshur would turn down free labor? The population here is dwindling. Those who've chosen to remain, despite the less hospitable climate, have suffered from lack of available workers. What better way to indoctrinate the Myren people than demonstration in the form of slaves to ease their burden. They'll not only prosper from the help, but they'll fall more quickly in line with our cause."

"A few select brothels might not hurt as well," Cutter said, his gaze locked on his new prize at his feet.

"An excellent idea." One Maxis wished he'd thought of himself.

He took his seat, stroked the black lacquered arm of his chair, and let the silence pulse between them. "Give it some thought." He waved at the food. "Talk amongst yourselves and tell me what you think."

Reese shot from his chair and paced along the farthest wall. Thyrus followed, ever the eager one for gossip, and Cutter fell in line behind him. The two men chattered with an almost cultish glaze to their eyes while Reese scowled at them from a distance.

Five minutes. He'd wait that long or until their muttered conversation died down. Still nothing from Reese, his eyes darting to the exit in one-minute increments.

"Tell me, Thyrus." Maxis stood and joined them. "Do you have any prospects we might consider for better relationships with the ellan?"

Thyrus wiped a meaty paw across his mouth, yet managed to miss the majority of what needed attention. "I think our best focus is Angus Rallion. He and Eryx went to blows only a month ago. Eryx found him guilty of treason for standing in Eryx's place during criminal trials and stripped the geezer of his rank. Angus has grumbled ever since."

"He's lucky." Cutter snatched a fresh morsel from the tray of goodies and strolled to where his slave still kneeled. "Eryx could have stripped his powers or hung him under the stamp of treason."

Oh, this was good. Of all the emotions to work with, revenge was the easiest to manipulate. Especially when it forwarded his own. "Lucky for us he didn't." He shifted closer to Thyrus.

Reese kept his place at the wall, ignoring the conversation. Too much distance. Something Maxis would need to work on.

Maxis handed Thyrus a much-needed napkin and leaned a hip against the table. "How do you feel about arranging a meeting between me and this Angus fellow?"

"Shouldn't be a problem." Thyrus shrugged, wiped his pudgy fingers and disregarded his face altogether. "Any topic in particular?"

"As a matter of fact, yes." Maxis handed Thyrus another particularly greasy hunk of meat. May as well keep his allies well fed. "I have some information about our malran and his visits to Evad. Something a man with a grudge might find very interesting."

$\mathcal{E}$ryx swiped the last beads of water from his body and tossed the towel to the floor. The damned thing was too soft for his mood. Every joint and muscle ached with fatigue. Feeding Galena energy while she anchored Lexi had stripped him to the point he shouldn't be able to stand—but he couldn't disengage enough for sleep. Not with Galena's warning about the sedative rattling round and round in his head.

Tradition in our world, sure. But in her book, you're a deceiving bastard. The fact that she was confident she'd handled damage control via girl-to-girl talk didn't matter. Nothing would until he talked to Lexi himself.

If she'd ever wake the fuck up.

He wrung the lingering water from his hair and a few of his knuckles cracked. Why he'd thought a shower was a better idea than hovering bedside was beyond him. Instead of clearing his head, his anxiety had jump a notch, his thoughts meandering the path of what he'd have to face if she didn't wake up.

He snatched a pair of silk black pajama bottoms. May as

well get dressed and wait it out. Maybe think positive and ask Orla to have some food ready.

A broken whimper eased beneath the bathroom door.

With a quick yank, he drew the pants up and threw the door wide. "Get them off me!" Her eyes sealed shut, Lexi raked her nails along her neck and thrashed beneath the sheets.

He pinned her free hand to the bed and healed a slow-seeping gash on her check with a swipe of his thumb. Other welts covered her neck and jaw, limited only by the fact her other hand was too tangled in the sheets to add more damage.

The wound mended and faded as he tackled the next batch of scrapes. "Lexi, wake up."

She writhed beneath him, her eyes still closed. "Bugs." Her head shuttled side to side. "Fire. Hurts."

Fine sparks of electricity snapped around them and an untamed gust of air swept the room. Whatever the cause for her slow and tedious transition, it was well and truly over now. She'd gone from an untapped Myren hull to a powder keg of energy—too much of a good thing trapped in an unprepared and unconscious body.

"I know, baby. You gotta wake up." He wanted to be gentle. Tried to ease the grip at her wrist while he unwound the sheet from her other arm, but the fine sheen of sweat covering her made the task a challenge. "You're on overload. Wake up. Let me help you."

Wind whipped around him, his once drenched hair drying fast beneath its fury.

"Make. It. Stop." She flung herself forward.

Air whooshed, and he slammed into the far wall with enough force to rattle the room. He shook his head, the edges of his vision fuzzy.

Lexi's roar still resonated through the room, carried on a

nearly constant stream of air. Even now, sitting upright in bed, she struggled to open her eyes.

Memories of his own awakening fired bright. The sluggish thoughts, the disorientation, the burn of strengthening muscles—the worst hangover of his life.

Lexi kicked at the sheets and took a fresh swipe at her now exposed arms, leaving another angry mark in the wake of her nails.

He shot forward and held her to the bed. "Lexi!" The command was strong enough to startle a corpse, but it worked. Her eyes popped open in time to let loose a ragged scream.

"Lexi, damn it." He shook her. "Look at me"

The arch of her neck slackened enough to level her gaze with his. Tears pooled in her eyes and her lips trembled. "Help me." Her haggard plea punched through his gut, fisted his insides, and twisted.

Repositioning so they were palm to palm, he laced their fingers tight. "Push the energy into me. Focus on my hands."

Tremors shimmered through her. "Don't know how." A bead of sweat slipped down her temple and her chest heaved on a ripple of sobs.

"Bullshit." He gripped harder and got nose-to-nose so she'd have no choice but to focus. Her blue-gray eyes darkened to stormy gray, nearly consumed by the black of her pupils. "You threw me across the damned room. Now push the energy into me. Do it. Now."

Her body bowed and a grated wail ripped through the room.

Wind lashed against his bare back, but the barest trickle of energy eased into his palm.

Lust. He shook with it, a pure compulsion fired by the stroke of her unique power. Sunshine and rapture. Innocent sparkle and shady sin. It licked along his skin with a thousand tiny tongues for the most erotic stroke of his life.

His lips were at her jawline before he realized it, the herbal scent that clung to her filling his lungs. "That's it." He nuzzled her earlobe. "Give it to me."

A fresh wave of energy answered. It shot up his arms and down his chest to cradle his balls. Praise The Great One, he was a fucking leech. He needed to keep his head. Focus on funneling the surplus of energy from her strained body. Drain her to a point she could function and think. Not coax them both into a sexual haze. Damn it if his dick wasn't hard enough to pound nails.

Lexi moaned beneath him, the throaty sound penetrating the carnal focus of his thoughts. She'd stopped thrashing. Had softened and taken up a hedonistic rhythm with her hips. Energy flowed from her in a constant, desperate pulse, euphoria and ache rolled up in to one heady rush.

"Eryx?" One word that conveyed so much. The edge of agony in her voice was gone. Replaced with confusion, hunger, and desperation.

"It's your energy." He stifled a groan and eased back. He shouldn't take advantage. Wouldn't take advantage.

She ripped her hands out from under his and a gust of wind and translucent sparks shot through the air. Her fingers bit into his flanks and yanked him close. "More."

Her energy cranked through him. He licked her lower lip. A trace of honeyed balm teased him. Taunting. "Be sure," he whispered against her mouth. "Be very sure."

She answered with hands fisted at his scalp and a quick nip. "Now." Her hips punctuated the demand. "More."

The two words triggered something. Freed an animalistic part of him he'd sensed, but dared not release. It shoved his conscience and reason aside to better study its prey—firm, sinuous flesh covered only by the thin stretch of a white cotton sheath, the dusky and hardened outline of her nipples straining against the fabric.

He gripped the neck of the gown, guided by the beast— and ripped.

COOL AIR ASSAILED LEXI. Her nipples hardened, heedless of the panic in her head.

Above her, Eryx tilted his head. Too shrewd. Too watchful.

She swallowed around the tightness in her throat and clung to his shoulders, his muscles a welcome anchor. She could do this. The past didn't define her. *She* defined her. Her choices. Nothing else.

"Don't stop." She flexed her hips, a silent encouragement, the silk of his pants a frustrating barrier for the erection sliding against her bare skin.

Eryx shifted toward his heels. Not so far she lost connection at his shoulders, but enough to lose the steady stroke of his cock between her legs. His palms skated along her upper thighs, spread wide atop his. His scrutiny wriggled beneath her skin, prodding for answers without uttering a single question.

No way was she going there. Not now. Not for a good long while. Distraction was better. And the sweet promise of his shaft buried deep.

She reached for the silk at his hips.

He batted the hand away and shook his head in a slow predatory glide. "Share your secrets when you're ready, but never hide from me. Not in this."

She nose-dived into dumbfounded and her heart leapt into her throat. "Eryx, I—"

"Don't care." He crept forward, hands at either side of her

head, his dark hair falling around them. "We talked about this. You need to say no, say it. You want me, then say that, too. But no evasion. No lies."

She nodded, his heat and the solemnity of his words too powerful to do more. He was right. The least she could do was suck it up and spill what she could handle of the truth. "You scared me."

His chin dipped in barely perceptible acknowledgement, but his eyes stayed locked to hers.

"But I still want this."

Those sensuous lips of his curled in a wily grin. He rose tall on his knees. "Show me. Put your hands above your head and grip the pillow."

Her heart tripped and her insides spun, but she did as he asked, her throat too dry to swallow.

Roughened fingers brushed the outside of her knees. "Say it again." His silver eyes burned into hers, his voice spilling across her in a wicked rush of heat.

"I want this." The admission wracked her, her voice husky and breathless.

For the first time since she'd balked, his gaze drifted down her body and a slow growl rumbled from his chest.

So exposed and vulnerable. She'd never needed touch this badly. Never craved this kind of carnal intimacy.

He splayed his palm against her belly and the muscles beneath clenched tight. "Send your energy through my hand." The ferocity of his voice ricocheted through her. "Focus on where I touch."

The fine hairs along her skin danced to attention, and something a step stronger than the brush of a feather leapt from her flesh to his.

He leaned forward and his breath fanned out around her breast on a low, throaty sigh. "Do you know how long I craved this?" He swirled his tongue around the turgid nipple and imitated the stroke with his finger at the other. The tips of his hair tickled her side and his spicy scent filled her lungs. "How many nights I ached to feel your skin under my tongue?"

She urged his mouth closer to her breast, his hair fisted in her nearly barbaric grip, but he refused to budge, keeping the touch light. "Damn it. I ache."

The bastard chuckled. Actually, chuckled. "Yeah, now you get it." His tongue painted a naughty path along her flesh, down one tight globe and up the other. He circled the other pebbled tip and looked up beneath thick black lashes. "I'll give you what you need, when you need it." He flicked his tongue against the peak. "Always."

Wet, delicious heat enfolded her nipple. Sent spasms straight to her belly and her mind to the moon. Passion weighted her eyelids, but she kept them open. Couldn't forgo the vision at her breast—his cheeks hollowing with each pull, eyes shut as though he savored every second.

Logic and common sense ceased to exist, buried so far down it couldn't find the light of day, much less interrupt.

She tried to form words—demands or curses. Anything to shove him past his leisurely feast and on to filling the aching void between her legs. But all that came out were husky sighs and scratchy pleas.

Hot muscle flexed beneath her hands. The pads of his chest, the ridges across his stomach, the V at his hips. With every touch, energy flowed between them, a mix of sparks and soft-spun cotton. She shoved at the offensive silk at his waist, but couldn't reach enough to push the fabric past his hips.

"Please." She scraped her teeth along the taught line of his shoulder, salt and an almost metallic taste on her lips. "Let me feel you."

Her nipple slipped from between his lips. He studied the

rosy tip, a salacious gleam in his eyes as he looked up. The hand teasing her thighs slid higher and he licked the other neglected tip. "Like this?" Two fingers slicked through her wet folds—once, twice—then thrust deep as his mouth clamped down.

"Yes!" No. God, it wasn't what she'd meant, but the stretch was perfect. A hint of what she craved, a spark for what promised to be explosive. She didn't know whether to tug him away and demand he comply, or press his mouth harder against her breast. "I want you inside me."

He lifted his head with one last lap at her nipple. "Not yet." He shifted back and pushed her knees wide, his stare so hot between her legs she thought she'd burn. "Not until I get a taste." His touch drifted over her bare mound and he licked his lips. He lifted her hips and his breath fluttered against her thighs. "So sweet. Perfect for my mouth."

A low, guttural moan grated from her throat, the porn-star kind she'd blush about when she remembered it later. Each decadent swipe of his tongue, the steady rhythm of his face between her legs, the brush of his hair against her thighs —she couldn't fight it. Didn't want to. Just gave herself over to the pleasure and laid her soul bare.

His hand flattened against her belly, stilling her hips. "Give me what I want." He growled the demand against her slick flesh and it resonated up her torso. His fingers rocked back and forth, demanding. "Give me a taste." The scorching heat of his mouth bathed her clit and he suckled deep.

Climax whipped through her, swift as the shout that ripped from her lungs. Her pussy rippled around him, her hips meeting each glide of his fingers. She urged him closer and widened her knees, the wicked pressure of his lips more important than air. Shame had no place here. Only touch. Emotion. Passion.

Eryx eased back.

She took her first full breath—then promptly lost it on a huff when he lifted his head.

His eyelids were heavy, his dark hair accenting the harsh angles of his face and lips glossy with her release. His fingers still thrusted inside her, slow and steady, a pace that eased her from the peak but refused to let her land. "That's honesty." He slipped his fingers from her entrance and cleaned them with a naughty swipe of his tongue and lips. "Sweet, honey-coated honesty."

A none-too-subtle ripple shuttled through her belly and another chunk in her emotional blockade tumbled into nothingness. How could she keep him out? Did she even want to anymore?

He rose over her. Sweat glistened on smooth muscles as he shoved the black silk past his hips. His cock bobbed, thick and ready against his abdomen, the base smooth and bare. "Still your call."

No threat, no judgment of any kind. Just a fierce strength in the line of his jaw. One that said he'd step away if she said no—even if it killed him.

"I want more." She flung the words out before she could overthink them. Maybe she'd regret it later, but she'd face her worst fears five times over if it meant having this moment to remember.

Like once will ever be enough.

She rolled her hips, the release of moments before eradicated by the sight of him stroking his shaft. Oh, no. A lifetime wouldn't be enough.

One hand propped beside her head, he rubbed the head of his cock through her slick heat. Slow. Teasing. His sexy, indrawn breath sounded above her. "You belong with me."

The claim brushed through her, tempting her to hope. She clenched her eyes shut. Didn't dare meet his gaze for fear she might actually believe it.

He gripped her hip, the tip of his staff poised and ready. "Look at me."

Oh, God. This would kill her. Leave her powerless.

His cock teased her entrance. In and out. Enough to entice, but not nearly enough to ease the ache. "Lexi."

She opened her eyes and his gaze rattled her soul. "You belong with me. Tell me you understand."

There was no way to move. No way to force the fullness she craved, and no protection for her heart. "Yes." A raged cry. Desperate. "Please."

He filled her in one hard press, stretching her still fluttering walls to the point of delicious pain. One perfect, primitive moment that reached beyond their joined flesh to coil around her heart. The head of his erection scraped against her tender flesh, back and forth in powerful surges. She was lost, deliciously unplugged from everything in the world but the man driving against her hips.

Need pounded from every quarter, an all-consuming demand for something beyond the promise of physical release.

"Eryx." She anchored her hand at his chest. His heart hammered beneath it. Her energy leapt to surround it, the move as instinctive as a toddler's need to walk, driving for a connection to ground her before she shattered into a million tiny pieces.

He shuddered and his eyes clenched tight, hands fisted against the mattress.

"Please." She was so close. Desperate for an illusive touch she couldn't identify, her nails scored the skin above his heart.

He met her gaze. He knew what she needed, the tortured slant of his eyes damning him even as his hips rammed in a wicked rhythm. He slid his hand between their bodies and circled her clit. Slick, perfect pressure. "Let go."

Her pussy clamped around his iron length and he slammed deep, catapulting her beyond suspicions and secrets into a bright abyss.

He reared back on a jagged bellow. Violet shards of electricity shot toward the ceiling and a crash of thunder racked the skies outside as his cock jerked inside her.

She rode the storm, arms and legs locked tight around him. Wind snapped and soothed their sweat-slick skin as she reveled in his weight. The slow, steady glide of his hips and each delicious aftershock.

The tightly coiled muscles in his shoulders eased and eager arms wrapped her tight.

A ragged breath shook from her lungs, her body thrumming on a steady hum. The pain from her awakening was gone, replaced with the pleasant ache in muscles too long ignored. For the first time in her life, her heart vibrated with connection. As though the grooves of her life had settled into their perfect notch.

Almost.

Eryx's guilty expression—the point just before he'd shoved her over the ledge with his clever fingers—replayed in her mind.

Whatever he'd withheld wasn't about deceit. Of that much, she was certain. But he was hiding something. Something she had every intention of finding.

CHAPTER 12

Maxis ducked inside Phybe's sheltered porch and checked the street behind him. Quiet, not a soul out in the early afternoon, the quaint warriorville cottages locked tight. Most families made their rounds to sanctuary and family dinners this time of day. The tradition was a bit too close to human ritual to suit his taste, but in this instance it came in handy.

Unlike the others, Phybe was home, a confirmation he'd made before setting out. No point in roasting his retinas with a wasted trip. He rapped on the evergreen-colored door and waited.

The door opened with a high-pitched groan, the entry shadowed and empty.

"Come in." Phybe's voice echoed from somewhere deep within the home. Whatever she was doing, her words held a bite he'd have never associated with her mousy demeanor.

The foyer was little more than a short hallway opening to a vaulted living room. Ivory chaises and fluffy sage chairs sat in casual arrangements. Matching rugs in conservative patterns covered a pale slate floor. Beyond it was a sliding glass door spanning the far wall, the entire length open wide to let in the blasted sun.

"Wesley." Phybe kneeled on the patio beyond the doors, clumps of near-black dirt scattered atop the sandstone pavers. She staggered to a stand and swiped the back of one soil-crusted hand across her forehead. "I wasn't expecting you. I look horrid."

Maxis strolled toward the mess of pots and overturned blooms. "You have a love of plants?"

"Praise The Great One, no." She motioned to a nearby chair beneath an awning, its weathered cushions indicative of too many hours in the sun. She resumed her place in front of her most recent horticultural victim. "The malran's sister is helping me keep my mind off things. She thinks blending my soul with Mother Earth will help heal my heart."

"I've heard it said she's a renowned healer. Perhaps she's right." Maxis noted the particular bloom teetering cockeyed in the center of the ruby colored pot. "Your choice of flower warms my heart."

A flush rushed her cheeks and she ducked her head. "I can't take too much credit. Galena brought them to me. I took the flower you gave me to my presentation to the malran. I told her a friend had given it to me and it gave me strength."

Maxis' gut cramped, the absent tapping of his finger along the armrest freezing midair.

Phybe gripped the edge of the clay pot so hard the petals shook. Her eyes were hidden behind a veil of pale lashes. "When she came by yesterday, she said she thought your gesture was lovely and wanted to enforce the sentiment."

"You told her about me?" He tried for a lighthearted tone. Difficult when sparks threatened to leap from his palm.

She ducked her head and scooped a pile of rich dirt. "Very

little. Only that I'd made a new friend and you'd seen me safely home."

Maxis sucked in a lungful of air and let it out, a good part of his temper sliding out along with it. "I take it the presentation went well?"

"As well as can be expected." With a wistful smile, she shoved the pot away and dropped her hands to her lap. The dreary tan color of her leggings was perfect for her work, but a drab blend for her already pale skin. "The malran was very kind. Assuring."

"So Galena was in attendance. Anyone else?" More direct than he'd intended, but the constant drift of the sun as it inched past the awning pricked at his attention.

She shook her head and swept piles of dirt toward the burlap bag at her right. "No. It was just the two of them." Her sardonic chuckle tinkled through the air. "At least until Serena showed."

"Serena?"

Phybe huffed out a tired breath and stood. "The malran's former lover. I knew nothing of her, but a few of the wives told me about her once I got home." She scooted the bag of dirt to the far edge of the patio wall with a flick of her wrist to guide her mental push. "They say she and the malran were an item many years ago. Apparently, he lost interest quickly, but she never did. Galena said the scene after I left was quite nasty."

"Intriguing." Maxis crossed one leg over the other. "Such gossip among the royals. Too bad he didn't have a current love to throw into the mix. Would have made for good entertainment."

Phybe situated herself in the chair beside his, and the sun angled off her pale hair in a blinding ray. "No. No, current loves. At least not that I saw. Which was fine with me. Serena brings enough drama on her own."

Damn it all. The woman needed to stay on point. He held out his hand. "And how are you?"

She placed her hand in his with a gentle sigh. "Tired. Every time I close my eyes, I see Saul's face. I wonder if he felt pain at his passing. How my future will be without him."

He barely registered her words, focusing instead of the full stream of memories from her time at the castle.

"Wesley?"

The question tapped at his attention. "Forgive me." He shook his head, feigning sadness to cover his intrigue. "Your comments brought to mind losses of my own. What did you say?"

"I asked if I could get you something to drink?"

"No. I was merely out on errands and thought to stop by as I'd promised. I think it's best I be on my way. One can never be too cautious with gossip. Particularly in your situation." He stood, eager to escape to the only slightly dimmer living area. "Of course, you're always welcome to come see me. It's more private there. Secluded."

Phybe avoided his gaze and didn't answer, hands clasped tightly in front of her.

"Well, then." Wasn't this awkward? "I'll leave you to your planting. I'll check on you again soon to see how you're doing."

She trailed behind him on his way to the door, but he didn't look back. With no sign of Lexi in Phybe's memories and too close of a call with the malran learning of his involvement, the trip was nearly a wasted one.

Then again, Serena Doroz with her long, white-blonde hair, vivid blue eyes, and loads of attitude trouncing through Phybe's memories had much potential.

Definitely a woman he could work with.

~

By the time they pried themselves from Eryx's bed, the red-rimmed Eden sun was well past noon. Lexi and Eryx trudged up a soft-sloping hill covered in Eden's shimmering green grass. Clouds capped the azure horizon.

Lexi's body buzzed, ready to kick ass and take on the world— including Eryx and whatever had his brow wrinkled to match a shar-pei. "So, what secret have you got tucked away this time?" Her sarcasm came off a little thick, teetering on self-righteous snark.

He shook his head.

"Oh, come on. No man I've ever known has thunderbolt sex and walks away grumpy."

He grabbed her arm and ground them both to a halt. "You've never known a man to throw the kind of bolts I do, and the thought of you post-orgasm with anyone but me doesn't improve my mood."

Whoa.

Okay. Maybe more finesse. "You know how I feel about secrets. I know you're keeping one. Or several. You ever thought about talking to me instead of tiptoeing around every issue in sight?"

He planted his hands on either hip and worked his jaw in slow circles.

"Let's try this," she said. "How many more whammies am I due for?"

He hung his head and rubbed the back of his neck. He'd plaited his hair in a mass of braids, the ends capped off in all manner of metal beads. In lieu of the jeans and T-shirts she'd grown to love, he sported a charcoal gray linen tank and pants. A spiritual rendition of Braveheart on steroids.

"Two." He looked up from his vacant perusal of the grass. "They're mine to wrestle. I'll share them when I'm ready."

She opened her mouth.

"We've already established you have secrets of your own,"

he said before she could speak. "The fact that Ludan knows every dark nook and cranny of your mind including those secrets makes me mental. The fact that they're significant enough to make you freeze when you're naked beneath me drives me to near murder."

Put that way, she couldn't help but mentally downshift and reevaluate. She took a deep breath and raised her chin. "You're right." The words tasted like shit. "Just promise me there aren't any others to rip the rug out from under me."

"I can't do that." His lips flat-lined. "Who I am in this realm affects you, but it's still about me. I'm asking you for patience. To get to know me before I heap on everything else."

A cool breeze tickled the side of her face. She lowered her eyelids and fixated on the sun's warmth, the crisp bite of grass as it hit her nose. "Does it have anything to do with this morning?" She locked onto his gaze. "There was something…" What words could she use? The words she had to work with wouldn't come together in the right formation. "Something missing."

He straightened and his lips parted. "Okay, make that three."

Son of a bitch. Seriously? She fisted her hand. She was faster now. Surely she could get at least one jab in before he stopped her.

His lips curled into a shit-eating grin.

Screw that. She'd go for a right hook.

"In my defense, there's not an unmated female Myren alive who knows the third secret, so sharing that one's non-negotiable." He resumed his trek up the hill.

She hustled to catch up. "What the hell does that mean?"

"It means exactly what I said."

"Sounds like a whomping pile of crap to me."

He shrugged and kept moving, but cast a wicked wink

over his shoulder. "Human kids believe in Santa Claus and the Easter Bunny, but I don't see you yakkin' that up. We're Myren. We have our traditions." He snatched her wrist, tugged her closer, and wrapped his arm along her shoulder. "May as well get used to it." He dropped a kiss to the top of her head as they reached the highest peak.

Wow. Just, wow. A deep valley ran below them, water the color of the sky back home running down its center with happy whitecaps bubbling against smooth gray boulders. At either side, black-trunked trees with violet leaves covered the mountain slopes. One thing was certain. Color schemes definitely ran the gamut in Eden.

"I love this spot." Eryx pulled her in front of him. With a contented sigh, he hugged her close and rested his chin on top of her head. "Graylin brought me here not too long after he built his place. Said every man needed a place to be quiet."

"Have you ever brought anyone else here?" She sounded about as foolish as she felt, but figured what the hell.

His lips grazed her temple. "Never wanted to."

God she wanted him. Skin to skin and sweaty as hell like they'd been this morning. Then again, she wouldn't mind kicking him in the shins a few times either. She tamped her chaotic emotions down. This place, this moment, was special. Sacred. She'd get her answers when Eryx was ready. Now was a quiet time. Maybe even a beginning.

Eryx's heartbeat thrummed steady against her back. A hint of something floral floated on the wind. Honeysuckle maybe, but a little sharper.

Prickles danced beneath her skin. Unexpected and out of place. The same cautionary flare that had saved her bacon off and on her whole life, only bigger. More pronounced and accompanied by the taste of burnt toast. Where the hell did that come from?

Eryx stared at the rushing waters below, his gaze distant.

Despite his relaxed shoulders and easy embrace, sharpness marred his features. More the look of a troubled man than one in sync with an idyllic landscape.

"Everything okay?"

He blinked, mildly startled, and refocused on her. "I was thinking about Graylin. I caught him with an odd look on his face while he was watching Orla this morning. I haven't seen that expression since before his baineann died." His eyes darkened. "She's been with The Great One for a long time."

"A baineann's a mate, right? But I thought Myrens lived a long time."

He turned her and pulled her close. "Doesn't make us exempt from tragedy. Ludan's uncle killed her. Went crazy one day and murdered her in cold blood."

"What made him do it?"

He shook his head and tucked a strand of hair behind her ear. "No one got a chance to find out. Ludan found him minutes after it happened and snapped his neck."

"Ludan could have looked, right? Scanned his memories like he did mine?"

"He claims he acted on impulse, trying to save his mother." Eryx's mouth twitched. "I'm pretty sure he knows though. He was always a little harder than everyone else growing up, but after that he was different. Colder."

Lexi stroked his arms and shoulders. The sadness coming off of him made her want to fidget. "I caught Orla looking at Graylin pretty intently, too."

He froze. "Intently as in angry? Or intently like waiting for something?" The world around her blurred and her senses drifted. The memory replayed with a clarity she'd never experienced before, though with it came emotions she felt as though they were her own. "Like she saw the raw man underneath."

He cupped her shoulders and edged her back. "That's a pretty precise observation."

Lexi shrugged and stepped away, uncomfortable with the whole petri dish level scrutiny. "I guess. It just came to me." She looked out over the beautiful scene, but couldn't focus on a bit of it. Not with his stare so heavy at her side.

"Fair enough." He nodded. "Then let's get on with what I brought you here for."

Thank God. "I though you brought me for the view."

He shook his head and a wicked grin crept across his face. "I thought you might like to learn to fly."

CHAPTER 13

*E*ryx swept Lexi into his arms and shot to the skies before she had time to argue.

Her garbled shriek rang in his ear, and it was a damned good thing he knew exactly where he was headed because the way she'd coiled her arms around his neck made turning his head impossible.

"Relax." He wedged a hand between her arm and his chest and shifted her down an inch or two. "This is supposed to be fun."

Lexi kept her face notched in the crook of his neck, her breath a steady pant against his skin.

He rolled so the ground lay below him and the slow, steady rush of wind hit her face. "Come on, hellcat. I felt you in your dreams. You loved flying there."

The fingers fisted at his shoulders eased a bit, and she lifted her head into the breeze. She peeked at the tall gray mountains below with their violet treetops and shivered. "That's a long way down." Fear lent a huskiness to her voice, but a tad of her snarky bite was back in play.

"You're safe." He squeezed his arm tight around her waist. "I promise."

She swallowed and edged out another inch. "I can really do this?"

"You're Myren. It's a birthright. Though some are better at it than others."

The way she chewed on her lip said she wasn't altogether convinced. "How?"

Laughter rumbled from his chest, the sensation that went with it lighter than he'd felt in years. "Always with the details." He rolled again so they were side-by-side and aimed toward their destination. "Trust me when I tell you, details will only make it harder. Go with your gut and you'll be fine."

"You're not going to drop me are you?" Her grip strengthened to the point he could barely breathe. "Kick me out of the nest, so to speak?"

"I think I have enough strikes on your naughty list without adding cruel and unusual punishment." He was playing with her. Joking and teasing without a care for the world, and he liked it. "We're headed to a flat stretch of land. I figured slopes and water weren't such a good idea for day one."

She nodded, but her eyes were clouded with wariness. Eventually, she craned her neck to look behind them then below to watch the view pass by.

He kept his silence, giving her the time to assimilate and him time to check on Ludan and Ramsay. *Everyone's in place?*

"Yep." Ludan, always the talkative one.

At least Ramsay was willing to give details. *"We've got five men at all points scanning for signs of movement, and we've had men on patrol since last night. No noted activity outside of wildlife. She's safe."*

"And where are you?" Eryx scouted the perimeter of their

route as they flew. Bit by bit, the mountains behind them gave way to weathered boulders, crumpled and veined with evergreen moss.

"We're a good quarter mile out. Ludan's the only one up close."

Ramsay hesitated for a second. *"You think she'll sense us?"*

Eryx wasn't sure what to think. Her quip about secrets rattled in his head and his sense of judgment hiccuped. Everything about her scattered his rational thoughts, muddying paths he'd long thought certain. *"We're about to find out."*

A long swath of emerald green with shards of silver stretched out before them. "I'll never get used to this." The awe in Lexi's voice filled him with a ridiculous amount of pride.

He shifted them both so their feet aimed toward the ground, slowed his descent, and held Lexi up so he'd take the brunt of the landing.

The ground rushed closer and Lexi tensed.

He landed with no more impact than a jump off a chair. "See? Not so bad." He lowered her to the ground. "Ready to give it a try?"

Her breath gushed out with a shaky laugh. "Maybe after my insides are settled back where they're supposed to be." Rubbing her bare arms, she scrutinized the low sloping hills in the distance.

"Cold?" Galena always favored the tank-styled tunic and leggings Lexi had chosen this morning, so he hadn't thought to suggest anything else.

She shook her head and scanned the lush valley in the opposite direction. Tiny white flowers dotted the rich green grass and wiggled in the steady breeze. "Do you feel that?"

"Feel what? Put words behind it."

She curled her arms across her chest, elbows tucked in

tight, shoulders tense. "I feel like I'm in the middle of a packed football stadium and everyone's watching me."

"Can you tell me where it's coming from?"

Lexi faced him. "That's a pretty leading question. Is there something I should know?"

Well, histus. He should've known she'd jump straight to suspicion. Considering everything she'd been through, he couldn't blame her. "No, I'm telling you to work with me and let me teach you."

She straightened, opened her mouth then shut it, sighed and closed her eyes. She pointed. "Over there."

Well, what do you know? Eryx turned toward Ludan's masked form. "You're busted."

Ludan wavered into view, his trademark disinterested frown in place.

Lexi pursed her lips and glared at them. "You could have told me I'd have a test."

"Defeats the purpose." Eryx hugged her. "The ability to sense other Myrens is a valuable gift. Not everyone can do it." He stroked her back, hoping to ease the tension.

She pushed away, turned in a slow circuit, and scanned the horizon. "Ludan isn't the only one, is he?"

Ludan stepped forward, eyes sharp on the skyline and arms poised for action.

Eryx eased in behind her. "How many do you sense?"

"A handful. Four or Five. Maybe six?" She faced him again.

No way. She was a woman, not a warrior. "Can you sense anything else? Reach out with your mind and see what information it brings to you."

She closed her eyes and the wind blew a strand of dark hair across her face. "I know one of them. It feels like you, but not. So I'm guessing Ramsay. The others are strangers. At least to me. But I don't feel anything bad. Just….loyalty?" Her eyes popped open. "Who are they?"

"That's fucking impressive." Ludan scratched his chin.

Eryx couldn't blame him. Assimilating what she'd pulled off was taking him awhile too. "You're right. Six men surround this area, one of them Ramsay, and they're a good distance out. Outside of the Forte family and mine, I don't know of anyone who can do what you did."

She might have been angry at the way he'd approached the lesson, but her stance shifted to something barely short of a preening peacock—one still gaining confidence its feathers were worth showing off.

Maybe he'd been right to stick with the traditional approach. "So are you ready to give flying a go?"

Lexi glanced at the landscape behind her. "In front of everyone?"

Eryx edged closer, but didn't crowd. He stroked her cheekbone. "They're to keep you safe. Until we find Maxis, we need them."

She wrinkled her nose and scowled. "Am I going to flop on my face?"

"Tell her about your first try." Ludan smirked and crossed his arms.

"Can it." Eryx said, but kept his focus on Lexi. "Picture it in your mind and let the energy do the rest."

She nodded and sucked in a breath.

He stepped back.

Her eyelids fluttered shut and her hands fisted at her sides. The soft drone of nature hummed and wind swirled between them.

He held his breath, anxiety wrenching the muscles along Eryx's forearms.

"Yeah, not working." Her shoulders slumped and she ducked her chin.

"At least you're not jumping off of rocks or tall ledges," Ludan said.

Eryx glared at Ludan and stepped between them. "You're not helping."

Lexi sidestepped and asked Ludan, "Who did that?"

Ludan didn't respond, but the way Lexi's lips spread into a sly smile told him Ludan had pointed at him.

Interfering family and friends. He couldn't wait until Ludan found someone he gave a shit about impressing. Payback would be a bitch.

He turned Lexi away from his somo. "You need to relax. If you tense up it gets harder."

"Easy for you to say. You're not the one learning with a bunch of strangers watching."

"Forget about them." He cupped her shoulders and lowered his voice. "Close your eyes and think about your dreams. Remember how it felt to fly."

The wind around them stirred, nothing too strong, but more than what Mother Nature generated on her own and crackling with untrained energy.

He eased back. "Just like that. Remember the feelings. How you took off. How you turned. What the wind felt like on your skin."

Lexi relaxed her head, faced aimed at the sky with her eyes still closed. Peaceful looking with the barest smile on her lips.

He lifted off the ground and hovered a few stories above her. Pale silver shimmers danced in a fine halo around her head and shoulders, power ready for release. "Now open your eyes and come with me."

Her chest lifted on a slow, deep breath and she opened her eyes. For a split second, her gaze clouded, then sharpened. She took two steps forward and shot into the sky. Overshooting his position, she squeaked and began to fall.

"Whoa!" Eryx snatched and steadied her against him. "You have to keep thinking. Autopilot doesn't kick in right away. It's like driving a car. When you've been doing it for years, you don't even think about it. But when you first start, it's all you can think about."

She laughed, not the least bit concerned she'd nearly tumbled to the Earth. "I did it." She braced her hands on his chest, the smile on her face enough to grip his heart and lock on tight. "I really did it."

Her warm breath fanned against his face. His thoughts scrambled and a raw, achy need pushed to the surface.

Her mouth softened and she rubbed her hand, slow against his heart. "You okay?"

Reason batted at the back of his head, shrieking to get back in the game. Now wasn't the time or place for selfish impulse. "I'm fine."

She lifted an eyebrow.

"I like seeing you smile." It was only a sliver of the truth, a speck of the impact she had on his heart.

Her face glowed, the tips of her cheeks a pale pink. She glanced at Ludan, still on the ground, but poised for action. "Can we do it again?"

"That's what we're here for." What he really wanted was to cart her home and practice at something much more carnal. He faced her forward instead. "Ludan will cover from below. I'll stay close."

She shot from his arms without a beat of hesitation. With every minute her movements smoothed. Her confidence radiated against his senses hot and heavy, slipping into her Myren nature as easy as a river found its course.

If she knew the type of relationship he craved from her, would she adjust to the idea of him as easily? He shoved the idea away before it could take root and tightened his distance to Lexi. He should be focused on her training, not postulating relationship suicide.

Every task he gave her she tackled, her enthusiasm and tenacity unhindered by the realm she'd left behind. And it was rubbing off. Not just on him, but Ludan and Ramsay too if the awe-filled commentary via link was any indication. Most people balked when it came to learning to land, but Lexi? She laughed and plowed toward it like she did everything else.

Her latest approach was faster than previous landings, arms high and opened for balance.

Eryx balanced on the balls of his feet, ready to catch her if she faltered.

Her energy sputtered.

He darted forward and swept her into his arms just as her knees buckled. "I let you go too long." His voice was gruff, the angry beat of his heart and the fact that his stomach was lodged in his throat making a lighthearted tone impossible.

Lexi draped her arms around his neck. "Hardly." A contented sigh hummed past her lips and her head relaxed against his shoulder. "But I am tired."

Eryx lowered her to the ground, but kept an arm around her waist. "That's burnout. Just like you had too much before, now you're running low. You need food and rest. Once you've acclimated, the extremes won't be so great."

Stomach rumbling in agreement, she pressed a hand against her belly. "I love it." Huffing, she leaned over and rested her hands on her knees and looked up at him. Her eyes twinkled and she smiled wide enough to show perfect white teeth. "For the first time in my life, I feel right. I think I could handle just about anything you throw at me today."

Could you handle the idea of being my mate?

The thought leapt up along with a growl he barely kept in check.

Lexi straightened, slow and purposeful, lines of concentration furrowing between her brows. "What was that?"

"What was what?"

"I could have sworn I felt your hand on my neck. And that cologne you wear." She motioned at him. "That leather and spice, toe-curling stuff. It got really thick."

Leather and spice, toe-curling stuff? "You think I wear cologne?"

"Stop it and focus." She sidled closer and rested her palms on his chest.

"I felt you, but you weren't anywhere near me. What were you thinking?"

A low warning hummed along his shoulders. He grasped her wrists. "I was thinking of you."

She pressed closer and her eyelids drifted closed. "Think it again."

The memory of her hand on his heart this morning—her energy diving into his chest in search of a link—exploded. He crushed his mouth against hers, desire obliterating every fragment of reason.

Ludan coughed behind them. "We done here?"

Eryx eased away from Lexi, her lips a shade closer to rose than pink from his kiss. "I think I've got this."

Ludan took to the air, leaving loose blades of grass swirling in his wake.

"You're afraid I'll run away if I know your feelings." Lexi's voice floated as easy as dandelion fluff on the wind.

He tightened his grip on her shoulders.

"You're afraid if you tell me what you want, I'll bolt."

White space. A giant bucket of questions with zero answers. That was all his brain offered. "How'd you get that?"

She grinned and her gaze glazed over. "I have no idea. I felt your touch and my brain went laser sharp." She met his stare again and the grin grew to an ear-to-ear smile. "Then I kind of heard it in my head. I think. Or felt it." She shook her head and choked out an awkward laugh. "It just was."

Everything inside Eryx ripped to a standstill. "You're an emotional empath."

"A what?"

"An emotional empath." It made sense. The physical sensations she'd called out, not real but tied with an emotion. Her assessment of Orla. Her ability to identify not only a Myren presence, but to specifically identify Ramsay and the loyalty of his men. How attuned she'd been to his wild moods. "Where Galena physically takes on a person's injuries, you take on their emotions. Emotional sensation manifested first as physical sensation, followed by insight."

"You're saying this is one of my gifts?"

"Most likely."

Lexi stepped back, hands absently rubbing her hips.

The distance she'd created bugged him. He itched to step forward and gobble it up. She was learning things about herself, not him. So why did he feel so exposed? "Does the gift bother you?"

"No, but you holding back does. My heart is on the line here, too." A statement with an undercurrent of realization. "I've never known a family or love like you have. Not until Ian. But I'm not afraid of it."

Like histus she wasn't. She'd put every kind of emotional wall between them she could since the minute he found her. Then again, Lexi had a penchant for tackling whatever she set her mind to. He reclaimed the distance she'd created and gripped her shoulders so she couldn't run. For a second, he could barely breathe, his words bottled in his throat. "This is no small can of worms you're prying open. Once it's out, I'll move nirana and histus to keep you in my life."

Her cheeks and jaw hardened and she lifted her chin. "Duly noted."

Ten years he'd searched. Dreamed and waited. And here he was, his soul perched on the edge of an emotional cliff. The muscles along his arms tensed and his throat croaked. "I want you as my baineann, Alexis. I've wanted it from the first time I found you in my dreams. I've wanted it since I first saw you in the flesh. I want you in a way a starving man wants food. In a way that is completely irrational and insane."

Quiet.

Her breath remained even, unlike his own. Her expression locked into a blank slate. He was tempted to read her emotions, but it seemed dishonest.

He laid her hand over his heart. "You've felt my emotions. Go deeper. Know my intent." The plea in his tone grated at his pride. Ramsay and Ludan would mock him for years if they ever heard, but he didn't care.

She closed her eyes.

Energy danced along his skin as she searched for answers words alone could never give. What if she railed against what she found? Could he handle it?

"Love," she whispered. Her eyes opened and tears pooled along the bottom edge. Was it fear that tightened her cheeks? Hope?

"It's been what's driven me to find you. What will drive me to keep you. Will you accept me as your fireann, Alexis? Will you take that chance?"

Perfect stillness. Even the breeze seemed to listen. His heart thundered in an uncomfortable rhythm and his stomach burned. What if she didn't want him in the way he wanted her?

She fisted her hand against his chest. "Give me time."

~

MAXIS DODGED an ellan scurrying from the council building and pressed his masked form tight against a massive marble pillar. The crowds were thick after the general session, a swarm of opportunities to misstep.

"Don't know why you bother with a hidden identity." Thyrus trundled upstream through the exodus just twenty feet away. *"Hardly anyone talks of your father these days. Anyone committed to the Rebellion keeps to Evanora's guidance and skips right over the old man's bumbles."*

Those bumbles had cost Maxis an incalculable loss of status and money—not to mention a good seventy years of time he could have spent ruling his people.

"Let's keep our minds focused on the task at hand." He edged his masked form tighter against the golden marble column. One inadvertent brush with passersby and the crowds would go wild with panic. *"Just pass the information on to Angus as we discussed."*

Across the main isle, Thyrus shrugged. Too lackadaisical and dangerous. A loose cannon in charge of a delicate job.

Maxis rolled his shoulders and breathed through his impatience. Taking over wasn't an option. Planning and building his infrastructure alone was one thing. Now was the time to cultivate relationships. To spread his influence among those who counted—no matter how much he hated the task.

"Mmmm," Thyrus grunted. *"There's our boy."*

Maxis nearly barked out a laugh. Boy wasn't the term he'd have used. A three-generation relic was more apropos. Angus' face was a wrinkled mess. Thin silver hair in short stumps of disarray shot out of his pale head. From his puckered mouth and the way he scooted about, obstinacy was probably the only thing keeping the old fart breathing. *"Stick to the plan. We only get one shot."*

Thyrus waddled forward and wiped his pudgy paws

along the sides of his ivory robe, the stiff, stark white of Angus' council attire making him look dirty in comparison. Thyrus thrust out his hand.

The old man sneered at the offered palm.

"Channel the conversation through the link." Maxis could barely hold still. He wanted to pace, or even hover overhead where he could move without fear of impact with others, but the stir of energy would give him away to guards nearby.

"Yes, yes. Sorry." Thyrus gave up on the handshake and wiped his palm on his robe. "I apologize for catching you on short notice, but I've come upon some urgent information I thought it best to convey as quickly as possible."

"Make an appointment with my page." Angus sidestepped Thyrus to leave. "He'll handle the details."

"I'm afraid it won't wait," Thyrus said.

Praise the Great One. Thyrus had actually listened to Maxis' instructions. And hadn't given up easily either. Traits he'd be wise to remember in the future.

"The information is sensitive. The type a man of your caliber and…situation could make use of."

The old man straightened, and his eyes pinched to match his scrunched up lips. "What are you implying?"

Thyrus shook his head and his jowl wobbled. If Angus' snide behavior bothered him, he sure didn't show it. Then again, Thyrus was a well-practiced lawyer, so he'd likely earned a thick hide years ago. "Not implying a thing. Merely offering a faithful servant a tool to further his purpose." He folded his hands over his protruding belly and gave a meek bow. "Assuming you're interested in hearing what I have to say."

Angus scanned the area. He stared at Thyrus, tapping one finger atop his clasped hands, and then flicked his wrist toward the far end of the pavilion. "Over there."

Thyrus loped in the direction indicated, either oblivious

or uncaring of Angus' shrewd study. Probably the latter.

Darting through the fast-moving throng, Maxis plastered himself along a nearby wall as Angus and Thyrus came to a halt.

"Out with it," Angus said, checking behind him one last time.

"Yes, well." Thyrus cleared his throat. "Our malran has made the acquaintance of a human. A lover, we believe."

"I don't give a damn if he fucks them all. What good is such information to me?"

Thyrus raised his hands in a calming motion. "We believe in this instance it's a bit more…involved…than simply relations."

Maxis almost laughed. Relations? Apparently, Thyrus had a hang up with words of a more colorful variety.

"It seems," he continued, "the malran may have actually brought the human here. To Eden."

Angus snapped to attention. "What do you mean *may have*? Possibilities don't interest me. Facts do."

"Already on it." Thyrus puffed his chest out. "We haven't yet confirmed her presence, but we've got men on the case. All we need is a sighting to prove it."

Angus stood there with his mouth pursed tight as a drawstring pouch. Maybe he'd died and shot straight to rigor mortis. "Say nothing of this. To anyone. If you find this human and gain your proof, come and talk to me. Otherwise, this discussion never took place." He shuffled off. No backward glance, no indication he'd even been interrupted.

Thyrus rocked on his heels. *"I'd say that went rather well."*

Angus wound through the crowds, the golden council walls a painful backdrop to Maxis' eyes.

Anticipation whirred. *"You did well, my friend."*

One step closer. All Maxis needed was proof and Eryx's world would come tumbling down.

CHAPTER 14

*L*exi high-stepped it down the hall to the room she shared with Eryx. Sconces blazed to life along the walls with each step, Eryx setting them alight with his mind to light her way. *Providing what you need.*

Ugh. Not something she could think about right now. His sure, confident strides sounded behind her. No matter how far ahead she tried to stay, his hunger burned inside her.

Stupid gift. Now that she'd somehow uncorked it, she couldn't get it turned it off—and damned if she wasn't a raging inferno as a result.

She'd thought asking for time would calm his fears. Maybe ease his foot off the throttle a little bit. But oh, no. She'd tugged the lion's tail, tossed out a slab of meat, and thrown the cage door open wide.

The door to their room whipped open and thudded against the wall.

She flinched, but kept going. "You don't need to be so melodramatic."

She'd gone for playful, but ended up sounding like Marilyn Monroe on a heaped-up dose of Spanish Fly.

Moving to the dresser, she tugged off her blue leather sandals. "Maybe we can rest later and you can teach me how to move things with my mind instead."

Eryx ripped his tank over his head and tossed it to the floor. Smooth muscles flexed under tight, tan skin.

She closed her gaping mouth. *Tugged the lion's tail indeed.*

"I thought I'd give you something else." He stalked her until her back met the wall and caged her with arms on either side of her head. "Something that will feed you instead of drain you."

He ran his nose along the column of her neck and inhaled, slow and deep.

Goosebumps prickled along her forearms and her belly fluttered. "I thought you said I needed to rest."

"You need energy. I'm going to give it to you." He nipped her earlobe then sucked at the same spot. "You said you've never known family or love." His hot breath brushed across her skin and his tongue traced the shell of her ear. "So I'll give you that, too."

A blowtorch, insane, leave-me-here-to-die-in-glory fire blasted from her insides out. Where the hell was her caution? Her worry?

"I warned you." He bit her lower lip and the sting zinged to her nipples. His hands abandoned the wall and caressed her back, her thin cotton tunic a nearly non-existent barrier. "You said you could take anything I threw at you." He whipped the tunic over her head and the indigo fabric sailed to the floor behind him. "Then you'll have me." His gaze lowered to her bare breasts. "All of me."

He claimed her lips and crushed her body to his, the heat of his skin alone enough to make her gasp. His tongue swept between her parted lips and brushed against hers. No remorse, no constraint. Just a man beyond the confines of control, focused on one, single objective.

Her.

His fingertips skimmed and teased the sides of her breasts, and the cotton of her leggings rasped against her hips in a slow descent.

How could he…

She jerked away from his kiss.

Her leggings continued their descent, pushed toward the floor by nothing more than his thoughts. His wicked fingers at her breasts never missed a beat.

"You gotta teach me that trick." Licking her lips, she raked her nails along his abdomen. A few inches and the right angle, and she'd have the hot erection tenting his linen pants cradled in her palm.

"I don't think so." He swept her into his arms and strode to the bathroom. "I can't show you all my tricks." He splayed her on a wide chocolate-colored chaise and stepped away before she could pull him close.

She shifted, uncomfortable. Down-soft chenille caressed her back, but the skin along her front? All tingles and tight-ness. Laying naked in front of him was one thing, but the power in his expression stripped away the deepest barriers.

"What are you waiting for?" Even her whisper seemed frantic against the tiles and Grecian columns.

"Enjoying you." He shoved his pants past his hips. They dropped to the floor with a whisper. "Persuading you." He planted one knee at the foot of the chaise, and gripped her knees. "Loving you." He spread her wide and lifted her hips, his greedy mouth on her before she could draw a steady breath.

Her lungs hitched and burned, the wet heat of his tongue making the need for air a secondary concern. She rode each stroke, surrendered to every lick.

The muscles along his shoulders strained and his dark head bobbed and circled with each swipe of his tongue. His sultry gaze lifted and locked with hers, gleaming with challenge. With slow deliberation, he held her stare, licked from her drenched entrance, and circled her swollen clit.

Holy shit. Every muscle locked and quivered, her entire focus zeroed on the bundle of nerves.

He sucked with a hungry groan and thrust two fingers deep.

She splintered, existing nowhere and everywhere in one moment. She arched, ablaze with fire and stretched to a perfect pitch. Her pussy milked him and waves of pleasure raced through every cell.

"That's it." His heated breath brushed her mound, sweet crooning sounds dancing across her flesh as he kissed her belly. He kept a steady, sinful rhythm between her legs. "Take from me."

Her muscles softened, his voice cushioning her fall back to reality. She grappled for a witty retort. Something to make her feel less exposed.

He straightened, his erection straining nearly to his navel. A self- satisfied grin tugged at his lips.

She stroked the soft fabric beneath her, craving his skin instead. She wanted more, craved more of the connection he'd started, to touch him as deeply has he'd touched her.

Could she?

Starting at her abdomen, she trailed her fingers in an erotic path to the valley between her breasts. "You know. I think I do feel more rested."

Eryx's gaze locked on the visual, the silver in his eyes lightening with flecks of white. The rise and fall of his chest increased.

Pushing up on shaky arms, she tucked her legs beneath her, the chaise tickling her skin. The springs groaned as she crawled toward him and paused, scant inches from his cock.

He fisted the base, ready, waiting.

She exhaled against his length, mimicking that glorious sensation he'd given her only moments before, and locked gazes.

He hissed and the muscles along his stomach tightened. His smug expression shifted to tight intensity.

With the barest caress, she pressed her fingertips against the hard columns of his thighs just above his knees, and skimmed her thumbs along the inner edge. His erection jerked as her hands drew closer, impatient with her slow intentions. With one tentative touch, she traced the most prominent vein from base to tip, and circled in the drop of precum.

A tremor rippled along his formidable body.

Her heart pounded in triumph. The silver centers of his eyes sparkled, the whites surrounding them a pleasant glow. His lips parted and his breath rasped past them in a slow, steady rhythm.

Oh, yes. She'd reached him. Maybe not as deeply, but getting there. She inched forward and savored his musky scent, sampling his taste with a swirl of her tongue.

Eryx's growl bounced from the tiled walls, and he gripped the hair at the nape of her neck.

"Careful, hellcat." His hips flexed so his shaft brushed her lips. "Teasing can go two ways…and I can hold out a long time."

Lexi's stomach vaulted and an electric jolt ran thick beneath her skin as she clutched the base of his staff.

"Take me in your mouth." He cupped the back of her head. Dark. Demanding.

Part of her bristled. Told her to sit back and prove her own power by refusing. A bigger part of her thrilled at the command. Yearned to submit.

Maybe she could have both.

Trailing in an unhurried path along the stark veins and

ridges, she sampled his hot, hard flesh. Her tongue. Her lips. Gliding along his slick shaft. Then, mimicking the pleasure he'd given her, she circled the crest, lifted her gaze—and sucked.

He thrust into her mouth with snarl, and his hands tightened in her hair.

She was lost.

The taste of him, salty and warm. His grated sounds. This was more than sex. It was intimacy. Two people mingled into one, combining every God-given sense. Inhibition flittered into nothing, her heart laid bare. She palmed his sack and tongued the tender ridge below the crown.

"Perfect." A reverent groan. "Fucking decadent."

She opened her eyes and found his gaze focused slightly behind her on the mirrored wall. Eryx loomed, tall and proud, his cock scant inches from her lips where she knelt before him, gripping his shaft. Her lips were red and swollen and her eyes glassy with lust.

"Beautiful." He guided her to face the mirror, his front to her back. "And mine." He skimmed her rib cage and palmed her swollen breasts. He raised them gently, the subtle shift in weight heightening her vulnerability. "You can't doubt what's between us. I won't let you. Not anymore."

Water spilled from a waterfall shower behind them, multiple faucets raining a gentle spray from all three walls.

She opened her mouth to question the water's source, but groaned instead when Eryx gave a gentle tug to both nipples.

"I used my mind." His teeth grazed her neck and a veil of humor laced his voice. "I'd thought by now you'd be used to it."

Steam billowed from the marble enclosure and swirled at her ankles in a sensual invitation.

"Now, let me take care of you." He stepped in first and eased her beneath one stream.

The rain-like pelts soaked her hair. Hot rivulets streamed around her breasts leaving them heavy and tight. "You're going to ruin me."

"That's the plan." He turned her to the mirror and picked up a bottle behind them, the open entry leaving their every intimacy bare for reflection.

The steam wound around her, lulled her and tugged her eyelids.

"Open your eyes." His sultry voice stroked her. "Keep them open."

A lemony scent bloomed in the thick heat. His soap-covered hands circled her waist and rubbed seductive circles across her belly.

"I want you to see us together." His hands grazed the bottoms of her breasts and her breath hitched. "Watch me touch you." His cock pressed along the crease of her ass. "Watch me take you."

A needy mewl slipped from her lips. He toyed with her nipples, and she angled toward the source of the pleasure. She couldn't get close enough, couldn't get enough of his hot hands against her slick flesh. She gripped his corded neck, and ground her ass against his straining length.

With a frustrated snarl, he turned her to a side wall and pressed her hands against the stone. He nuzzled the space behind her ear. "Don't move." His warmth disappeared, and a cool gel drizzled along her spine. He worked the silky substance at the small of her back, but withheld any other contact. Seizing her hips, he lifted. "Arch for me."

She answered in the most primitive of ways, angling her hips in invitation.

A low rumble of approval wrapped around her, but still he didn't move close. He traced the curve of her ass to the seam at the top of her thighs and nudged her legs apart. "Wider."

Erotic. Sensual. The order sent goose bumps everywhere. Never had she felt so exposed and alive. Out of balance and perfectly placed at the same time. "Eryx, don't leave me like this." Every nerve ending protested his lack of touch. Shivered with a need she wasn't sure he could ever sate.

He grazed the back of her knees. Crouched behind her, he faced her blatantly exposed core. "Shhh." His whisper landed against her center a second before his devious tongue.

Ache was too inadequate a word. Soul wrenching, needy desperation was close, but still lacked the necessary weight. Her hips flexed up and back, but Eryx kept her locked in place with a ruthless grip on her thighs and devoured her sensitive flesh.

"Eryx. Please," she wailed, begging for mercy and fulfillment.

He pulled back with a volatile hiss. A second later his cock teased her pussy. "Look at us." A sultry predator, staking his claim. "Say it. Tell me what you want."

She almost wept, his slick shaft poised at her entrance, prodding but not giving. She quivered despite the heat. Lust clouded her vision. "Take me. Please."

His erection pressed deep in one, powerful thrust. Her pussy rippled with a mixture of pleasure and pain. It was perfect. Completion in its most literal sense.

Their carnal image in the mirror hypnotized. His dark skin against hers. His long fingers gripping her waist and his head thrown back in pleasure. The steady flex and release of his ass as he pumped in and out and dragged her toward sweet oblivion.

He lifted his head and met her stare in the reflection. One hand snaked between her slick thighs and circled her clit in time with his hips. "Let it come." His jaw tightened. "Now." He pressed her swollen nub, plowed deep, and shoved her into an orgasmic free fall.

Her knees shook and her channel flexed. A steady, delicious pulse.

Eryx rode his own release, his cock jerking inside her as his hips rolled and bucked.

She clung tight to the wall and savored each stroke, willing her heart to find a steady beat. Her legs buckled.

Eryx caught her, cradled her tight against his chest, and sat with a *thunk* on an overlarge bench behind them. Water spilled over them with hypnotic warmth, a gentle massage to guide them back to Earth.

Lexi trailed the droplets of water against his chest. His heart thumped steady beneath her ear and water spattered against the tile.

How was someone supposed to land from something so profound?

He kneaded her nape. "Don't overthink it. Accept what I offer. Give me what you can."

Such simple, yet profound words. Given without demand for anything in return.

She didn't know what to say. For once, her doubt-laden thoughts lay eerily silent beneath a cinder block of emotion. Was this really all she could give? When this amazing man offered everything?

"I know what I want to give you," she whispered.

His heart stuttered beneath her ear and his steady caress along her spine hesitated.

Water trickled down her arm. She splayed her fingers wide over his heart.

She was safe.

One deep breath.

One simple sentence.

She absolutely could do this. "My answer is yes."

CHAPTER 15

*M*axis perched on a rocky ledge at the height of his training grounds and observed Reese with the new recruits below. Despite Asshur's cooler temperature, most had shed their shirts mid-drill. Their bodies shone slick with sweat even with the cloud-covered sky. They ducked and weaved and counterattacked in smooth kicks and punches. Their hesitation and strategy still needed work, but their grunts and shouts promised staunch determination.

If only the rest of my plans would fall in line.

The nagging thought tapped his impatience and shoved him to his feet. Four days since he'd spied Eryx with Lexi and still no sign of her anywhere in Eden. Sightings of Eryx abounded, but there'd been not so much as a glimpse of the dark-haired woman from Evad.

Doubt waggled in the back of his mind. Maybe Eryx had contained his interludes to some remote corner of the human realm. For all he knew, the man had a damned harem locked away in Timbuktu.

He waved off his doubts and sent a mental summons to Reese. Second-guessing himself was a waste of time, especially with the other options he could work with. The bit he'd learned from Phybe about Serena promised an entirely new and intriguing angle for his schemes—and he intended to leverage every last thread he could find.

He situated himself on a nearby rock. Stone the color of burnt adobe stretched out, a wasteland, barren and dismal. Only sparse outcroppings of spindly, gray bushes broke the dull terrain. Thanks to the somewhat constant rain in this region, the men stirred very little dust as they drilled, but if a drought were to occur, the place would be a dust bowl.

Reese landed on the hard rock. "What do you want?"

Maxis ground his teeth. *Remember his value. Patience.*

"You'd do well to remember who you're speaking to, strategos." Maxis emphasized the title and bared his teeth under the guise of an empty smile. "The army you're training is young with very limited loyalties. You could be replaced. Rather quickly."

Reese placed his hands formally behind his back, but the move screamed of mockery.

Maxis pushed from his seat. "I have an assignment for you." He peered over the ledge to watch the men once more. "There's a woman we'd do well to court. Welcome her into our fold, so to speak. Her name is Serena Doroz." He faced Reese. "I understand she's spent considerable time in the malran's bed. Are you familiar with her?"

Reese cocked his head. "Gossip about the malran's love life isn't a topic I follow."

Maxis paced with slow steps along the ledge. "Apparently, this lady was involved with the malran some time ago and is a bit distressed she's been unable to regain his interest. Keeps throwing herself at him in hopes he'll take another bite."

Reese's face hardened. "How does the malran's discarded lover have anything to do with me and my efforts to train an army?"

Maxis waved over his shoulder and headed in the other direction. "The two have nothing whatsoever to do with each other. This is a new effort. One that will pay off for us handsomely if we play our cards right." He paused directly in front of Reese. "Find this woman. Work your way into her good graces. And her bed, if it furthers our cause."

"And that gets us what?"

Plenty.

Evanora's ruthless, deadly reign proved it.

"The emotions of a jilted woman can fuel enormous power. Serena may be a laughing stock at court, but she allegedly has free rein in the castle. Why not use her access when it suits us?" Maxis resumed his seat and crossed his legs. "You're a handsome man, and the woman can't be too ugly to have caught the malran's eye."

Reese's mouth opened and shut—twice.

"You never know," Maxis said, "she may end up being the perfect woman for you."

Reese stared a few moments more before nodding his head—not altogether convincingly. "I'll make some inquiries."

Maxis smiled and savored the agreement. "You do that, strategos. You do that."

"Oh, Lexi." Orla's muffled voice sounded from deep inside the closet. "Wait until you see this."

Lexi ignored her. Or tried to. She still hadn't learned to turn off her senses and Orla's happiness had pelted her nonstop ever since Eryx announced the upcoming mating. This had to be how parents felt after too many hours locked in a room packed with sugar-saturated four-year olds.

"Are you ready?" Orla's voice fairly twinkled behind the bathroom door.

A hell of a question. When Lexi had told Eryx she'd marry him, she'd thought there'd be time to adjust. To make plans and settle into her new life. Not leap into wedded bliss the next night. So, no, she wasn't ready. Not really. "Sure, bring it out."

Orla swept into the bedroom Lexi shared with Eryx, a jaw-dropping gown of black velvet draped over one shoulder and her arms. "It's beautiful, don't you think?"

Lexi plunked into the armchair behind her and her heart leapt into her throat.

She was getting hitched.

Tonight.

To Eryx. The dress proved it.

"Don't you like it?" Orla hustled over and let the bottom of the dress fall toward the floor to better display its grandeur.

"It's beautiful." Lexi brushed the velvet surface and the fabric whispered a soft greeting. Platinum clasps with delicate filigree were spaced in six- inch segments from the neck to the sleeves, holding the front and back of the gown together. Magnificent rubies adorned the center of each clasp with diamonds embedded at the edges.

"Do you love him?" Orla's voice changed, levity replaced with concern. A tremble of fear.

Lexi dropped her hand to her lap and fiddled with the edge her robe. "I thought I did. And then he left for…" She waved toward the door. "Whatever secret stuff he had to do. Now I keep asking myself if I even know what love is."

She surged upright and resumed the path she'd worn off and on all afternoon.

Orla laid the gown out on the bed, her footsteps soundless. She snatched Lexi by the elbow on her next pass, and spun her around. "Turn your silly mind off and answer my question with your heart. Do you love him?"

She thought of waking in Eryx's arms. The intensity and comfort of each touch. The sincerity of his actions, and how her disconnectedness from life had ended the day she'd met him. "I think so."

Orla raised an eyebrow.

"Yes." The admission shook her to her core. A fine sheen of sweat broke out along her spine and her head felt light enough to fly off her shoulders.

Orla stroked Lexi's cheek, and her cornflower blue eyes filled with understanding and sadness. Or was it pity? "Then why fight it?"

"It's just so…fast."

"Is it?" Orla took both of Lexi's hands in hers and pressed them tight together. "He looked for you for years. If you know he has your heart, why waste precious time?" She released Lexi's hands and lifted the sleeve of her loose silver gown. The dull-gray image of a Rowan tree covered the space from her wrist to her elbow, its roots intricately twined around her arm.

"This was my mate's mark." She sucked in a ragged breath and gazed longingly at the faded image. "The marks pale when our other half moves to nirana, but when they're alive, they're a glorious, bold ebony." She met Lexi's stare, eyes wet and mouth trembling. "My fireann was taken from me when I was far too young. We had no children when he died, and I thank The Great One every day for the gaping hole Eryx and his family filled when they took me in."

She let the sleeve drop and gripped Lexi's shoulders. "There are days when I would give anything to have one more day. If you know this is right, then charge in and don't look back. Drink up every minute of your love with no regret."

Rattled from the strength of Orla's emotions, Lexi's shoulders curled inward of their own accord, like the action might somehow better protect her heart. "I don't know how."

"Oh, sweetheart. The answer's easy." Orla pulled her into a hug. "You let Eryx teach you."

Such warm, heartfelt words. They radiated out across Lexi's soul and cocooned her spirit in a soft embrace.

Orla held her for long, patient moments.

As soon as she could pull a steady breath, Lexi stepped away. The dress lay on the bed, waiting. A fairy tale promise —if she dared to take the leap. "Okay. Let's do this."

Orla whooped with delight, all solemnity washed away under the happy clap of her hands.

The dress slipped over Lexi's head, and the silk lining slithered wickedly against her skin. "I'll never get used to this no underwear thing."

Orla's chuckle was downright naughty. "Admit it. *Au naturel* feels better. Right?"

A knock sounded on the door.

"Perfect timing." Orla smoothed out the velvet along Lexi's shoulders. "We're just finishing up, Graylin. Come on in."

The door opened without a sound.

Orla stepped to the side with a Vanna White motion. "Doesn't she look beautiful?"

Graylin strolled into the room, hands clasped at his waist. He hadn't deviated from his usual tank and lounge pant combo, but this time the fabric was as black as the velvet of Lexi's dress. "Radiant." He kissed Lexi's knuckles and winked at Orla. "Eryx is a lucky man."

A pretty pink dotted Orla's cheeks.

Graylin's lips tilted in a sly smile.

A sweet, innocent moment—and here she was, a gawking intruder. Stepping to Lexi's free side, Graylin settled one hand in the small of Lexi's back and motioned toward the door. "It's customary for a woman's mother and father to walk her to her soon-to-be mate. I hope it's not presumptuous of Orla and I to ask for such an honor in their absence?"

Orla looked up from her study of the floor and smiled hopefully.

"Are you kidding?" She was about to walk headlong into the single biggest step of her life without so much as a clue what to expect. If they were offering to stand beside her for the first few steps, she was very much on board with the plan. "I'll take all the help I can get."

He nudged her forward. "I know you're nervous, but you should know all Myren women go into a mating with exactly the same knowledge you will. It's a tradition. A very worthy and important tradition."

The candles along the hallway flickered, the subtle twitches and turns of the flames a fair representation of the nervousness skimming beneath her skin.

Graylin's mouth pursed, the line between his eyebrows etched deep. "Tonight will be about Eryx proving himself. Demonstrating the manner in which he means to act as a mate. How he intends to provide for you, care for you, protect you and, most importantly, love you. Your task is to observe each action, each nuance, and determine if he is worthy of your commitment."

She took the first steps toward the main level and rifled through the meat and potatoes of what he'd shared. The concept of Eryx putting himself out in such a formal way sounded beautiful, but Graylin hadn't given much in the way of her responsibilities. "What about me? Don't I need to do the same for him?"

Graylin halted. "Praise The Great One, no." He shook his

head and urged her into motion. "It's a man's honor to display his intent in a mating."

So she was supposed to just sit and watch? Do nothing? Say nothing? The idea wouldn't jibe with the world she'd grown up in—at least not in her neck of the woods. "Shouldn't a woman have to prove her own intentions in a marriage?"

"Mating," he corrected almost absentmindedly. "And a man would never take this important step if he hadn't already deemed the woman ideal for him alone." At the top of the stairs, he steered her toward a section of the house she'd yet to explore. "Our culture is much different from the one you grew up in. Women here are revered and cherished by their men. This is his night to show you how important you are."

Revered. Cherished.

Her footsteps slowed from the weight of the words. They curled through her, not uncomfortable, so much as unfamiliar. But they fit. With Eryx, they fit.

"So." She hesitated, thoughts scrambled. "What am I supposed to do?

A hallway lined with deep chocolate panels stretched out before them and soft gray stone lined the floors.

"You decide," Graylin said. "You move forward or you walk away depending on what you garner from his actions. Not that ascertaining his true intent should be troublesome for you given your new gift."

He pulled her to a stop at the end of the hall, the closed doors ahead of them symbolic in a way she couldn't escape. It was all she could focus on—the thick slab of wood with its distressed markings, and the commitment that waited on the other side.

"There is one thing I will tell you." He fixed her with a this-is-really-important stare. "If you can't give yourself completely into Eryx's keeping, trusting him without question, you shouldn't go with him tonight."

The solemnity of his voice sent goose pimples along her arms. The content of his words gave her absolutely nothing concrete to stand on, but the weight behind them wrecking balled into her gut. "And, the eight-hundred pound gorilla you're trying not to talk about in this conversation is?"

"That's it." He straightened and squared his shoulders. "Suffice it to say, I love Eryx as much as I love my son, and I seek to protect him. I'm sure your senses are telling you there's more to it, but some things in this world you have to figure out on your own. Tonight is one of them."

The door opened.

Graylin stepped back.

She stood alone, perched on the precipice of something huge, yet utterly intangible. Her imagination ran wild, snippets of what her future might look like if she stepped forward or if she ran.

The smell of leather and worn parchment fluttered across her face. Books lined the far wall, and brocade chairs in taupe and crimson sat at conversational angles on thick patterned rugs. A glance at a corner window showed the Myren sun nearly nestled beneath the horizon, leaving a musky purple sky in its wake.

"Time for you to choose, Lexi." A verbal nudge from Graylin at her back, though neither he, nor Orla, joined her.

An easy tug issued from the space around her heart, the pull strengthened by the memory of Orla's quiet, heartfelt talk. She wanted this. Pitfalls and unknowns in all.

She sucked in a slow, deep breath. With trembling legs, she stepped across the threshold, turned, and drew up short.

Eryx stood near a mammoth fireplace, his torso covered in a thin mesh that looked like chainmail, but stretched across his skin like a fine fabric—similar to the one Ramsay had worn her first day in Eden, but with sleeves to the middle of his forearms. His pants were soft black leather, as were his boots. The braids he'd worn the day before were gone, his sable hair unbound and reaching midway down his back—just the way she liked it. The thickness against her fingers, the slide against her skin, the whole package reeked of power and screamed, *"Wait until you see me naked."*

He prowled in her direction.

Heat blasted her as though she'd walked through a wall of flame.

Take. Protect. Love.

Eryx's emotions, lust and raw possessiveness, but she felt them like her own. Powerful and barely restrained, so violent she stepped back.

Safe. The thought pushed through her mind and an invisible, silk cocoon wrapped around her. No matter his needs or emotions, Eryx would put hers first.

"Alexis." His whiskey voice. A slow delicious burn. "Let me show you my heart. Take my hand and come with me to the home that would be yours as well."

Heavy, sensual magic wrapped around them. His formal words, his voice, his eyes, even the hand he held out in offering, hypnotized. A perfect moment without so much as a touch.

She tingled, her newfound energy dancing beneath her skin. The wash of his emotions tugged at her spirit with a heady pull, but she was loath to move into the next moment too quickly. She'd never get this moment back. No way was she rushing through it.

She slid her hand into his open palm. A perfect fit. Two pieces meant to be together. His warm, strong fingers enclosed hers, and he pulled her into the shelter of his arm.

She stepped forward on shaky legs—and surrendered to the unknown.

CHAPTER 16

*L*exi flew high above the Myren landscape, the night sky peppered with twinkling stars and streaks of silver energy. Wind nipped her cheeks with the barest sting of autumn. Cold temps weren't her favorite, but tonight she didn't mind. With Eryx's heat at her back and the scorching grip of his emotions, the cooler air was a relief.

"Am I ever going to get to fly on my own again?"

Eryx's arm tightened around her waist and he nuzzled her ear. "When I have fewer control issues." His provocative rasp dragged invisible fingers down her belly, and she wriggled against him.

From there, they stayed silent, the quiet accentuating the erotic tension between them. Eryx guided them toward a stretch of darkened buildings and brought them to land alongside a towering rock wall. He steered her forward, still quiet. Almost brooding.

Thick, spongy grass with its veins of silver sparkled in the moonlight, their footsteps registering no more than a whisper. The perfume of unseen blossoms hung in the air, tinged with a salty, elusive scent. "Where are we?"

Eryx kept his pace, focused on an indefinable destination ahead. "Havilah." His emotions snipped along her arms, as clipped as his response.

She puffed out a frustrated breath. A perfect, magical night and her Prince Charming gets a dose of manstration.

Figured.

Eryx halted before a wrought iron gate anchored to a wall of solid rock. He gripped her chin and gently angled her face to his, the slant of his features etched with regret. "I'm sorry. I'm distracted." His eyes searched her face. "If I talk less, it's because tonight is about feelings. I need you in tune with yours."

A hint. Subtle, but there, his eyes a little more narrowed than normal with a read-behind-the-lines look to them. A quick tap of her emotional radar—worry, hope, fear…a well full of love. Beautiful and understandable, but not a lick of help.

She petted the strange fabric covering his pecs, the slick/rough texture pleasant yet foreign. A part of her, some illusive place emanating from the space around her heart, wanted to reach out. To connect and console. "I'll try."

He brushed his lips against her temple. With the gear he wore, the leather scent was stronger. "I know you will."

The gate groaned open.

He grasped her hand and pulled her through the opening.

A sharp, humid gust buffeted her face and pushed her hair off her neck. The tang of salt settled against her lips, and anticipation skittered along her collarbone. Salt water. Had to be. Anticipation tingled in her cheeks. She'd never seen the ocean. Always wanted to—even had a passport ready to go—but had never had the chance.

A fire roared to life not fifty feet away, the pit large enough to roast three pigs. Around it were loungers and thick futon-like cushions, their coverings a mixture of snowy-white, taupe, and silver. Unique, yet tropical looking plants dotted the secluded paradise, and white sand paths spread out in intricate veins. All of it sat high on a flat bluff, a white- capped sea tossing in the moonlight beyond.

Beautiful.

Eryx led her toward the most sumptuous of the cushions —thick, white, and the size of a king-sized bed, situated with the stormy water on her right. Lexi sank into its comfort, reclined into a mountain of pillows, and stretched out her legs. The fire sent licks of warmth against one side of her body to offset the whip of wind at the other.

"Are you warm enough?" Eryx scrutinized her with an unsettling intensity.

She petted the velvet gown against her leg in a nervous twitch. She folded her hands in her lap and straightened her posture. She didn't belong here. Didn't know how to act. "I'm fine, thank you."

Disappointment whipped across his face, but he banked it quickly and pivoted away.

"Eryx?" She squeezed one hand with the other, blood pulsing a protest in her fingertips.

He paused beside a nearby table and glanced back, his face schooled in polite question.

"The fire's nice, but the wind's a little cold."

Eryx's smile flamed to life, it's strength as bold as the fires he'd lit moments before. With swift steps, he grabbed a fluffy, white blanket from a nearby bench. The covering billowed out above her and settled across her lap.

She curled her feet under her thighs and ducked her chin. "I didn't want you to move us. I've never seen the ocean before."

Eryx knelt on one knee, tugged her feet back out to a full stretch, and tucked the blanket around her. When satisfied with his work, he cupped the side of her face and grazed his thumb along her cheek. "Never tell me what you think I want to hear. I can't provide for your needs if you don't share them."

Her heart pole-vaulted high enough to clear the moon and Graylin's words echoed through her mind. *Tonight will be about Eryx proving himself. Demonstrating the manner in which he means to go forward in your life together as mates.*

She trailed her fingertips along his forearm. Even with such a light touch there was no missing his strength. Power held in check by fierce discipline. She rested her hand over his at her cheek and pressed a soft kiss into his palm. Definitely something she could get used to.

Maybe that's why you're so afraid.

He drew away and rose. "Are you hungry?"

Thank God. A topic she could deal with.

"Are you kidding?" Genuine laughter escaped. "I've been starved ever since the awakening. Seems like all I've done is eat." She shifted to one side and ran her hand along her hip. "I'll be big and fat in another two weeks, so you may want to reconsider this baineann thing while you've still got time."

"You won't get fat." His gaze followed the line of her curves. "I'll make sure you burn the energy you need." He turned with a sultry wink and left her smoldering body to cool. From a nearby table he lifted a platter full of bite-size meats, fruits and cheese and placed it beside her.

Her stomach grumbled and she popped back two of the treats in quick succession. The sharp tang of the cheese exploded and the meat's spice left a trail of warmth on her tongue. She could ooh and ahh over the foods here all night.

Eryx handed her a glass of red wine. "Go easy on that. Our wines pack a bigger punch than what you're used to. I'd like to know you chose to be my mate with a clear head."

Lexi laughed and bit into a new selection.

No response. No movement.

She glanced up.

Eryx watched her. Avid. Concentrated.

Great. He probably thought he was hitching up with a frat boy. She swallowed the morsel, dropped the bite pinched between her fingers back onto the platter, and reached for a napkin.

"Don't do that."

She wiped her fingers on her napkin and pretended she couldn't devour at least half of the food. "Don't do what?"

"Don't shut yourself down. Don't try to be someone you're not."

She focused on the cushions as a slow heat spread across her face. She traced the stitching along one edge. "You were staring."

"I was appreciating." His voice stroked across her in a devilish glide. He sat beside her and settled his hand above her knee. "I don't want the woman you think I want. I want you."

Her skin tingled in response, every nerve ending standing up to take notice. "Even when I stuff my face and giggle?"

He smiled, warm and smooth. "Especially then."

A spark of mischief fired and she pursed her lips, her best playful. She sidled her hand toward the tray keeping her gaze locked to his, grabbed another bite, and alley-ooped it between her lips.

"That's more like it." He gave her backside a playful swat and shifted to sit at her feet. After he'd arranged a pile of pillows behind him, he fished under the blanket and curled warm fingers around her ankle. With deft movements, he removed her sandal and massaged her foot, his thumbs working deep at the arches.

Lexi scrunched deeper into the cushions and moaned. "I thought you wanted me with a clear head."

"Perhaps I should modify my intent." His gaze took a

languid trip along her body. "If anyone's going to muddle your mind, it'll be me."

Her heart jackhammered and the muscles along her thighs fluttered. He turned his attention to her other foot, every action unhurried. Seductive.

They talked about the time he'd spent looking for her. About the events of her life during the same span. Every moment lulled her. Eased the last bits of her anxiety into nothingness.

After she'd eaten most of the food, he tucked the ends of the blanket back under her feet and stood. He traced the side of her face and furrowed his brow.

The taste of birthday cake and sour milk overcame her, followed by a surge of love and fear.

Emotional sensation manifested first as a physical sensation, followed by insight.

All of a sudden, Eryx's explanation made sense. And how sad was it he felt fear when she was a languorous pile of velvet and skin?

He strode to a small table near the fire pit and grabbed a long, mahogany box about six inches thick. The odd shirt he wore stretched and pulled across his chest as he situated the box at the edge of the pit, arranging items she couldn't see.

She let go, imagining the point in the night where she'd be able to touch the hard muscles beneath the silky-rough surface.

Eryx lifted a dagger from the box.

Lexi's lustful thoughts tumbled off track. The weapon had to be as long as her forearm. Maybe bigger. Rubies and sapphires embedded the ebony hilt and the silver blade gleamed.

She straightened away from the pillows, poised to leap.

The barely perceptible tightening of his arms told her Eryx was aware of her change in focus. Hell, he could probably hear her banging heart. But he kept his eyes averted, focused on whatever task he was about instead.

He sucked in a deep breath, laid the dagger on the ledge, and shoved the sleeve of what he'd called a drast past his elbow. A gust of wind pushed his hair away from his harsh face, the flames casting his golden skin in a fiery glow. He reached for the weapon. In one, smooth move, he sliced the blade deep along the inside of his arm from elbow to wrist.

Her stomach plummeted. She jolted forward on the cushion. "Eryx!" A muscle flinched at the back of his jaw.

She froze. The wind whipped around her, the fire a steady burn along the side of her face.

He stretched out his hand toward the pit and his blood flowed thick and crimson, sizzling against the hot metal basin.

Her heart constricted and pain shot through her body. Was it her pain? His? What the hell was she supposed to do? He didn't move. He just stood there, waiting. Breathing.

Tonight will be about Eryx proving himself. Surely that was the key. She cursed Graylin and stupid traditions and swore if she ever had a daughter, she wouldn't go into this mess so ill prepared. She tried to swallow, but her throat wouldn't cooperate. Reclining into the cushions with jerky movements, she clenched her trembling hands together in her lap.

A sigh escaped Eryx's lips, taking his tension with it. He lifted his head and addressed the heavens. "I vow to the Great One to love and provide for this woman until I leave this life. To see to her needs and the needs of those she holds dear. To protect her at all costs, even to the point of death." His gaze shifted to hers, void of all barriers, exposing his soul.

She fisted the cushions, seeking some purchase to hold her in place. The need to be with him, hold him, pounded from every quarter.

"No other will be placed before her and she will be cherished until I breathe no more." He waited, quiet, blood still seeping from his wound.

Lexi didn't know whether to weep or bind his gash. How was a woman supposed to appreciate such a vow from a man when his blood was pooling up and he did nothing to stop the flow?

As if sensing her concern, Eryx motioned for her.

Lexi shot forward, torn between verbally flaying him and asking a million questions.

He focused on his arm and slid his free hand along the deep gash. The lines between his brows were deep with concentration, but the blood dwindled and the flesh mended. When blood no longer flowed, he held out his arm and displayed the jagged pink line along his arm. "You see? Everything's fine." He grabbed a damp cloth from the ledge and wiped at the blood.

Lexi snatched the cloth from his hand and took over.

His mouth opened.

"Not a word, Eryx." Her arms shook so badly it took every ounce of focus to wipe gently across the wound. Her throat was dry, barely able to generate words. "I sat through that. I watched while blood poured out of a four inch deep wound on the man I love, and trusted he knew what he was doing. So, let me do this."

The wind lashed out and whipped her hair into her face. Her heart beat so frantically it hurt.

"Say it again." His voice rumbled like thunder, and this time the wind coiled around her in a way it shouldn't have been able to, caressing every intimate place at once. The nature of her trembles transformed into something far more pleasant.

"Which part? The words I said out loud or when I called you a dipshidiot in my head?"

"The ones you said out loud."

Lexi kept her head down and swept the cloth against his skin once more. She laid it aside and finally managed to swallow. All she needed now was one, solid breath.

She squared her shoulders and met his waiting gaze. "I love you."

Eryx's emotions slammed into her. Joy. Pride. Gratitude. Lust.

His arms banded around her and one hand cradled the back of her head. "I've loved you since before I knew you. I've loved you since the first time I saw you in my dreams and heard your laughter. No one will fit me the way you do."

He kissed her. Not a kiss of stormy passion, but one of devotion and awe. His firm, full lips stroked and coaxed hers over and over in an unhurried glide, each wine-spiced brush of his tongue luring her deeper into surrender.

Too many years, she'd held herself aloof. Kept people distant. With this man, there would be no more holding back.

He eased away too fast.

Loath to let him go, she opened her eyes, intent on provoking her insatiable man to finish what he'd started.

A predator stared down at her. Hungry and determined. If she thought the night was downhill from here, one look at Eryx's face said the ride was about to get intimately bumpy.

A spear of pleasure shot squarely between her legs. She licked her lips and savored the taste of his kiss. "There's more isn't there?"

God, she sounded like a thrill-seeking, breathy nympho.

But Eryx's voice was all grit and sensuality. A sensual smile crept into place. "Oh, yeah. There's more."

CHAPTER 17

*E*ryx wrapped Lexi close and shot them into the air on a barrel roll. Her stomach was still somewhere on the ground in a quivering mess, but she couldn't care less. His lips slashed against hers, not bruising, but fierce. His need resonated through her emotional gift and layered on top of her own.

The land streaked by beneath them, and the air swooshed along her skin. She didn't know how far they traveled. Didn't try to gauge their destination. Though she dimly wondered how he could simultaneously navigate and deliver such an all-consuming kiss.

He shifted their bodies to land and eased his embrace, the swipes of his tongue against hers more succulent than gluttonous. They landed and he set her away with a mischievous grin. He turned her so she looked out from the top of a hill. "I wanted your first view to be the best."

She gasped so hard the cool air stung her throat, and a sparkling rush of awe tickled along her collarbone. It was a castle. A real life, honest to God, castle.

Not a single light shone from inside the estate, yet the

pale-colored rock walls looked pearlescent in the moon-shine. Whitecaps sparkled in the background, and the crash of waves pounded her ears. An elaborate garden of blooms fronted the majestic scene, their stems bobbing in rhythm with the sea and wind.

Eryx's chest lifted and fell against her back. "Welcome home, Lexi." He extended his hand, palm out, and hundreds of torches blazed to life, illuminating the garden and grounds in all their splendor.

Eryx nudged her forward.

She shut her gaping mouth and forced her legs into motion. The torchlight rivaled the sun and exposed a kaleidoscope of color. The white sand path looked as soft as baby powder and, for a minute, she thought about ditching her sandals in favor of bare feet.

They neared the balustrade lining a raised patio and her heart gave a happy squeal. Ivy covered the railing and inched its way toward the castle walls.

A sensation tapped at her shoulder, like a tentative child nudging for someone's attention.

Eryx halted.

She followed his sharp gaze to a large rock beside the path. Behind it huddled two patches of red-haired young-sters shaking with barely restrained laughter.

"Boys." Eryx's authoritative voice whipped across the short distance. He darted a quick wink at Lexi before resuming his mask of passivity.

The giggling stopped and two boys, who looked all of seven or eight, rose from behind the boulder, their eyes wide and lips twitching with a mix of fear and giggles.

Without a word, Eryx flicked an imperious hand toward the gardens.

The boys scrambled to take their leave, but their delighted chatter hung in the air.

"They were only curious. You didn't have to run them off." It was a light reprisal. A natural banter she'd heard between other couples that shared a good stretch of history —and didn't that concept warm her in a hearth and home kind of way?

Eryx inhaled. A slow sexy one that stroked her libido with a promise of intentional seduction and purposeful delight. His wicked eyes sparked from behind hooded lids. "Tonight I'm busy feeding someone else's curiosity."

The groan of opening doors sounded behind her.

She whipped around. Two arched panels of distressed wood, thicker than two fists, beckoned her into the darkness beyond. Trailing her fingers against the rough surface, she crossed the threshold. The scent of flowers from the garden, lemons, and earth tickled her nose. Only random shafts of moonlight and flickers of the torches beyond filtered through windows.

Eryx settled his hands on her shoulders and his warmth wrapped around her in the stillness.

Candles flickered to life to display a grand foyer. Magnificent didn't cover it. Iron sconces lined the stone walls, the rock running a spectrum from pale gray to near white. Thick rugs in warm, neutral colors covered the floors, and a window big enough to let a semi pass through graced the front.

He led her up an enormous staircase and through an intricate weave of plush hallways. No matter how much she gawked he didn't rush her, letting her soak in every detail.

The corridor ended before another set of colossal wooden doors, similar to those at the front entrance, but unique in their details. Candlelight glinted on the fine mahogany, and etched on each side was a winged horse, reared back in fury with wings stretched up and wide. She'd seen the image before, but—

"These will be our rooms."

An odd way to phrase it. "Will be?"

"This space hasn't been occupied since my parents died. I didn't want to be here without my mate."

A week. She'd known him less than that, but so much had changed. Twice now she'd walked through unknown doors for him, first the portal, and then meeting him tonight. The fact that she stood in front of yet another symbolic entry wasn't lost on her, and with the track record she'd had so far…

The doors opened.

Adrenaline ignited her newfound Myren energy and propelled her forward. She glanced back to Eryx, still at the threshold, his eyelids heavy over his swirling silver irises. He looked like a bull ready to charge. Strangely, it didn't scare her. In fact, her confidence fairly sang with empowerment. If she had a red cape, she'd have wielded it only to provoke him further.

With a slow, libidinous grin, Eryx approached and candles flared throughout the room.

Splendor surrounded her. The same stone walls, yet deeper in color. A stormy gray to match the color of his eyes. Rich, velvet drapes of deep red fell from towering ceilings and pooled on floors covered in thick, black rugs. And in front of her was a mammoth bed, covered in the same sinful red hue, and perched on a raised platform that reminded her of some kingly dais. The whole scene incited all manner of wicked thoughts.

Eryx closed the distance between them, his footsteps silent on the plush rug. He moved in behind her and leaned close, the tickle of his lips against her ear and the heat of his breath sending shivers through her.

"It's not too late to run." His voice caught, and his emotions crackled against her newfound senses.

She shook her head, muscles shaking with excitement. "I'm done running."

He slid his hands from her shoulders to her wrists. He circled the last jeweled clasp on each sleeve, sampling the texture of the gems with the pads of his fingers. "I'd have chased you anyway." With a flick, he triggered a mechanism and released the clasps, freeing the fabric so the front and back sections fell away from each other.

Only her wrists were exposed, but her heart hammered in expectation.

Eryx said nothing. Only hovered at the same spot, his lips and steady exhalations feathering against her neck. He scraped along her exposed skin to the next set of clasps and released them. Then the next. Each drag against her skin ratcheted the volume higher on her lust. Each release detonated a tiny bomb of ecstasy.

Only one set remained fastened at her shoulders. Cool air teased the skin along her arms.

He skimmed the exposed flesh in an achingly slow descent. "Turn around." Gone was his soothing, husky voice. In its place was a command that brooked no leniency.

Her abdomen twitched and moisture pooled at her core. She complied but kept some distance between them, lifting her chin to meet his gaze.

Crouching before her, Eryx lifted the hem of her gown and reached for one foot. "Hold on to me." He removed each of her sandals, his touch at her ankles both tender and erotic. When he stood, his gaze trailed up from her feet. His arms hung loose at his sides, still as a predator poised to strike. He flicked his fingers.

The last clasps snapped opened and the heavy fabric dropped to the floor.

Lexi's breath caught, the cool air a salacious stroke against her skin.

By the smirk on his face, he knew he'd caught her off guard. "Get on the bed."

His authoritative tone sent a trill through her body. Even worse, she wanted to obey. She lifted an imperious brow anyway. "No seduction tonight?"

His silver eyes smoldered. A stream of air swirled around her nipples and sliced between her legs. "I've already done that or you wouldn't be here. Get on the bed, Alexis."

Lexi fought the order this time, her shaky exhalations loud in the otherwise quiet. The tendrils of wind increased at each pleasure point until desire won over pride.

She didn't make it easy on him, though. She sauntered to the bed, hips swaying with each step. She crawled across the silk and rolled to her back. Resting on her elbows, she bent one knee provocatively and lifted her gaze.

Feminine pride and power fired hot. Her sexual red cape had definitely done its job. Eryx's drast lay discarded on the floor and his bare chest heaved. The gray of his eyes glowed and sparkled.

His ragged voice seemed more animal than man. "I'm raw tonight. Too long. Waiting."

She refused to be daunted and trudged her chin up a notch. "Should that frighten me?"

He unfastened his leather pants and shoved them down. "Do you think you should fear me?"

The answer came to her quickly, unfettered by her usual doubts. "No. You wouldn't hurt me."

Candlelight danced across his tanned skin, the muscles accented by shadow. He gripped the base of his cock and her mouth ran dry. "Will you take me then? Uninhibited? Trusting me to care for you?"

His words and the visual impact shot a ripple of pleasure through her belly. She was spellbound. Utterly entranced."Yes."

He stalked to the bed and nudged one foot with his knee to kneel between her legs. His touch drifted over the tops of her feet before he circled the insides of her ankles. "Spread your legs."

She nearly came from the words alone, her sex needy and drenched. She hesitated, more from the sting of insecurity than defiance. What he asked would leave her defenseless. Exposed in the most carnal of ways.

His knuckles grazed the insides of her calves. "Give yourself to me."

The rasp of his voice, and the spear of pleasure that raced up her thighs, worked its magic and she spread her knees wide. She reached for him, unconsciously seeking some form of anchor in the storm of sensation.

"No." Unseen hands pinned her wrists above her head, the pressure formidable, but not so much to cause discomfort. His eyes tightened to a stern slash. "Tonight you take. I give."

He inched his knees closer and drug his index finger in a circle around her belly button. "Beautiful."

Her muscles quivered beneath his touch.

He drew a slow, debauched path toward her mound. "Stretched out." His gaze flicked to hers. "Helpless."

Panic ricocheted with the fervency of a five-alarm siren. She tugged at her arms and lifted her leg to kick.

And froze.

Eryx stared. Intent.

Christ.

He knew. Knew her deepest fear and still wanted her submission. Her lungs burned and, despite the bite of fear on her tongue, she ached for his touch. Could she do this?

Yes.

The answer pushed from the depths of her soul and her hips lifted without another thought, a ragged moan slipping from her lips.

His finger resumed its slow descent and she bucked against him, her legs widening further. He parted her slick folds and stared at her undulating body, watching his ministrations with rapt attention. "Let go." A surge of power circled her clit and Lexi gasped. She couldn't breathe around the overpowering rush, the wave of pleasure enough to short-circuit the last trace of rational thought.

Two fingers slipped inside her entrance and his free hand held her hips place. "Don't fight it. Take my energy. Let it take you where you want to go."

The sensations didn't *take* her anywhere. They dragged her, catapulted her into another dimension where sensuality ruled with an iron fist. The silk tips of his hair tickled the inside of her thighs. Wet heat surrounded her core and she exploded. Shafts of light burst behind her eyelids and her back bowed from the bed. Wave after wave crashed through her while Eryx feasted from her core.

She relaxed in gradual degrees, muscles shaking as they found their way back from her sexual peak.

Eryx's grasp slid up to her shoulder blades, urging her breasts toward his tantalizing mouth. The swirls of energy around her core regained in strength and the same temptation built at her breasts. His lips closed around one nipple.

Lexi moaned, her passion vaulting to meet his once more. She lifted her arms, prepared to fight his restraints, but found them gone. She rested her hand against his heart. "Eryx, please. I need you."

But she needed more than just him inside her. She needed something else. Something deeper. That same drive for an indescribable connection she'd felt before only stronger and unrepentant.

He released her sensitized nipple and sat back on his heels. His cock nudged her core and swirls of energy rushed around each pleasure point.

She wriggled her bottom, desperate for his fullness.

Covering her hand with one of his own, Eryx pressed it hard against his chest. With his free hand, he trailed a slow path along her abdomen, between her breasts, to lie against her own heart. "Alexis, look at me."

She undulated her hips against his rigid length and opened her eyes—though it took some doing.

Strain etched his face and sweat beaded his brow. Hunger raged behind his molten eyes.

"Eryx, now." What the hell was he waiting for? Every nerve ending screamed with a mind-numbing mix of pure agony and pleasure, the swirls of energy at each pleasure point now twice as intense.

"Know you have my heart." His words were rough, barely formed. "Know I love you."

He thrust deep.

Sweet, delicious fullness stretched her walls. She rocked upward, greedy for every inch.

A swooshing sound filled her ears and reality shifted. The room vanished, replaced with the nothingness of dreams and her incorporeal body—and it was falling. Plummeting from some unknown height. Space screamed past her with nothing to grab onto.

She fought. Tried to regain balance. Tried to reach for Eryx's physical presence in her altered state, but met only air. Only dusky space surrounded her.

And panic.

Everywhere.

In some peripheral sense, she heard a shout. Male. A wail of agony that scraped along her spine.

Eryx. In pain.

The wind swept by her, the free fall never ending. The muddled mire of confusion and the thick press of dread pressed on every side.

God, he'd done so much for her. Taught her. Pushed her to trust him. He was hurting and she couldn't help him.

That was it.

Trust.

Certainty leapt in her heart and billowed out along her chest and arms. She let go. Surrendered to the free fall and accepted her fate.

The swooshing sound came again. Like the exit from a long dark tunnel on a fast moving train into open air.

Strong arms surrounded her and snatched her from her nosedive. She was back.

Eryx's hips hammered against her core, and she sank her nails deep into his flanks. She pried her eyelids open and nearly wept. It was the most carnal, delicious sight. Eryx's tanned hand at her heart, her legs spread wide, his cock slick with her wetness, tunneling deep with each thrust.

His gaze lifted from the point where their bodies joined and he slipped a hand between them. One rasp against her swollen clit and her world splintered. Her strangled cry filled the room.

Eryx's garbled growl followed right behind it. His hard length pushed and pulled against her convulsing walls, layering fine tremors on top of each clench and release.

He shouted and his pelvis slammed home. His cock throbbed and jerked within her, the flex and release of his abs against her belly a perfect mirror of the ripples fisting around his shaft.

She held fast and rode the pleasure, tears mingling with the sweat at her temples.

"You're mine, Alexis Shantos." His velvet lips brushed her forehead, his skin hot against hers. *"My baineann. My malress."* The words rumbled through her mind, possessive, but comforting.

She floated back to Earth. Had she heard him in her head? Or had she gone batty from pleasure?

"I'll think about that later." She wriggled beneath his weight and nestled close.

The blackness of sleep crept along the edges of consciousness and an answering chuckle filtered through her mind. *"Sleep, my baineann. Sleep."*

CHAPTER 18

Galena sidestepped a servant with a loaded tray of champagne flutes and angled for a better view of Phybe. Galena hated the formal gatherings so often thrown by the wives of Eryx's warriors and, judging by the tight frown on her face, Phybe wasn't a fan either.

The quaran hosting the night's festivities had invited far too many guests for the size of the room. With so many heated bodies she could barely breathe. Despite the strapless cut of her lightweight gown, the back of her neck and the valley between her breasts were damp with sweat.

If she'd been smart she'd have piled her hair on top of her head rather than leave it straight, heavy and thick down her back, but then the gossip would have started. With the Myren tradition of bound hair equating some form of relationship, she couldn't so much as braid a small section of her hair without setting tongues afire.

A French braid spilled over Phybe's shoulder. Unlike some of the power-hungry women in the warrior's camp, Phybe appeared to have truly loved her mate and refused to acknowledge that fate had unwoven their lives.

Galena navigated the crowd, smiling and chatting as necessary. With every superficial conversation a fresh layer of fatigue set in. If it weren't so important to keep appearances, she'd have left hours ago. Duty wasn't something so easily set aside, though, and like it or not, she had a role to fill. The decorous princess—proper and loyal. Never mind she might have wants and needs of her own.

Her eyes settled again on Phybe. Some of the snippiest women in the warrior clan surrounded her, their laughs obnoxious against the drone of chatter, their gowns ridiculously ostentatious for the simple affair.

Phybe was the exception. Her understated sky-blue sheath hugged her curves and she rarely joined in the conversation, her gaze locked on the balcony, twirling the stem of her crystal flute between her fingers and thumb.

Galena was only five steps and two polite, yet empty conversations away. Maybe she could do them both a favor.

A woman draped in a ballet pink chiffon gown swept in to join Phybe's group. "Juno says Ramsay refuses to downgrade the high alert status until Maxis is found. Seriously. As our strategos, you'd think Ramsay would make better use of our men's time. The Lomos Rebellion's been dead for years."

A simmering burn fired in Galena's belly. The outspoken, shortsighted bitch needed a serious reality check.

"Momma! Momma!" Clopping footsteps pounded against the slate floors, punctuated by hard breaths. Two young boys dressed in loose black pants and white tanks ground to a stop beside one woman. Twins, both beaming smiles with mops of flaming red hair that spiked haphazardly in all directions.

"Momma, I saw the malran." The one who'd spoken pushed his tiny shoulders back, eyes bright with mischief. "He had a woman with him."

"Really? That's interesting news." A calculated grin tugged

at the mother's lips as she met the other women's gazes. "I wasn't aware the malran was courting anyone."

"Oh, it's beyond courting, I assure you." Galena stepped into the fray and stood alongside Phybe.

Phybe smiled, the first one Galena had seen all night. "Galena, it's good to see you."

Galena nearly giggled at the wide-eyed looks Phybe's familiar comment garnered. Nirana forbid the shy girl actual have connections beyond their elite circle. May as well rub the surprise in while she had the chance. "How did the practice run with the krocious flowers go? Are you ready to give your green thumb a run in my garden?"

Phybe ducked her chin and a sweet blush crept across her cheeks. So genuine and kind among the vain and shallow. Her fingers tightened around the stem of her glass. "I think I made more of a mess than anything. I'm willing to—"

"Did you say the malran was serious about someone?" The lady in pink inched closer to Galena. The greedy little bitch.

Galena pulled the glass from Phybe's grip and sat it on the tray of a passing servant. She focused on the odious woman in pink and worked a little of the imperial bullshit she'd learned from Eryx. "I did. She's a wonderful woman." She let the subtle taunt of unshared information dangle in the huddle and turned to Phybe. "Would you like to come with me for a fresh drink? With all of these people, I find a cool beverage helps keep my temperature down."

Phybe's mouth parted and more than one woman behind Galena gasped. "I'd like that."

Galena steered Phybe by the shoulder and tossed a careless departure over her shoulder. "Ladies, if you'll excuse us?"

Like she'd wait for a response. Better to leave the gossip-mongers behind to do their thing.

"Thank you for the respite." Phybe's words rushed out before they'd even reached the small serving bar.

"You should have told Eryx you weren't getting along with the rest of them," Galena said. "He would have found another solution for you."

Phybe shook her head.

"Phybe, you looked like you'd rather watch grass grow. You're nothing like them at all."

Phybe shrugged and reached for a fresh drink. "There are certain people you simply can't walk away from if you're to be accepted by the group as a whole."

Funny how similar their situations, yet still different. Phybe did what was expected to gain acceptance. Galena did what was expected because no one considered she might want something else.

Galena sipped her drink. The citrusy punch tickled her throat and she smacked her lips. "I suppose we all have our political tightrope to walk." The crush parted enough to let in a faint breeze and Galena turned into it.

"Is it true the malran has a new love interest?" Phybe asked.

The curiosity caught Galena off guard. At least it was genuine and not coated in malicious intent as the other woman's question had been. "She was a lost Myren and Eryx found her. She's only recently gone through her awakening."

"Is it serious?" Phybe's eyes sparkled.

Galena almost laughed. Still, Eryx's business was his own. "We'll see." The crowd near the doorway shifted and voices rose in surprise.

Ramsay's tall form strode through the door, two of his elite guard close behind him.

"Phybe, I hate to leave you, but I need to check in with Ramsay."

Phybe took a step back and held her glass close to her chest, a wave of sadness washing across her face.

Galena laid a hand at the top of Phybe's arm. "I know the idea of gardening doesn't exactly thrill you. Have you any other hobbies? Things you've longed to do, but never before thought to try? Now might be the perfect time for you to step out and try something new."

Phybe's lips tipped into a shy, self-conscious grin. "Not really. Saul had planned to take me sightseeing around Eden once he'd earned time away. Other than that, I was focused on making our home."

"Then maybe you should see that goal through." Galena tightened her grip until Phybe met her stare. "Get out. Tour our lands. Havilah is beyond beautiful. Brasia is a frigid mess, but breath taking. Have you been to Cush?"

Phybe shook her head.

"Then, go there. It's golden and busy and a shopping dream. Heck, I'll go with you."

Phybe smiled ear to ear.

Galena hugged her tight. "You'll be fine, Phybe. Make your own way and don't let those nasty women crush you." She paused, an uncomfortable tightness gripping her throat. "Be who *you* want to be."

Ramsay walked by and jerked his head toward the balcony beyond.

Galena relinquished her shy friend. "I expect to see you at my cottage in the next few days with at least a few exciting stories, agreed?"

Phybe nodded and Galena shuffled off to see what her brother was about. She'd definitely need to talk to Eryx in the next few days, though. Phybe might not be willing to ask for other arrangements, but Galena had no problem demanding them.

CHAPTER 19

$\mathcal{E}$ryx woke to the barest hint of morning sun, the exhaustion of his mating to Lexi replaced with a deep contentment. Now he understood why the ritual was kept secret from unmated Myren women. If they had even an inkling what transpired, some might surrender to the bond without trusting their mates, mistaking hopes and dreams for a true foundation. Others, like Lexi, would forgo the exchange altogether, for the pain it dealt the male.

She nestled closer, her legs tangled with his.

Oh yeah. He'd pony up the pain nightly to wake in this same spot.

He rubbed the welts lining his chest, a starburst pattern centered over his heart where Lexi's energy had surged into his body. She'd made him work for the bond—and left behind a mark his male pride wouldn't mind showing off for as long as it took to heal.

But that wasn't the best part.

He shifted to better see her arm resting on his chest, and a feral surge of possessiveness fired in his veins. The Shantos

Pegasus reached from her wrist to nearly her shoulder, the ebony mark bold against her lightly tanned skin.

His malress. The picture of her standing before the ellan, her crowning, and their acceptance, slammed to the front of his imagination. He couldn't fucking wait. Leaving her first thing in the morning post-mating he could do without, but seeing the shocked faces of his councilmen? That would be a decent consolation.

Unraveling himself, he paused long enough to enjoy the sinful lure of his mate twisted in the crimson sheets. Dark hair. Tan skin. Maybe the ellan could wait an hour. Or three.

His erection twitched in agreement.

Then again, she hadn't so much as stirred when he'd slipped from the bed. She'd been through more than most people could take in the last few days and deserved some rest.

And the truth.

The realization backhanded him hard enough to rattle his bones. She was bound to be pissed. Especially after the trust she'd given last night.

He squared his shoulders and sucked his pride up tight. He'd do what was right and let his woman take whatever hide out of him was necessary to get back in her good graces. Just as soon as he handled his council.

He padded across the thick black rugs to the bathroom bathed in the soft streams of morning light. The oversized, platinum mirror lured him. He lifted his hand to trace the angry starburst pattern of streaks—

What in histus...

He leaned closer to the mirror and stretched out his arm. His heart took off in a pounding jog and a heady buzz kicked in beneath his skin. Lexi's mark ran the stretch of his arm—a sword twined in ivy. The hilt sat near his wrist, embedded with jewels and ancient markings, accented with fine filigree. The blade reached to the tip of his shoulder.

When a Shantos male takes a mate bearing the mark of a sword wound with ivy, so shall dawn a new era in Eden.

Her mark was the epitome of the prophecy, and it was exquisite.

He could already hear the ellan. The populace in general. They'd be all over the place, some rejoicing and predicting great things, others sure their civilization was doomed. Either way, he and his new baineann had a political roller coaster in front of them.

He flexed his hand, his muscles rolling beneath Lexi's mark. Adrenaline pushed through him in a steady pulse. They could throw whatever they wanted his direction. He had his mate and was more than up to the challenge.

He plaited his braids back in place. Funny how they meant so much more today. For years he'd worn them as a sign of his commitment to his people. Now one brave woman took precedence over them all.

He pulled his council attire on and hesitated. Usually, he'd forego the silk overcoat in favor of only the platinum silk tank and pants, but today he needed to throw his punches carefully. He snatched the overcoat and padded to the bed.

He kept his voice low so as not to rouse her too deeply from sleep. "Lexi."

"Mmmm?" She snuggled closer. Her dark lashes remained closed, sultry crescents against her skin.

"I need to take care of something, but I'll be back before you wake up."

She cracked one eye open before closing it again on a moan. "I thought husbands stayed home the morning after they get hitched."

Oh, yes. The intimacy of waking up with Lexi every morning was a luxury he'd definitely enjoy. "I won't be gone long. I promise." He sucked in a slow, steady breath. Better to lay some groundwork now. Something to keep him honest when he got home. "And we need to talk when I get back."

Both eyes opened this time, caution pushing out the fog of sleep. "Everything okay?"

He kissed her softly. "It will be." She started to sit up, but he urged her back against the mattress. "It's time to share some things with you. That's all."

She relaxed and her gaze softened.

He traced her lips. "No more secrets between us."

A shadow seemed to cross her face.

Had he accidentally stumbled across whatever it was Ludan had seen in her past? "No more secrets from *me*. You'll tell me what you need to when you're ready."

She burrowed into the silk sheets, a silent thank you and a silly smile on her face. The kind a woman got when a man gifted with her with unexpected flowers. "Hurry up and get back."

He kissed her temple, lingered long enough to breath in her sultry scent, and pushed from the bed. He nearly tripped on Ludan sprawled outside their closed doors in a wingback chair that hadn't been there the night before.

Eryx closed the doors behind him with his mind. "I thought I gave you the night off."

Ludan stood and twisted, the crack of his spine echoing down the hall. "You ordered me the night off. Doesn't mean I had to listen. No telling what Maxis is willing to try where you're concerned." He jerked his head toward the doors guarding his chambers and grinned. "You weren't exactly alert."

"Well since you're here, watch out for Lexi while I go to council." He headed for the stairway, but Ludan held him back.

"Screw that. My job's with you. Have Ramsay get her protection."

Eryx faced his somo and his chest tightened. If he was going to test the waters with anyone, Ludan was a damned fine place to start. He shrugged the overcoat off and put his arm on display. "Today, you stay here."

Ludan's defiant posture dropped and his jaw went slack.

"I need to know she's safe. Shit will hit the fan the minute this is public."

Ludan's aloof demeanor faded and he studied the symbol.

"I'll be back in a few hours. If she wants to get out, stay with her."

Ludan nodded at Eryx's chest. "She make you work for it?"

Eryx lifted the tank to show the ragged welts. He knew damned well he was smirking the same way he had when he'd got his first weapon and couldn't care less.

"Oh, yeah. That hurt." Ludan stretched back out in the wingback and crossed his arms across his chest. "I got this. But hurry up. I want details."

Eryx stalked down the hallway. "If anything happens, I want to know."

Praise The Great One, the shock on Ludan's face had been priceless. And Ludan had given not one word of argument once he'd seen the mark.

Eryx cleared the castle doors and took to the sky, centering his thoughts for the confrontation ahead. Somehow he had a feeling his ellan wouldn't be as short on words.

CHAPTER 20

*L*exi stood before a floor length mirror, naked, skimming her fingers down the symbol on her arm. A winged horse, like some fantasy depiction of the mythical Pegasus, but dark as midnight instead of white. Reared back on his hind legs, the creature looked back over his shoulder, defiant, wings arched high to touch her shoulders. His long mane twisted up and around her arm as though caught in a fierce wind, and the tail ribboned down her forearm to her wrist.

Claimed.

Possessed.

Even without Eryx here, his mark promised the most devout protection.

Unease scampered through her belly. She'd seen the mark before. Nowhere near this in fine, or this large, but there was no mistaking its similarities to the painting on Graylin's wall.

Voices stirred beyond the chamber doors and a polite knock sounded.

Lexi's heart picked up. Her gown lay in a heap on the floor. No way she'd get the two halves back together in a decent span of time. Across the edge of the bed was a black silk robe.

Okay, so leaving her on the first day of their honeymoon with a mark that scared the hell out of her wasn't the smoothest move, but Eryx's thoughtfulness counted for something.

She donned it and quickly cinched the belt, swooped to retrieve her discarded gown, and hustled to the door.

"Surprise!" Galena raised both eyebrows in an are-you-going-to-tell- me-the-details kind of way, her hands clasped excitedly at her chest.

Ramsay and Ludan stood to the side with knowing smirks. The drast and leather pants combo didn't surprise her on Ramsay, but Ludan wearing the same outfit did. At their necks and wrists—cuffs and torcs with the exact image covering her arm.

"Hi." A lame greeting, but overall pretty impressive considering the possibilities swirling in her head.

"If you're too tired we can come back." Galena stepped away from the door.

"No." Lexi opened the door wider and motioned toward the cement truck-sized fireplace and the sitting area fronting it. "I think company to keep me occupied might not be a bad idea. Anyone know when my husband's due back? I need to talk to him."

"Fireann." Ramsay sat in a crimson and gold wingback.

Galena backhanded Ramsay's shoulder on her way to sit beside Lexi. "I wouldn't provoke her if I were you. You're a dead ringer for the idiot who left her here alone. She might decide to slug you instead." She focused on Lexi and tilted her head. "Everything okay?"

Lexi nodded. The tail of the winged horse peeked out from her sleeve. Surely the mark was a coincidence.

Galena edged closer, the deep teal of her loose fitting

linen pants and tunic a defiant color amidst the mostly red and black room. "Did you have a good night?"

Lexi almost laughed. If Galena was shooting for nonchalant, she'd missed it by about two football fields.

Both men raised one eyebrow at Lexi. Synchronized, silent commands.

She clamped her mouth shut, deception bitter on her tongue. The whole mating secret custom didn't sit well. Hell, she wasn't even sure she'd worked through it in her own head. "I think I can safely say it's a night I'll never forget."

Galena's face fell and her shoulders slumped. She shot a venomous glare at her companions. "Killjoys. I'll find out."

More with the smirks from the high and mighty men.

Galena tossed her head and gestured at Lexi's arm. "So, let me see."

Gathering the sleeve of her robe, Lexi displayed the mark for her small audience. "It's beautiful, don't you think?"

"It's magnificent," Galena whispered, reaching for an outstretched wing.

"It's huge." Ramsay surged to his feet for a closer view.

Ludan stayed where he was, arms crossed with an I-know-something- you-don't-know stare. "Wait until you see Eryx's."

Galena and Ramsay stopped their inspection to glance at Ludan.

Oh, hell. She'd probably gone and done something to screw the whole mating thing up. "Is it okay? What is it?"

"Nope, not going to ruin it." Ludan shook his head, completely unrepentant.

Lexi swallowed, but the lump in her throat wouldn't budge. Knowing her luck she'd left him with Mickey Mouse ears. "Is there something wrong with it?"

"It's impressive." Ludan's face softened a touch, but his grin stayed in place. "I just don't want to ruin the surprise."

She zeroed in on Ramsay. "Don't most look like this?"

Ramsay resumed his sprawl in the wingback and laughed hard enough to rattle the knickknacks. "Hell, no. Most reach the elbow at most. Yours screams, 'I mated a bad ass!'"

"Eryx's shouts, 'Don't fuck with my baineann.'" Ludan slid forward in his sly, prowling manner, eyes still locked on Lexi, and stopped in front of her. "But then, such a mark would be appropriate for a malress wouldn't it?"

Galena gasped.

Ramsay's smile flat-lined.

Ludan held out his hand, palm up.

Maybe company had been a bad idea. Not knowing what else to do, Lexi laid her hand in his.

His callused fingers wrapped around hers and he dropped to one knee. He bowed his head and laid a chaste kiss to her knuckles. "As I have pledged my loyalty to our malran, so do I pledge to you, our malress."

Apprehension swirled around her, chilling her to the core. "Malress?"

Ludan rose, silent.

Her three guests stared at each other, gazes darting back and forth.

Damned telepathy. Now they weren't even bothering to hide when they did it.

Ramsay laughed, a good-natured one that broke the room's tension. He stood and ran his fingers through his sun-streaked hair. "Eryx's gonna kill us." He sauntered forward, snatched her hand from her lap, and dropped to one knee. "As I have pledged my loyalty to my brother, our malran, so do I pledge to you, our malress." He peeked at her and winked. "And my shalla."

Ramsay stepped back and Galena pushed forward to both knees. She scooped Lexi's trembling hands into hers. Her Caribbean-colored eyes bore into hers, solemn, peaceful.

"You are my shalla and my malress. My skills and my loyalty are yours to call upon."

Lexi looked from one person to another. "I have a feeling I'm going to regret this question, but what's a malress?"

"Eryx is our malran, Lexi." Galena gave her hands a gentle squeeze. Her voice slipped around Lexi, cool and tranquil. "The interpretation for malran in Evad would be king."

White noise. Lots and lots of it.

"You're now his mate," Galena added. "Which makes you the malress. Or our queen."

"I'm not…" Every word she reached for fizzled into nothing. She closed her gaping mouth, licked her dry lips, and tried again. "He said a malran was a leader. I thought he was an ambassador, maybe a senator, or something. I didn't know—"

"And he didn't want you to." Galena squeezed Lexi's ice-cold fingers. "But not for the reasons you might think, so try not to be too harsh when you judge him. He's high-handed and overbearing at times, but he's still a man."

"Ah, Lena." Ramsay whined petulantly from the couch. "Don't go mending bridges for him. It was gonna be fun watchin' Lexi hand him his ass on a platter."

So playful. Light-hearted as he always seemed to be. Didn't he get what a colossal problem this was?

"I don't know how to do this." Lexi leaned closer to Galena, nearly pleading. "I'm not that kind of person. I mix drinks and have decent street smarts. What the hell was he thinking?"

"You're wrong." Ludan's words slashed out, and from the look on his face she was about two pouts shy of a lecture to rival his father. "You're perfect for Eryx and will make a strong queen."

"But I—"

"For you to doubt yourself is to doubt Eryx and his judgment." Ludan prowled forward. "Do you honestly think he would take a mate who would fail his people?"

"You've gotta get over this doubting thing, Lex," Ramsay said, totally at ease with the fact his brother—a king—had shacked up with a no one.

Galena settled close to Lexi's side and draped her arm along her shoulders. "Sounds like you're the only one doubting you."

Christ, how was she going to handle this? A new realm. A new race. A new role. Her life had turned into one big Etch-A-Sketch.

The room grew silent and the stares of those around her, no matter how kind, stifled normal breath. She stood and angled for the bathroom. She had to get out. To move and think. Do something.

Ludan blocked her path, head tilted in a silent question.

She huffed and stepped around him. "Don't worry. I'm not running." Pushing open the elegant doors, she added over her shoulder, "Just working on that ass-handing thing Ramsay wanted to see."

ERYX STRODE into the council hall amidst the steady rumble of curious voices. It wasn't a cozy place. More like a high-domed museum with gold walls and filigreed platinum hieroglyphics from their earliest days.

Long ivory cushions lined the lower level, one in front of the other, with an aisle left open down the middle for the lower statesmen. Those more established in the hierarchy were already perched in the boxes jutting out from the circular ledges above.

He nodded at some he passed, smiled at others. Some he avoided at all costs. His race was at a tricky place in its life-span, stuck between the antiquated ways of old and the promise of new ideas. One way or another, what he was about to share was sure to knock a whole lot of people off the fence.

"Surprised you want anything to do with us." The voice scraped at Eryx's nerves and drew him to a stop.

"Angus." Eryx openly perused the councilman's stark white robe. "I barely noticed you without your colors."

Angus flinched, not that Eryx had expected otherwise. The reminder of how Eryx had revoked the man's rank only months before hadn't been intended as a subtle jab.

"Colors don't make the man." Angus waved at Eryx's platinum council attire, a symbolic representation to the metal reserved for use by the royal family alone. "If they did, you might be worth something." He harrumphed and shuffled off in a decrepit huff without another word.

Eryx stormed toward the front of the room. He had more important things to think about than a bitter old man stuck in the dark ages. Things like coming clean with his mate and sharing their roles within the Myren race. The weight of all the information he'd withheld sat heavy in his chest, and he wanted it gone. The faster he got this task behind him, the faster he could bare it all. Though, looking back at things now, he couldn't quite figure out why he'd taken the tight-lipped route to begin with.

The room settled to a dull murmur the moment he reached the dais. As he turned, the more junior members of his council settled to their knees, while those in their boxes reclined in their sumptuous chairs.

"Dunstan," Eryx said.

Head high and clutching his official tome of records, the council page stepped forward.

"Call this special session to order."

Dunstan gave a solemn nod and faced the room. His voice

rang out the customary call to order with a layer of pomp and circumstance that made Eryx ache to pace.

When the formalities were done, Eryx let a punctuated silence fall across the room. "I've called you together for an important purpose that will catch many of you by surprise."

A trill of whispers floated along the council floor.

"I know many of you have been concerned with my time away. My presence today marks the end of my necessary absences and the dawn of a new and exciting time for our race."

"And you expect to give no explanation of your deeds in the human realm?" Angus screeched from the rear of the room, his place among his peers the lowest of them all. He slowly stood. "While your councilmen have been faithful servants of our people, you've gallivanted about with those not of our race and left us here to toe the line. And you expect to return to our good graces without any account?"

Eryx tensed and his blood pounded through his fists. He should have killed Angus for his treasonous acts when he'd had the chance.

With long-standing years of practice, Eryx pushed the fire building in his throat deep into his belly. "You act as if I've been completely absent, Angus. I believe my responsibilities have been thoroughly filled regardless of my activities elsewhere. In fact, I'm certain only a few months ago we clearly established which of us is malran and which is not. Unless you'd like to formally challenge me for the right?"

The grossly public putdown fired a ripple of murmurs along the council floor.

"I do challenge you." Angus straightened as tall as his stooped form would allow, his body shaking with fury. "I challenge your time in Evad. I challenge your adherence to the tenets of The Great One. Have you or have you not brought a human among us, breaking the most sacred of laws our race is meant to abide?"

Gasps shot out from all angles of the room.

Eryx took one slow breath after another. Focused inwardly on the quiet, solemn place in his soul, and thanked The Great One for the repeated releases Lexi had gifted him with the night before. Otherwise, the sparks of electricity and flame from his temper would have fried more than half of his council.

"Far from it," he answered, the words deceptively smooth considering his emotions. "I brought your new malress." He pulled his over-robe from his shoulders and tossed it to the floor. "I did bring a woman to Eden from the human realm, but she was one of our lost. As you can see by the mark I now bear, the woman in question is not only very Myren, but is also now my baineann and your malress. My call for special session was to advise you of this change in keeping with our traditions and to announce her presentation tomorrow."

Mumbled comments trickled among those present, then faded to dead silence as each member grasped the significance of his mark.

"Her name is Alexis Shantos. You will receive her at session tomorrow and confirm her rightful place as malress. Together we will begin the new and promising years to come for our race."

A cautious smattering of applause and rumbling voices rolled across the room.

Eryx exhaled, slow and cautious. He opened his mouth to call the session to an end.

"Malran." Angus' voice was stronger than Eryx had heard in years. "I'm interested to know how you managed to confirm she was Myren before you divulged our race."

Eryx's fisted his hands and prayed for guidance. He definitely should have killed Angus when he'd had the chance.

CHAPTER 21

Lexi stepped beyond the castle walls into the brilliant Myren sunshine and most of her tension released. The chill outside from the night before was gone, dew sparkling off every surface in the morning light. Flowers dazzled under the light of day, a perfect balance of wispy pastel petals and vivid, sharp-edged blooms. The air shimmered, and her lungs sang with a mix of sweet and exotic perfume from the garden.

She tilted her head back and closed her eyes against the sun's warmth as she walked. "I love it here. It's like a fairytale."

Ludan's lazy footsteps swished in the soft sand path beside hers. "Since when are you the fairytale type?"

The ocean roiled beyond the castle bluff. God, she could relate. Nothing in her life felt settled right now. Nothing except Eryx. Her anchor in the center of the chaos.

"Every girl dreams of fairytales. Some of us are just more realistic than others." She crooked one eyebrow at him. "Which is rather ironic when you consider the last week of my life."

Her closet had proven to be a fairytale, too. The thing was as big as her entire apartment in Evad and packed with gowns in bold colors. Some were casual, made of comfortable, soft fabrics. Others were elaborate and covered with jewels, guaranteed to make any number of female jet setters swoon.

She'd chosen a comfy gown for her walk, but Galena had shoved it back in with the others and insisted on a blood-red number trimmed in black. It fell from one shoulder and clung to her curves, leaving the Shantos Pegasus well exposed.

She'd brushed out Lexi's hair and made her promise to leave it unbound. When Lexi asked why, she'd shrugged and said, *"Trust me."*

"Before Galena left," she said to Ludan, "she told me to call her. Did she mean I could talk to her telepathically?"

Ludan scanned the far edge of the garden. "She did."

"I thought it was only for family. And people you're linked with."

"She's your family now. Once you've mated, you gain the family links of the person you've mated as well." His gaze kept roaming, never stopping for long on any particular spot. He tucked her hand protectively around his arm, the bare skin of his elbow warm against her fingers.

Odd how the touch of another man felt awkward. "Can I talk with you that way?"

"Not yet. Eryx and I are close enough to be brothers, but we don't share blood." His gaze flicked to her fidgeting fingers, then back up. "You'd have to share a link with me."

"Will you teach me how?"

Ludan halted and a rare, wicked grin crept into place. "What the hell. He's already gonna rip me for ratting him out. May as well have a little more fun."

"Ludan?" An airy, cultured female voice flittered from behind them.

Ludan stiffened.

Bitterness scented the garden, heavier than lemon, but lighter than vinegar. Out of place with all the flowers.

Irritation.

On the bright side, she was getting faster with her new gift. The downside, they were kicking in over a woman.

Ludan pivoted, a solid wall of muscle between the woman and Lexi. "Serena."

Not a greeting, but an accusation.

"I came to see Eryx." The stranger paused. Sand crunched as the woman shifted. "Who's your friend?"

Ludan's shoulder blades bunched beneath his drast.

The fine hairs along Lexi's arms and neck rippled to life.

Oh, hell. It was Ludan's emotions. Pissed as hell and ready to pounce. Not a good sign for things to come.

"Eryx isn't here," Ludan said with an *all the better to eat you with* drawl. "I'll introduce you to his baineann though." He stepped back and angled himself so Lexi's marked arm was on full display. "Allow me to present you to our new malress, Alexis Shantos. Lexi, this is Serena Doroz, an *old* acquaintance of Eryx's."

Two seconds and Lexi hated her. Cerulean blue eyes, pale blonde hair to the small of her back, and soft pink lips. The type of woman who could bring a man to his knees with little more than a crook of her fingers.

In a nutshell, she was perfect.

All of a sudden she was fourteen again, gangly and inadequate, keeping to the shadows where the mean girls wouldn't see her.

Well, screw that. No Barbie doll was going to knock her off her fantasy life. Not without a decent catfight. She squared her shoulders and offered her hand. Emotion to rival a blowtorch blasted her, and her knees nearly buckled. She struggled for breath, the weight of Serena's feelings as heavy as a smoke laden room.

"A proper welcome is in order, Serena." Ludan stepped closer and towered over her.

Serena's ire spiked another notch.

Lexi's legs wobbled. God, she was going to kill Ludan. Slowly. With a spork. Just as soon as she could get away from the beautiful Satan and her pissed off mood.

"Of course." Serena coughed less than delicately. The ocean breeze teased her long, powder blue tunic, the chiffon panels lapping at her matching silk pants. "Forgive me, my malress. I was unaware Eryx had taken a mate. I was with him only a short time ago."

Bitch. She'd had more powerful digs thrown at her in kindergarten. Eryx was hers and she'd flay Serena before she let her anywhere close to her man.

Assuming she could stay upright.

Beads of sweat formed along the back of her neck, and the muscles along her back shook with fatigue. Her vision turned dim and fuzzy.

Serena dropped as smooth as a feather to both knees and bowed her head, her near-white hair framing her devil/angel face. "It is my great pleasure to meet you." She rose without waiting for a response and faced Ludan with an oh-so-haughty smile. "I suppose I'll have to speak with Eryx another day."

"That won't be necessary." Lexi snapped a little straighter. She gripped Ludan's forearm in a way she hoped would cause him to follow and strolled past Serena with the proudest stride she could manage. "I'll convey your request. If Eryx is interested in what you have to say, he'll send for you."

Serena gasped as they passed.

Even with Serena behind them, malice shredded her from the inside out. Her lungs seized, but she kept walking.

Fifty feet away color finally registered in her vision, but still no focus.

Stay upright, keep walking, and breathe,

It was the best plan she could come up with. Except maybe pray the woman would storm off in a huff.

"She's gone." Ludan's voice seemed far away. Muffled. His hand settled on her back and his heat spread across her skin in a wave of strength.

Her sight sharpened. She gulped in air, coughing and sputtering, greedy for oxygen. "She was really pissed."

"Serena's been a thorn in Eryx's side for years. Their thing's old news. Didn't last. She comes around every now and then, convinced he'll change his mind. He banned her from the castle a few days ago—for all the good it did."

On trembling legs, Lexi angled toward a wrought iron bench nestled by tall grass capped with cotton-ball tops.

"The anger impacts you more?" Even his cool curiosity came out with the strength of a dominant.

She rested her elbows on her knees, let her head fall forward, and stretched her neck. Her temples pounded. "Apparently, so."

Blissful quiet, only the hum of wind and happy birds.

Ludan's feet shifted in front of her. "If it's any consolation, you rocked the queen bit."

Lexi looked up.

Pride filled his gaze, so powerful it shook her to her toes. "It's not often Serena gets the setback you dished out."

She sat up and reclined with a throaty chuckle. The cool iron fairly sizzled against her heated skin. "It is a consolation. A good one. No woman likes confronting an old girlfriend."

"Lexi?" Eryx's voice.

She sighed. *"Too bad he wasn't here a few minutes ago."*

"What's that supposed to mean?" Eryx said.

Lexi sat ramrod straight. No way did she hear him in her head. She was imagining things.

His answering demand whipped through her mind. *"You're hearing fine. What happened?"*

"Hmm. Guess that answers how telepathy works. And don't get snippy with me." Could she add a snarl to her thoughts? *"I've had a hell of a morning."*

Eryx's sigh of resignation feathered through her head. Maybe sounds were possible. *"I take it I won't find you warm in our bed?"*

She gripped the slats of the iron bench so hard her fingertips turned red. It was either the bench or Ludan. The latter didn't seem fair since it was really Eryx's neck she wanted to choke. *"Oh, no. I'm up and about. Greeting my people, so it seems."*

"I see you've got telepathy down." Ludan's low voice, spoken aloud, startled her.

"How could you tell?"

"You have a shitty poker face." His mouth curled in a sarcastic twist. "Plus, he's bitching in my head. It wasn't much of a stretch."

Eryx landed not ten feet away with an earth-rattling boom. He jerked his head at Ludan. "Go."

Ludan blinked, slow and lazy. An intentional move that flipped Eryx the bird without lifting a finger. "Think not. Too risky." He headed toward an arbor less than thirty feet away. "But I'll give you space."

"What happened?" Eryx strode toward her until his towering form threw her in complete shade. He scanned her in a quick but thorough assessment.

Lexi folded her hands in her lap with a mock sigh. "I've had a lovely morning, thank you for asking. How was yours?"

Eryx crouched before her. He hung his head on a heavy exhale then looked up, his gaze resolute and sincere. "I'm sorry. You shouldn't have learned about who I am from my family." He wore cuffs around his wrists and throat—the same as Ludan and Ramsay.

After the workout she'd endured via Serena, she was too tired to muster much of a fuss. "I think I understand." She traced one wing of the horse etched into the platinum surface, a perfect match to the one along her arm. "Everyone deserves to be loved for who they are, not what they are."

Eryx stood, pulled her from the bench, and wrapped her up tight. His leather scent still clung to his skin, though it was silk that caressed her cheek.

"I could have done without meeting your ex though," she said.

The muscles along his chest went cinder block rigid. "Did she hurt you?"

Her eyes slipped shut and she melted deeper into his strength. "I think it's safe to say the fair Serena is not pleased with my newfound status, but she'd very much like the plea-sure of your company." She leaned back and found his brow creased with worry. "I've also learned angry emotions are extremely unpleasant. Especially when they're directed at me."

Eryx massaged her neck. "I haven't been with her in a long time."

Eyes burning from fatigue, Lexi cupped the side of his face. "Everyone has a past. I just don't want to run into her again anytime soon."

His expression shifted, the look of a guilty boy gauging how much he could fess up. "You're not angry about being malress?"

Her inner radar pinged with the promise of an incoming sucker punch. "Angry isn't the word. Anxious maybe."

He ran his fingers through her loose hair and a muscle

near one temple twitched. "Ludan said you held your own quite nicely."

She rolled her eyes and rested her forehead against his chest. "Nothing like a crash course."

He angled her face toward his. "Then buckle up because I've got two more bombs for you."

A growl ripped past her throat and she stomped a good three paces away before she faced him. "More?"

His shrug was so typically male she wanted to scream. "Nothing too bad."

She raised her eyebrows and waited.

"Your presentation to the Myren government is tomorrow."

She raised them another notch.

"A tidy chunk of Myrens will show up to see it."

She straightened and a slow throb started at her temples. "What else?"

He studied her a second then shrugged out of his silk coat. An incredible sword marked the entire stretch of his arm. *Her* mark. Elaborate symbols with a Celtic flair were etched into the hilt, jewels nestled above and below the grip. Its blade resonated with power, and ivy twined around it, tapering off near his shoulders.

She shuffled forward, eager to trace the fine lines. Her hand shook as she made contact.

Memory snapped its fingers and plastered the picture from Graylin's sunroom on the wall of her mind. Her stomach nose-dived, and she swayed.

She lifted her gaze to Eryx. The only words she could find the same as those she'd use if she'd run out of liquor on a busy night. "Oh, hell."

〜

MAXIS STROLLED the main hallway of his grandmother's vast estate, hands clasped behind his back. Each footstep echoed off the white marble, but otherwise the grounds were still as winter snow. Gray and gold veins ran along the slabs beneath his feet.

His plans weren't moving. Not like he'd hoped. Ramsay's troops scrambling to find Maxis tickled him shitless, but it also kept his spies too far from the castle for any sighting of Lexi. Reese had all but disappeared except for a few grumbles about locating Serena.

He stopped at the end of the hall. Evening sun slanted through the windows behind him in a dramatic angle. Everything was ready. The warriors' quarters, the estate, his receiving room. Soon Brasia would be the home of the malran as Evanora had intended. Only a few loose threads to tie off.

The main entrance rattled open in the foyer beyond, then slammed shut with a hollow *boom*.

Maxis strode toward the sound, his clipped steps hammering against an equally confident stride headed in Maxis' direction.

He turned the corner and nearly slammed into Reese. "What in histus are you doing here?" Even at low decibels, Maxis' voice rumbled along the stone floors and walls.

Reese's gaze roamed the tall, domed ceiling with its sky murals and gold edging. "Nice place." It wasn't a pleasantry. A rabid dog near to starvation would hold less bite.

Maxis didn't mind. He had teeth of his own. "Not on par with where you grew up?"

Reese's green eyes took on a lethal edge. "I'd take my homestead over your pomp and bullshit any day."

"Then why are you here?"

He sneered at Maxis and meandered to the wall of windows overlooking the rear grounds. The mountains rose in the distance, covered by a blanket of snow with a soft rainbow of purples, pink, and yellow thrumming beneath. "I thought I'd make use of our new link and seek you out. Share the latest and greatest news."

Maxis' pulse leapt. Reese seeking him out for any reason was a move in the right direction. That he brought news made it even sweeter. "And?"

Reese turned from the window. "I'm out on the bit with Serena. The woman's a short-tempered shrew. If she means so much to the cause, you court her." He took a few steps toward the entry.

Maxis stepped into his path. "Giving up so soon?"

"Hardly." Reese chuffed out a derisive chuckle. "I finally found her, only to walk in on a ridiculous tirade. I've got better things to do."

"And what's got her in a snit?"

A slow, sinister grin split across Reese's face. "Seems the malran's claimed a mate. The news isn't settling all that well." He sidestepped Maxis and continued on his path. "So I'm out."

Maxis scrambled, clawing for some piece of his plan left untouched.

A few steps from the corner Reese stopped, stomped one booted foot on the floor, and held up his hand. "I almost forgot." He spun and flashed a smile that said he hadn't forgotten a damned thing. "Your ellan lackey? Seems he's got a bit of a temper, too, and accused the malran of breaking the sacred tenets during special session." The crinkles around Reese's narrowed eyes deepened. "Come to find out, the human you've been looking for? She's no human. She's Myren. And your new malress."

CHAPTER 22

*L*exi stared from a high, slender window of the council building in Cush into the streets below. Specks of gold twinkled from the ivory and tan brickwork roads that wound through the town.

From the sky, the capital had looked more like a low-sitting cloud than a city, the rounded rooftops sparkling with silver, shimmering tiles atop high stucco walls of ivory and white. Mix Moroccan style with a sci-fi flick, and you'd end up with a region like Cush.

An ironic smile tugged at her lips. If someone had told her she'd be flying into a city on a real-life Pegasus a week before, she'd have tabbed them out and refused them any more liquor. Never mind the fact that she and Eryx could have flown themselves. Oh, no. They had to do it with an extra bit of flair on a winged horse that was black as sin. One more holy cow on top of a heaping pile of jaw-dropping events.

Alone for the first time since she'd woken, blissful silence surrounded her. The cavernous chamber echoed the tiniest sound. Even her breath ricocheted from the hard surfaces.

Ancient-looking gold symbols ran a thick swath on each wall. Their raised surfaces lent a formal elegance to the otherwise smooth gray texture—Celtic patterns whispering of mystical secrets. The ivory furniture dotting the room held the only other color. No rugs, no pictures. Only cold, flat gray. Beautiful, but still cold.

She strode to the full-length mirror for one last check of her appearance. Her sandaled footsteps tapped along the way and her dress hissed behind her. She stared at the mysterious woman in the mirror and marveled at the work Orla and Galena had done. They'd amplified her blue-gray eyes with smoky, sexy colors across her lids. Her skin shimmered in even the dimmest light from the diamond dust they'd brushed all over her body.

Her hair hung in one simple braid, plaited by Eryx before he'd left the women to their ministrations. He'd huffed something about Galena not being trustworthy before he'd left them alone and Galena had laughed herself silly explaining the Myren custom of bound and unbound hair—the former indicating commitment and the latter signifying openness to the opposite gender.

She smoothed the front of the magnificent gown. Delicate, platinum mesh that shimmered with every infinitesimal move. The design was simple, yet deliciously sexy. One full-length panel in the front with a halter cut top. Another draped from the small of her back to form a short train behind her. All that held the two pieces together were black silk knots at her sides, leaving the sides of her legs exposed. Embedded in the mesh were diamonds of varied sizes.

Two sharp knocks boomeranged around the room.

The modicum of calm she'd nurtured in the last five minutes fizzled.

The door opened a crack. "Lexi? You decent?"

Ramsay. Not Eryx.

God, she could sure use his touch right about now. "Come on in. I'm ready." A complete lie, but she sucked it up and smiled anyway.

Ramsay and Ludan ambled into the room, Ramsay whistling his appreciation and making a show of looking her up and down. "You know, if you weren't my brother's woman I'd definitely hit on you."

"You hit on all the women." Ludan crossed his arms and braced, feet shoulder width near the door. Never an animated man, his scowl seemed even worse than normal. A tiger locked in a too-small cage. Maybe it was the clothes that pissed him off.

"Do you guys always run around in silk jammies at these things?" She tried to hold back her laugh, but it filtered out between her words any. To be fair, they weren't any different than Graylin's attire, except they didn't do the over-robe like him. Just the tanks and loose fitting pants in a light silver color. Still, on these two? Totally hot.

Ramsay reached for her elbow. "Don't start with the jammie thing. Ludan's more of a Levis man. Getting him to suit up for council is tough on a good day." He steered her toward the door and leaned in close with a wink. "Silly or not, they make getting naked a breeze."

Ludan stepped close to her exposed side and they padded into the eerily quiet hall. Her train dragged against the stone floors to fill the air with white noise, and the blood in her veins surged to match its pitch.

The men steadied her at the first stair down and every step after cranked her heartbeat up one click. By the time they reached the landing, every council member in attendance would be able to hear its exacerbated rhythm.

"Lexi." Eryx's voice settled her, warmed and comforted from the inside out. *"This should be straightforward. No matter what happens, you can say or do nothing wrong. We are equals."*

She couldn't answer. Her mind and throat may as well have been coated in ice. She jerked a nod, and then remembered Eryx couldn't yet see her.

Ramsay chuckled and covered her hand resting on his arm with a loving pat. "Just keep your senses turned down or off like we practiced. You'll be fine."

They halted behind two closed doors the size of a three-car garage back home. The two halves parted outward with a groan and a stream of cool air slipped eagerly between the cracks to fan her heated face.

Oh...wow. Myren big wigs didn't mess around when they went high town.

A domed ceiling spanned at least three stories. Gold and ivory walls with platinum detail woven into intricate symbols circled the perimeter. Half of the building had theater-looking boxes that jutted out from the wall, and thick ivory cushions lined the main floor with an aisle down the center.

Every space was taken, people kneeling and waiting with stiff backs, their breathing the only sound. At the end of the aisle two large ebony chairs sat on a dais. Sunlight poured from the glass dome to shine on the stately fixtures in a natural spotlight.

Eryx stood between them, his presence so strong and confident it reached her at the rear of the room. His eyes matched the color of the stone floors. Dangerous. Daring.

Ramsay and Ludan stepped forward together.

She followed reluctantly and every head turned in her direction. With rigid formality the crowd stood and followed her progress.

A clammy sheen covered her face. Probably a pasty flu-white she'd be ashamed to have caught on tape. Thank God for the lack of electronics in Eden.

Eryx wore the same council garb as Ludan and Ramsay,

though his matched the platinum of her dress. His braids hung down his back and a thick band of platinum circled his head.

A crown.

An honest to God crown.

Panic speared through her belly. The urge to wipe her sweaty palms on her gown pricked at her instincts. She wiggled her fingers instead and focused on the regular intervals of tribal etchings and black diamonds adorning Eryx's circlet.

They reached the dais steps and Ramsay pulled her to a subtle stop. The swoosh of fabric and moving bodies whispered behind her.

She cast a surreptitious glance over her shoulder and found the council members on their knees with heads bowed. She faced Eryx, heart hammering.

A grin flickered at one corner of his mouth. His voice rang out like a God. "Rise."

Her libido poked an eye out from its hidey-hole. *"Wow. That was hot."*

Ramsay's laughter chimed in her head. *"Really? You think that's hot?"* His voice shifted to a considering tone. *"Is it a dominant thing? 'Cause I'm pretty comfy in that mode."*

"Ramsay!" Eryx's warning had bite. With a lazy, pantherlike grace, he descended to her and his gaze heated. He held out his hand, palm up.

Lexi slipped her hand in his and almost moaned at the fire his touch ignited.

"We really need to work on what you think out loud," Eryx said. *"Or at least make sure you channel it to only me."* He led her up the stairs and faced the crowd.

The rustle of bodies stilled.

"Dunstan," Eryx said, "are all ellan present?"

A younger man dressed in a crimson robe stepped from

the front row, an oversized, and well-worn book tucked under one arm. "They are, my malran."

Eryx gave the man a curt nod and addressed the council. "In accordance with the mandates which govern our society as created by the ruling family and the council representatives for the Myren regions, I come to you today to present my baineann and your malress-elect, Alexis Shantos."

He shifted behind her and rested his hands on her shoulders. "As evidenced by the Shantos mark she bears, my spirit has called out to hers in the most sacred of Myren customs and she has answered, placing her trust in her fireann and pledging her life to the betterment of our civilization."

A young female with shoulder length chestnut hair and kind eyes rose from the crowd. "Alexis Shantos, is it true you freely dedicate your life in the same manner as your fireann, to serve as malress, working for our people until you pass from this life?"

Lexi's throat worked around several knots and she fought the urge to cough. "I pledge to support my…"

"Fireann." Eryx and Ramsay both chimed the reminder simultaneously in her head.

"…fireann in his efforts to guide all Myrens as his conscience directs him." She took a deep breath and tried not to stammer. "For myself, I want to aid individuals, no matter where they're from."

A rumble issued through the crowd, some heads bobbing in agreement, some eyes sharpening in displeasure. Some faces utterly bored.

An elderly man with a pompous voice scratched from the rear of the room. "Is that to mean you support humans as equals to the Myren race?"

More hushed comments and rumblings.

The same man droned on. "The malran advises you hail from Evad and know nothing of our culture. Perhaps humans preside higher in your estimation than those of us here in Eden."

Lexi hated the scraggly, thin-haired man in the back row already. If the tension in Eryx's fingers at her shoulders were any indication, he wasn't high on Eryx's list either.

"It means I will not ignore or belittle those who are from Evad," she answered before Eryx could. "There's every possibility more of our people are lost in that realm, unaware of the beauty in Eden." Inspiration fired. "I've lived a quarter of a century unaware of my heritage. While I am deeply proud of the home I've found, I won't ignore others who may be lost if I can find a way to bring them home."

The man dismissed Lexi entirely, and turned his gaze to Eryx. "And what of her lacking education on our culture and customs, malran? Who do you plan to teach and guide her in our ways? She is grossly uninformed and cannot possibly be responsible for guiding our council."

Lexi tried to hold a bland expression. She was married to Eryx and didn't pull that kind of snark on him. Was the old man a complete idiot?

Eryx's lethal drawl coiled through the room. "Surely you're not implying the council will have anything to do with her instruction on our ways, Angus. I don't recall any point in my or my siblings' upbringing where an ellan was responsible for educating us in the ways of government. Those lessons were provided by my parents and Graylin Forte. And, as I recollect, only weeks ago I had to educate you on the subject of treason. I think I'm more than competent to educate my baineann."

Silence fell thick on the room and eased Lexi's tension. At the rate Angus had been going, Eryx was bound to snap. Given the things Angus had said, Lexi wasn't altogether sure if she'd break the fight up or cheer Eryx on.

The young woman who'd risen earlier spoke up again and

directed her voice toward the page. "Dunstan, I move that Alexis Shantos be accepted as the rightful malress."

Two males stood and seconded the motion.

"A motion stands before the council." Eryx's voice rang through the room. "If any oppose, speak now."

Blessed silence.

The muscles around her rib cage released their tight grip. Now all she needed was a beer, super spicy wings, and some cheese fries.

Eryx sucked in a deep breath behind her. "Dunstan, make note that on this day, Alexis Shantos is accepted unanimously by the ellan council as the rightful malress and will remain so until such time as she passes this life to nirana."

Dunstan scribbled dutifully in his mammoth book, while the woman who'd made the motion shuffled forward with a thick, silk, ivory cushion. She placed the pillow on the floor directly in front of Lexi and stepped back, her eyes respectfully downcast.

"Kneel, Lexi."

She nearly moaned at the sinful stroke of Eryx's voice turning the space between her legs into his own, personal slip and slide. Didn't the man know he was supposed to be serious right now?

Kneeling, she bowed her head on instinct.

Footsteps clipped across the hard floor, a distant giggle from a child outside the only other sound. Eryx's feet came into view.

"You're mine, Alexis. My baineann. My malress." He placed a circlet around her head. It tightened by slow degrees, adjusting the size by manipulating the metal as he'd taught her to do with the metal beads that bound his braids. He held out his hand and guided her up, his velvet lips brushing hers with reverence and promise. Reluctance etched his face as he

stepped away. "Members of the council, behold your malress."

A polite and curious round of applause kicked in.

The woman who'd brought the cushion forward now kneeled in front of her and grasped Lexi's hand in her own. "I pledge you my loyalty and devotion, and welcome you as our malress."

Lexi opened her mouth to speak, at least to thank the kind woman, but she stepped away quickly, replaced with another polite face. And then another. An endless stream buffeted only by Eryx's steady presence. He looked happy. Maybe proud. For the moment, she was, too. Every inch the princess from her secret fairytales.

The last of the line neared and Lexi contemplated where she might pilfer her much-earned beer.

Angus knelt before her.

With rough, dry hands, he grabbed hers and pursed his wrinkled lips. "I welcome you as our malress." No pledge of loyalty. No promise of devotion. Only a disingenuous welcome.

Lexi opened her senses and sampled his emotions. Her knees almost buckled and bile rose in her throat. Whatever else she might have done right today, she'd rubbed this man past the point reason.

MAXIS STEPPED from the shadows of his balcony perch. The royal couple disappeared behind the farthest bend on the main council passage and the throngs lined up for the formal procession filled in behind the band of warriors at Eryx and Lexi's backs. Shouts and cheers settled to a dull rumble of gossip and predictions, some craning their necks for one last glimpse of the prophetic mark.

He'd damned near flayed the messenger when Reese had finally gotten around to sharing that little tidbit. Yet, seeing the touted symbol on Eryx's arm with his own eyes went a long way toward assuaging his anger. True, his original plans might be little more than dust, but he could adjust. Myrens were a cautious lot, prone to superstition with a more-than-hyper fear of the unknown. A perfect situation—if one knew how to spin it.

A couple argued by a nearby lamppost, a sight that scratched his inner predator behind the ears. Convincing Reese to partake in one last meeting with Serena hadn't been without challenge, but had definitely been worth it. So much emotion on her face, her stance shaking with fury while she gestured wildly. Raw ire. Perfect for him to work with.

The knotted crowd loosened, and Maxis put his modified plan in play.

"There's a cootya one street over."

Reese stood passively next to Serena, no indication of Maxis' mental communication showing on his face.

"Meet me there with Serena in twenty minutes," Maxis added.

Reese placed a hand at Serena's back and gestured toward the cootya, his face a passive mask of nothingness. No mental response, no glance in Maxis' direction, just acquiescence.

An odd sensation stirred behind his breastbone, one he was loathe to accept but couldn't afford to ignore. He needed Reese. Wanted more than mere compliance.

He shook off the sentiment and ambled into the crowd. The cafe he'd selected was an open-air environment, a stucco roof jutting out over a smattering of tables where patrons could look on the throngs of people beyond. With the crowded streets, his anonymity was a near certainty, so he pressed toward the cootya, and kept to the shade wherever possible.

"I don't care who you want to meet, I'm ready to go." Serena's petulance pounded the stone walls as Maxis entered. "Give me one good reason why I should stay."

Reese maintained his facade of ennui—or maybe he truly was bored to tears.

Maxis approached, his footsteps camouflaged by the rumble of other, chattering customers, and leaned in close. "Revenge."

Serena spun in her chair, more righteous indignation in her elegant frame than fear. The air around her hung thick and heavily charged.

"It must rankle to be replaced with a human-raised no one," Maxis said. "I'd say the malran deserves a lesson or two."

It was a risky punch of provocation on his part, but at this point the risk was worth it.

A regal bearing settled around her. "And who are you to suggest such a thing?"

He sidled closer, offering his hand. Her fingertips tickled his palm, barely deigning to touch him. "My name is Maxis Steysis."

Her mouth parted.

He curled his fingers around hers and held her wary stare. Her presence was intoxicating, and his eyelids weighted with unexpected desire. "It appears you recognize the name." He pulled her hand to his lips, grazing her knuckles a second longer than was appropriate. "So you know I'm inclined to be *sympathetic* to a beautiful woman scorned."

"I've heard the stories of Evanora." She smirked and folded her hands in her lap, the picture of gentility, though her eyes were sharp enough to cut diamonds. "She wielded quite a bit of her own power by the time she died—without the help of any man."

"As could you." Maxis pulled a chair out. "Should you choose to seize the opportunity."

The cootya workers bustled behind the counter and shuffled plates and glassware to waiting customers. Cutlery pinged against thick clay plates and the soft lilt of laughter floated from a distant table.

Serena held her silence. Her gaze flicked beyond Maxis' shoulder to the milling people in the street beyond and straightened to a haughty stance. "What are you looking at?"

Maxis pivoted in his chair to see who had captured Serena's attention, then shot to his feet.

"I thought your name was Wesley." Phybe's voice trailed off, both accusing and injured.

Maxis darted forward without thought, Phybe barely more than an arm's reach.

Reese intercepted his path. With a subtle inclination of his head, he noted the heavily populated shop. "Not now."

Frantic footsteps scampered along the dusty sidewalk, the visual blocked by Reese's hulking form.

His strategos glanced over one shoulder and his face hardened. "I'll find her."

Excitement kicked Maxis in the chest and he smoothed the front of his shirt to cover it. More than mere compliance from his strategos. Finally.

"*Find her,*" Maxis said. "*And make sure we never see her again.*"

CHAPTER 23

*L*exi plunked next to Ludan on the fire pit ledge and fiddled with the hem of her red tunic. Morning pinks and corals coated the horizon and workers trickled in to care for the castle. Eryx was already gone. "Is it always going to be like this?"

Ludan peeled the edge off a long lilac flower petal that looked a lot like a palm tree leaf. "You mean the council stuff?" He snapped off the end and formed a square corner, tossed the scrap over his shoulder into the pit, and shook his head. "Nah. He's just tap dancin' around Angus' claims." He set the colorful strip aside and restarted the process with another.

"Guess I've stirred a lot up, huh?"

Ludan gave her a sideways grin, but didn't pause in his task. "You could view it that way. Or you could see Eryx's got another shot to neutralize Angus and find Maxis. It had to be Maxis who tipped Angus off." He threw his latest scrap in with the others and scanned the skies and garden—the same visual sweep he did every few minutes.

"You're worried about him." Kind of a *well duh* observation, even without her newfound spidey senses sending prickles up and down her arms.

"Eryx can handle his own. I'm only backup." He weaved the strips into odd-patterned knots. "It's you we're worried about. It'll be fine as soon as we find you a somo and get you trained."

"It'll be better when I'm not so helpless." She stood and clutched the stone rail bordering their private garden, the same place Eryx had sworn his blood oath. The ocean churned beyond and the breeze lifted her hair off her neck. "Why can't you teach me?"

Ludan stayed bent to his task, but jerked on a huffed chuckle. "Because when a man finds a good woman, they're protective. He wants to be the one who teaches you. That and he's still yanked 'cause I nabbed your memories." He stopped and looked up. "You gonna tell him what happened?"

She turned into the wind. Those memories couldn't stay hidden much longer. Eryx had come clean with her. The least she could do was drag her own baggage from the closet.

"I think he already knows." She lowered her head and rubbed the coarse, gray stone. "Maybe not the details, but the gist of what happened."

"It wouldn't change how he feels. Not like you think. And details make a difference to a man like him."

No way was she going there. Not today. She strolled toward Ludan and tried for a diversion. "We never did get around to linking."

Ludan's mouth parted on a sly smile. "You sure you want to do that without Eryx here?"

"He's my mate, not my dad."

The smile grew. "Atta girl." He tied off another knot and held up a circle about the size of her wrist. "Here."

With the knots he'd woven, the simple lilac strips had

become an intricate mix of pale to deepest purple. "What is it?"

"A bracelet." He stood and brushed flower scraps from his pants. "Used to make 'em with Galena when we were kids."

A giggle slipped out, the image of Ludan traipsing dutifully behind Galena simply irresistible. She still couldn't get used to him in the warrior's get up, but it fit his personality more than the council jammies.

"Don't laugh," he said. "Galena's fierce when she sets her mind to something." He grabbed her hand and fitted his palm against hers. "You ready?"

Lexi nodded and focused on their joined hands. "What do I do?"

His laugh was warm. Out of sorts with the boredom he usually affected. "For starters, relax. Close your eyes." He lowered his voice. "Feel for my energy. Give it a visual."

A tingle darted through her palm. In her mind's eye, a ribbon of light—a perfect match to his arctic blue eyes—winded up her arm. "It's like what I feel with Eryx."

"It damn well better not be," Eryx said from behind her.

She jumped and tried to pull her hand away, but Ludan clamped down tight, the sensation still dancing up her forearm.

Eryx's hands curved around her shoulders and he bolstered her in front of Ludan. "Send yours into him." He pressed chest to hips against her back, his voice a rasp at her ear. "Wrap it around the image and let the fibers weave together."

She shivered, embarrassed at her obvious response. Hard for anyone to blame her though. With Ludan's intimate connection spearing through her palm and her mate tight against her back, even a nun would swoon.

As Eryx coached, she visualized her mental handshake and wound her stream of energy around the one Ludan provided. The strands circled each other, her own tendril a slate blue. They meshed in a sudden grip and snapped tight.

"Now get out of my baineann, Forte."

"Unwind your panties." Ludan took a polite step back and planted his hands on his hips. "You get her a somo who doesn't crank your attitude and she won't need me. Until then, one more line of contact doesn't hurt."

"It was my idea." Lexi ran her hand up Eryx's arm and his bicep flexed beneath it.

Eryx pulled her close and dropped a kiss at the top of her head. "I shouldn't have made you wait."

"I get it." She pushed away. "But I'm ready to learn how to throw one of those fireballs now."

Ludan and Eryx exchanged one of those puzzled looks reserved for the male species. Eryx rubbed his chin and the stubble he'd yet to remove scratched in the windswept quiet. "Not sure that's doable. Not like what you saw us do anyway."

"Why not?" She shuttled her gaze between them. "I thought everyone could manipulate the elements."

"They can, but only for basic needs like building a fire— or defense at best," Eryx said. "Most female gifts manifest as nurturing skills, like Galena and her healing. Or you with emotions."

Ludan eased himself into a chair near the fire pit and propped his booted foot on the ledge. "Yeah, but she's not just any female."

Eryx nodded and rubbed the back of his neck. His brow wrinkled up. "You sure you don't want to start with something smaller? Like move a pillow or something?"

Stupid. Fucking. Men. "You won't let me leave the house without you or Ludan and you want me to start with moving a pillow?"

Eryx smiled, a big one, full of teeth, then finally had the

good grace to duck his head a notch. "Fire it is then." He turned her toward the pit and motioned at the dry wood stacked in the center. "Jump in and see where it takes you."

Lexi peeked at Eryx, some of her enthusiasm stifled under a damp blanket of doubt. "Is there a trick to it?"

"No more than when you learned to fly." Eryx pressed behind her as he had days before. "Your body calls the element it wants and the mind directs it."

Lexi closed her eyes. The image of the fire pit, alive with flames on the night of their mating leapt from her memory. Deep reds and oranges. Long, fat flames, curled at the end. Random sparks as the wind pushed and pulled around it. She imagined the streams routing through her chest, held one hand out, palm up, and pushed.

Wind gusted. Flowerpots tumbled onto the patio, their broken clay mingling with rich soil and crumpled petals.

Ludan raked the mess to one side with the side of his foot. "Not fire, but not bad for a first shot at air."

Lexi wrinkled her nose at Eryx. "Sorry."

He shrugged and patted her shoulder. "It's your home now as much as mine. Just be sure to point away from the house."

"Gotta say, the wind bit looked promising." Ludan ambled out of the line of fire. "Kind of a *don't piss off Mother Nature* feel."

"But it's air," she whined.

"Hey. Don't underestimate air." Eryx squared her to the fire pit and leaned in tight. "Now, try again."

She screwed her eyes shut, and tried again, leaving the wind element out of her mental image. A fat stream of fire arched from her outstretched palm and landed short of the waiting pit. A sizable scorch crackled in what had been soft, green grass, and a cloud of smoke lingered above the sweet scent of fresh cut hay. Weird. She expected something more like a grass fire back home.

"Kinda lame." Ludan's gaze gleamed with a challenge.

Oh, she'd totally take that dare. No way was she leaving the boys to throw their muscle around without a little fight. Closing her eyes again, she recreated the landscape, targeted where she wanted the flame to go, and Eryx and Ludan's positions.

Tiny threads wavered across the image. Gossamer and flitting in the wind, they seemed connected to Ludan and Eryx. Maybe a visual connection to their links?

Focus. Think about that later.

She narrowed her mental aim on the pit, and pushed a visual stream of fire in its direction.

She opened her eyes and a fist-wide stream hit its target. "Yes!"

"Good." Eryx hovered over her shoulder, his voice urgent. "Now, throw a stream all the way to the edge of the bluff. Do it now. Don't think."

Eyes open this time, she aimed far and poured every shred of focus into a narrow blaze.

Whoosh.

Not quite to the bluff's edge, but close.

"It's about as far as Galena can throw, which is saying something." Ludan found his chair again and gave her a stern glare. "I think wind's your thing, though."

"Eryx." Ramsay dropped from the sky and shook the ground. Another man she'd never seen before landed shortly behind him. "We gotta talk. Jagger's got news."

Eryx released her and greeted the stranger with a warrior's clasp at the forearms. "Jagger."

The guy looked like he'd been birthed by the sun. Golden eyes, warm brown hair with honey strands at the top, and skin that glowed. You couldn't call him pretty, though. Not with the pronounced slant of his cheeks and jawline. Fierce, like some avenging sun god.

Ramsay shifted, an uncustomary tension in his face.

Lexi waved them off. "Y'all go. I'll practice." Rather than give anyone time to argue, she faced the pit. Their voices rumbled behind her. Nurturing skills didn't bother her, but doing anything average rankled. Surely she could find a way to make the stream stronger.

She drew the garden's image, this time focused farther out. The ocean and the rainbow painted horizon.

As they had before, the pale-white, nearly translucent strands wiggled as if vying for attention. Ludan, Ramsay, Eryx, Jagger. Each of them reached out—

Wait a minute. She wasn't linked to Jagger. So why was it there? She angled toward the castle, eyes still closed, and found more strands, less defined than those nearby. A complex spider web pattern shooting out in all directions.

She faced the ocean again. Maybe she'd been doing it wrong. She reached out with mental fingers and touched those streams closest to her, channeled a vision of fire, and stretched out her palm.

"Holy shit."

"That's impressive."

Ramsay and Jagger's exclamations rang out behind her.

And man, were they right. She'd not only reached the bluff, but had thrown a stream of fire to make what Eryx had done at the Waffle House look like a softball.

Eryx came up behind her. "How'd you do that?"

Lexi glanced at a smirking Ludan, then back to Eryx. "I'm not entirely sure." Not a complete untruth, but with the way everyone was looking at her, coming clean on what she'd done didn't seem such a good idea. At least not in public.

Eryx draped his arm across her shoulders and tugged her

tight to his side. "We'll figure it out." He kissed the top of her head. "Jag's right, though. It was damned impressive."

"We need to follow up on this, Eryx," Ramsay said. "If Jag's right about the men he's seeing in Asshur, we gotta get on it before Maxis can cover his tracks."

She nudged Eryx in the ribs. "Go handle your business. I'll stay here." She noted the tight line of Ludan's lips. "And take Ludan with you."

"I'm not leaving you alone." Eryx's levity disappeared, replaced with the hard edge that usually got him what he wanted.

She had hard edges, too. Lots of them. "The castle's guarded right? So, I'm safe. Take Ludan, figure out your business, and give me some time alone. I'm not used to being shadowed all the time. Makes me feel like I'm two."

"We could use his input," Ramsay said. "But we need to get a move on."

Eryx tilted her face to meet his. "Promise you'll stay here. And don't leave the grounds. For anything."

Lexi rolled her eyes. "Bad guys. Everywhere. Got it." She waggled her eyebrows. "But I can fry 'em now from a decent distance."

"Don't get cocky, hellcat." He kissed her forehead and headed for the waiting men. "And keep that blowtorch pointed away from the house."

CHAPTER 24

Stomach rumbling, Lexi wandered toward the kitchen. Eryx hadn't lied about her needing more food. Especially after two non-stop hours of target practice —and that messy elemental weapon experiment with water.

Off the main corridor, a castle worker dusted a twenty-foot table. Lexi smiled and waved.

The young woman averted her gaze and wiped the shiny surface double-time.

Same response she'd had from everyone. A little lacking on the welcome wagon side of things, but she couldn't blame them. Not with her prophetic calling card splayed on Eryx's arm.

On the bright side, she'd wielded electricity, fire, and wind with little, if any, hesitation by the time she'd stopped, her aim finally somewhat predictable. But Ludan was right— wind was definitely her thing. Her distance sucked, but no way was she hooking up with those strands again until she talked to Eryx. For all she knew, it was bad Myren mojo.

Crap. She drew to a halt in the foyer, retracing her steps in her head. Must've been the left hallway instead of the right. She huffed and redirected.

A flash through the giant picture window stopped her. In the garden beyond, a tall patch of amethyst blooms shook, rattled by something dark at its base. Silver hair peeked above the top.

Orla. She changed her path, her steps lightened with the promise of company. The white sand path sparkled in the noonday sun and the scent of varied blooms danced in her lungs. Sweet. Spicy. Citrus. All mixed together with the bite of tangy ocean salt.

Rounding the corner, she drew up short and nearly stumbled over a set of youthful legs with bare feet. "Oops. Sorry."

With a handful of errant weeds, Orla looked up from the flowerbeds, and a pretty girl with loose pigtails crawled out from behind a tall patch of wispy grass.

"Lexi." Orla dusted her hands on her apron. "I thought you were in the gardens with Eryx."

"Nope. Been solo most of the morning. The boys went to play war." Tired of tiptoeing around the strangers in her new home, she held out her hand to the girl. "I'm Lexi."

The girl took Lexi's hand and ducked her head in a shy, but polite semi-bow. "I'm Jillian." Though small, her sunny smile matched her yellow tunic and leggings. "I live here with Orla."

Lexi took the cautious hand offered and a vague familiarity brushed her senses. "It's nice to meet you."

Dark blonde hair, tiny freckles along her cheeks and nose, and a prominent bone structure that looked awkward on her young face. She'd grow into those bones though. And mixed with those hazel eyes? The boys wouldn't know what hit 'em.

Hazel. Expressive. She'd seen that—

"Wait a minute." Lexi looked to Orla then back to Jillian. "How are you related to Orla?"

With the exuberance of youth, her eyes lit up. "Oh, I'm not. She takes care of me. I've lived here with Uncle Eryx and Uncle Ramsay ever since I can remember." As quickly as she'd brightened, her features locked up tight. Her gaze darted to Orla. "I-I mean, they're not really my uncles. I've just always called them that. If you'd rather I didn't…"

Lexi opened her gifts a fraction. A lost, wayward soul. Happy, but still disconnected. She squeezed Jillian's arm in reassurance. "My being here doesn't change a thing. Maybe we could spend some time together and you could help me get to know everyone? Every time I get close to them they duck and cover."

Jillian clasped her hands behind her back and a blush pinked her cheeks. "I'd like that."

A dog padded out from behind the wall of tall grass, his long coat a color flitting between lilac and gray, maybe periwinkle. The only break in the surprising shade was a streak of pearlescent white shimmering down his spine. It ambled forward and nudged Lexi's wrist with a cold, wet nose.

Jillian's laugh flittered with the same lightness of the petals dancing in the breeze. "Oh, now you'll come out."

"He's beautiful." Lexi petted the top of his head. "What's his name?"

"Samuel." Jillian crouched and dragged her hand along the white streak at his spine. "Uncle Ramsay got him for me."

"He's a menace." Orla stood and rubbed the small of her back. "We're finishing up here. If you're not practicing your new skills would you like some lunch?"

"That's where I was headed. I got lost on the way to the kitchen and found you instead."

"Perfect." Orla tossed her spade into a battered taupe tote made of some sturdy fabric and motioned at a handful of tools strewn on the path behind her. "Jilly, get those gathered and I'll get these in the shed."

Lexi joined in to help and snagged the bag before Orla could. "I'll put them up if you'll tell me where they go."

Orla nodded, picked up her sack of weeds, and pointed down the path at a shed set near the garden's edge. "Just over there. While you do that, Jilly and I will start on the food. Anything in particular you want?"

"What was it you made yesterday? The pastry with the peach and caramel sauce on top?"

Orla and Jillian both laughed, but it was Orla who answered. "That's lasta. And it's normally for breakfast, but what the heck." She looked back at the weed-free beds behind her. "We've worked for it right?"

"Absolutely." Lexi took off for the shed, motivated by the promise of Orla's treat almost as much as she'd been eager to learn to throw a fireball. She rummaged through the rows of tools, found an empty spot for the tote, and stepped into the nearly noonday sun.

Serena's sing-song devil voice stopped her only a second before her anger fired against Lexi's sense. "I'd hoped I'd be able to find you."

Lexi clamped down on her sensory gift and braced. "What do you want?"

Evil burned in her exotic blue gaze. "Maybe I wanted to atone for my behavior the other day."

"My guess is you don't apologize for much. Sniffing around for my fireann is more like it."

"You use that term pretty easily for a woman who knows nothing of our race." The classic catty tone. A verbal blade slipping from its sheath. "You're right, though. I don't give a fig about your feelings. And Eryx will be mine."

"Like hell."

"Really?" From the folds of her gown, she revealed a slim, gold box no bigger than her hand. She held it out to Lexi with an unspoken dare. "I've got something here that says otherwise."

Lexi stared at the box, then at Serena. "Games?"

"Hardly." She covered the lid with her free hand. "See for yourself." She lifted the top. A gold shield lay on a bed of white felt.

Dread tingled through Lexi, and her stomach lurched.

Don't react. Breathe slow and steady.

"What is it?" With a little luck, Serena would be too hopped up on vengeance to notice the tremble in her voice.

Serena's head cocked. "You don't recognize it? I thought surely you would. His memories made it look like he was proud of his time as a... what do they call them in Evad? Policeman? Hasn't he shown you this?"

The shiny gold emblem winked from its innocent bed. The black TPD emblazoned across the middle sliced her gut open wide. Dread thickened to fear, but no way was she showing her cards to this bitch. "I don't know who you're talking about."

"Oh, darn it. I'm so bad with names." Serena touched one finger to her chin and surveyed the sky. "Ike….Isaac…" Her eyes popped open and her head snapped upright. "Oh, I know. Ian."

Fuck.

Serena paused, all dramatic effect and Grinch smile. "He wouldn't admit he knew you either. It's rather cute the way you two try to protect each other. Does Eryx know about him? Surely you two weren't intimate. He's so *old* looking."

Lexi's nails bit into her palms, the need to seize Serena's perfect neck and squeeze nearly more than she could stand. Her temples ached from the press of her clenched jaw.

"Your friend's tucked away in a villa on the outskirts of Cush. All you have to do to get him safely back where he belongs is to meet me there tonight."

Lexi straightened as tall as she could. "I realize you hold me in the lowest regard. But no one, not even a human-raised Myren, would be stupid enough to walk directly into a trap like the one you're suggesting. And you grossly overestimate the pawn you're using as bait."

"So, you wouldn't mind if I give the order to slit his throat now?"

Lexi clamped her mouth shut, unable to let such devastating words loose.

Serena chuckled. "I didn't think so. I'll give you the location and you'll be there tonight, alone, at sunset. And think twice before you share your plans with your precious new fireann. I've got political connections and an army at my disposal. All it will take are a few, well-placed words in the right ears and you'll be the lone instigator of a full-fledged war." Morbid delight glittered in her azure blue gaze. "I'm sure your subjects would be thrilled to know their new malress was the sole reason for bringing a new era of suffering and death to our people."

Serena rattled on with her instructions.

Lexi kept her silence. There had to be some way to deal with this. Some way to cut the shrew off at the pass and get Ian someplace safe.

When she was done, Serena stepped back into the shadows and shimmered into nothingness.

An overly perfumed breeze brushed past her.

Serena whispered in her ear, "I'll see you tonight, my malress."

Eryx stomped from the kitchen toward the garden and tamped down the silent fury racing through his veins. Orla and Jillian had pounced as soon as he'd landed with a frantic download of what had happened in his absence. Not that their words were helpful. Serena might have dropped in and rattled Lexi to the point of visual agitation, but no one seemed to know what was said. With Serena, it couldn't be good.

He stepped out into the late afternoon sun. Lightning pierced a wooden crate propped against the fire pit. Another three crates sat on the ground—if one could still call them crates. Hacked up scraps of wood and piles of ash was more like it, and the air reeked with the stench of smoke. "That crate must have really pissed you off."

Lexi spun to face him. Her crimson tunic was damp down the center and clung to her torso. Two splotches of dirt or ash marked one cheek and her forehead. "I didn't hear you come out."

"I see that." He started forward, cautious. Curious how she'd play whatever she was up to. "You've been at it awhile?"

Lexi nodded, a little too emphatically. "Getting lots better."

"Looks like it."

She tucked her hands behind her back and shifted her feet. "How was the meeting?"

Ah, so diversion was her tactic. "We modified our focus area. Patrols have gone out." He hugged her and the fine hairs along his arms lifted, a flagrant indicator she'd been at her drills too long. "You stop and take a break today?"

Lexi's head bobbed up and down, but her eyes didn't quite meet his. "I had lunch with Orla and Jillian."

He waited to see if she'd add anything else.

Nothing.

"Come on." If she wouldn't talk to him, he could at least take care of her physically. Tucking her against his side, he steered her toward the house. "If you don't rest, you're going to pass out."

Her head whipped up, eyes wide. "Shit. I forgot about that." She focused on the ground so hard he was surprised he couldn't hear the gears inside her head grinding.

And that was it. Not so much as a peep the rest of the way to their chambers. She crawled on top of the bed and curled onto her side, her back to the door.

In that moment, there seemed more distance between them than before he'd first seen her in dreams. His blood simmered with frustration, and a slow, steady squeeze gripped his heart. How was he supposed to help her if she wouldn't let him in? After their mating, he'd thought they'd be past this point.

With clipped steps, he snagged a throw off the bed. If she wouldn't talk, he'd just take what he needed from her memories. He spread the blanket over her and settled on the edge of the bed. "Talk to me."

Lexi kept her eyes shut and pressed her lips together so tight, the color shifted from berry to white.

Stalemate. Now what in histus was he supposed to do? Take her memories, or trust her to share when she was ready?

So still and silent, curled in a fetal position beside him. In one week, she'd been thrown more life-altering loopholes than most people walked through in a lifetime, and not once had she shut down like she was right now. The fatigue bit was bullshit. Whatever was eating at her was bad. Raw, barely dammed emotion—and it ripped him from the inside out.

And there's your answer.

If he stole her memories, he'd be no better than the people who'd hurt her in her youth. Not to mention he'd single- handedly kill what trust they'd forged. He let out a sigh and tucked a stray strand of hair behind her ear. "You're not in life alone anymore, Lexi."

A tear fell and a deeper crimson wet spot bloomed on the silk beneath her temple.

He stood and strode for the door. Better to leave before he could change his mind and do or say something he'd regret. The cold sting of the metal doorknob matched his heart.

"Eryx."

His heart kicked at the sound of her shaky voice. He braced and faced her.

Her face was tight, fists full of the comforter beneath her. "We need to talk."

OF ALL THE strategies and outcomes Lexi had contemplated since her run-in with Serena, not one had played out like this. The details she'd shared with Eryx had rushed out, peppered with a number of colorful metaphors to make a biker blush.

Eryx pulled her into a hug tight enough to crush her lungs. No ranting. No shifting into war mode. Just held her. His voice shook with what her senses confirmed as bone-deep relief. "Thank you for trusting me."

A stuttered breath. "You knew."

Eryx pinned her chin between his thumb and finger and lifted. "Jillian and Orla jumped me the minute I got home and told me Serena had been here, but didn't tell me what she said. I almost took your memories. I realized I needed to trust you the same way I want you to trust me."

Stunned, her knees nearly buckled. Tears spilled down her face and pooled in the hollow of her neck. Never since she was fourteen years old had she had anything worth crying about, but this man—this man was everything to weep for.

He wiped each tear and brushed tender kisses along her brow, her nose, her cheeks. "We'll find Ian."

She hiccupped around a sob. "But the Rebellion, we'll start a war."

He smiled. The arrogant, self-confident, deliciously wonderful man actually smiled. "The Lomos Rebellion will take on a life of its own no matter how we approach this. Whether we see to Ian's safety or not won't stop any plans Maxis wants to put into motion."

With that, he swept Lexi into his arms, settled them both on a chaise in his adjoining office, and sent a mental summons to Ludan and Ramsay. Half an hour later, his study was a hive of covert strategy—five quarans representing each region, Ramsay, Ludan and Jagger.

Lexi perched on Eryx's lap, all too conscious of her bedraggled appearance and the intimate pose the two of them made during such a serious discussion. No matter how many times she tried to escape for her own chair, Eryx held her tight with an arm around her waist.

"There's zero activity near the villa to distract from our movements. You'll have to use a limited number of warriors with strong stealth abilities to get inside undetected," one quaran said. "You've already noted Maxis exhibited skills unknown to us before. If he's gained the ability to detect masked Myrens, then sending too many in would tip him off."

"I don't know." Jagger shifted in his chair at Ramsay's right. "With the increase in men I've seen in Asshur, all built like warriors, it's possible they'll stage an ambush."

Another quaran chimed in. "Are you sure the human is there? Surely we won't risk our warriors on the words of a scorned woman?"

"One life—any life—is too precious to chance." Eryx's icy stare pegged the quaran who'd spoken. "If it were someone you loved, would you want me to ignore the situation?"

No one expected a reply, least of all Eryx. He looked to Ludan, sprawled in an oversized chair, one foot propped carelessly on the edge of the coffee table. "What's your spin?"

"Hostages and weak points were always his family's M.O. Doesn't surprise me he'd take that tack. Question is if Ian's still alive?"

"And how Maxis knew to find him," Ramsay added.

A fresh wave of nausea hit her.

"He must have been on our tail in Evad longer than we thought. Maybe saw us together inside," Eryx said. "Maxis isn't much on human ways but even he's got to be able to track a tag."

Ludan sat forward and rested his elbows on his knees. "Makes sense." He didn't sound like he was sold on the idea, though.

"You gotta assume it's a trap." Ramsay leaned a hip against Jagger's wingback and crossed his arms. "We scout the area first. If it's clear, we send the best people versed in masking first. If the whole thing's a ruse, we back out and regroup. Never let 'em know we were there. If the shit's real, we nab Ian and bolt."

"A diversion of some type might be convenient." A third quaran stepped into the fray, his voice almost whiny compared to the other masculine tones. "If they're expecting the malress, why not have her approach the villa and we provide backup?"

"No." The word dropped like an anvil.

The room stilled and each man gazed off at indistinct points around the room.

Lexi itched to pace. She tried to push from Eryx's lap, but his arm wouldn't budge.

Maybe it was the tightly leashed power in the room making her antsy. They were each powerfully built, capable of impressive destruction. Yet they all stood motionless, their minds grinding for options.

"Ramsay and I will go." Eryx's tone left no room for rebuke. "No one's stronger at sensing and shielding from other Myrens than we are. Jagger and Ludan are on backup."

Panic and anger bubbled in Lexi's gut.

The arm around her waist tightened further, as did Eryx's voice. "I need two guards, highly regarded, advanced skills. They'll be here with Lexi. I want the best."

The whiny-voiced quaran stepped forward. "I've got a newly promoted man well suited for such an assignment. His skills are exceptional, and he's moved quickly within the ranks. His loyalty is unquestioned."

Eryx's chest rumbled against her. "Anyone else?"

One of the yet unspoken quarans stepped forward. "I would be proud to offer my son, my malran. He's up for promotion to elite and has always shown outstanding initiative."

Eryx's gaze slid back to the wimpy sounding fellow. "Not sure I should trust a man so willing to throw my baineann to the wolves."

"Eryx." Lexi didn't make a full escape, but did manage to angle for a glare. "What he suggested makes perfect sense. I think you should reconsider."

"No." Eryx's response was even more clipped than the last. He eyeballed the two who'd offered warriors for service. "Get them here. And tighten castle detail. If they're not warriors, staff, or family, they're not welcome. Understood?"

"Yes, sir." The quarans' voices rang in unison.

"Ramsay, have a battalion with specialties in hand-to-hand on deck nearby. Don't disclose the final location unless the shit hits the fan. All plans will be kept to the individuals in this room. No one knows about this operation until it's over and Ramsay or myself give the order to share it further."

"We've got about an hour and a half before sunset." Jagger's voice was smooth compared to Eryx's harsh commands. The gold damask of his wingback framed his sun-streaked hair. "I'll need every minute to scout."

Eryx nodded, his thumb a steady back and forth motion at her stomach. If he knew how close she was to puking he might rethink the action. "Everyone out. Wait in the foyer."

The men strode from the room under a cloud of murmurs. Eryx rested his hand atop her white-knuckled fist.

Blood pulsed hot and thick beneath Lexi's skin. With every breath, her arguments built and battered against her tightly clenched lips.

Eryx's gaze held hers. Chagrined, but resigned and ready to battle. The office latch slid into place with a reverberant click.

Lexi launched from Eryx's lap and spun to face him. "You can't do this!"

The leather of his chair cracked in the silence as he reclined. His silver eyes darkened to liquid metal. "I can. I will." Pure, smooth dominance. A predator who'd planned his attack.

Lexi's teeth snapped together with a painful clink. "At the very least you need to let me go with you. Let me be a diversion. You can't leave me here while you're out fighting my battles."

Eryx shot forward, captured her hand, and made a show of twining their fingers together. "This isn't only your battle, Lexi." He tugged her so she stood between his knees. "It's been my family's battle for generations and now it's impacted you." He raised their joined hands and skimmed her inner wrist with his lips. "Because of that, I need to do this."

The contact raced up her arm. "Then I should go, too."

"No."

Lexi opened her mouth to argue.

Eryx laved her tender skin and her mind tripped. He blew against the wet path he'd left on her skin. "You're not ready yet. What you did today tells me you're warrior material, but we don't yet know to what extent. Putting you in this situation is unacceptable." His teeth scraped at her thumping pulse. "You'd know that if you stop to think for a moment."

Lexi jerked her hand away and spun for escape.

Eryx surged from the chair. His arm snaked out to cage her against him. His free hand gripped the back of her head and angled her face to meet his fierce gaze. His hot, elevated breath clashed with hers. "I know this isn't because you don't trust me. If that were the case, you'd have gone out to handle this on your own. You also know you need to develop your skills or you wouldn't have worked yourself to the point of exhaustion today. So what's eating you?"

A direct hit. A question she wasn't sure she had the strength to face. She squeezed his shoulders, so defined and solid, and dropped her forehead to rest on his chest with a haggard moan. "I don't want to lose you." The tears started again, the fear banging around in her belly pushing out ragged sobs. "I just found you. I don't want to lose you." The words cracked as they passed her lips. If she'd had to walk naked in the middle of Times Square she wouldn't feel this exposed. "I love you."

He lifted her chin. The implacable hardness of his eyes softened. "You won't lose me. I'm not that easy to get rid of. Between the four of us, we're damned near unstoppable. No one can sense or shield their presence better than my family's line."

"And if it's an ambush?"

"Then we'll know and abort for a different attack."

Lexi hugged his neck and plastered herself closer. Her ear settled over the solid rhythm of his heart. Her own wasn't as steady. It hammered like cement shoes in a clothes dryer.

Eryx stroked her spine, his confidence evident in every stroke. She trusted him, knew he and his warriors were the most skilled to handle a man like Maxis. Still, no one was infallible.

One tiny mistake and she could well lose the two men she loved most in her life.

Calling the rendezvous spot a villa was pushing it. Eryx had seen shacks from the Underlands in better condition.

Jagger shimmered into view just behind the tree line shielding them. "I combed the perimeter. It's clean. The quarans were right, though. Gonna be rough masking without other people to throw off our movements."

Damn, but it was good to have Jagger back—and the tracking skills that came with him. Giving him leave to handle private affairs in Asshur had been the right call, but if war lay ahead, they'd need every man they could get of his caliber.

Wind gusted down the open field between them and the domed structure, and a black, barely attached shutter clattered against the weathered stucco walls. "Any movement?"

Ludan shook his head, gaze rooted to the open windows. "Nothing but our backups and they're at least five hundred feet out."

Another one of Ludan's handy gifts. His sensory reach doubled that of most warriors.

With a curt nod, Eryx faced the other men. "Ramsay, you're the one linked to our backups, so you're on mass communications. Everything else stays between you, me, and Ludan. Circle to the other side and come in opposite me. Jagger, watch his back."

Both men flashed out of sight, wind swooshing the fallen leaves into a flurry as they took to the sky.

"Lexi?"

She hummed a gentle response. It was kind of amazing how quickly she'd learned to communicate this way, not to mention the other skills she was determined to learn in short order.

"We're about to go in. If you need me, all you need to do is reach out. Remember, you can call Ramsay and Ludan too."

"I'm fine." Spoken like a truly pissed off woman.

"Go downstairs and find Orla. Or look for Jillian. It'll keep your mind off things until I get back."

"Waiting's not my strong point." Her grumble promised all kinds of retribution when he got home.

On the bright side, making up would be fun. *"Mine either. You can make me pay for it later."*

"Giving me time to plan isn't a smart move." She hesitated, then a tiny crack broke through. *"Be careful."*

He savored the words. Relished in the fact that he had a mate. Someone waiting for him at home. Depending on him. If she hadn't shared Serena's treachery…

A chill racked him from the inside out. He slowed his breath and centered on his instincts. Now was the time for action. To save his baineann's friend and, hopefully, cut the head off the rebellion snake. *"Ramsay?"*

"In place."

"Let's go." Eryx eased from their cover and drew his shields in place. Air and earth layered across the outer edges of his mask and blended his presence with the landscape.

By the time they reached the dwelling, the sun touched the horizon. If the house held any occupants, they'd be looking for Lexi now.

"I'm in." Ramsay said.

Eryx eased through an open window and waited for his energy to settle. *"Second that. Nothing in the main room. Scan the top floor and I'll work toward the center of this level."* One sharp movement and anyone with a decent level of tracking could find them.

He combed the first floor. Zero. *"Anything?"*

"Not yet. One last room," Ramsay said.

"Ludan? All clear?"

"Clear." Ludan sounded almost disappointed.

"Shit. Eryx contact Lexi and get up here!" The echo behind his voice changed. He'd switched to mass communications. *"Lock the castle down. Secure the malress!"*

Eryx reached out to Lexi and shot with lightning speed to his brother's location.

Absolute silence through his connection to Lexi. The empty nothingness brought his world to a screeching halt. Roaring for Lexi in his mind, he rounded the corner.

A police badge with a note held Ramsay's attention.

We told her it wouldn't be wise to talk with you. Now we have them both.

LEXI SAT in the middle of her massive bed, knees pulled up so her chin rested on her crossed arms. If she was smart she'd do something productive. Take a bath, or change her clothes. Anything but pout.

With a pitiful huff, she scooted toward the edge of the bed. Better to let Eryx focus. With a little luck, Orla would still be in the kitchen and up for some meaningless chitchat.

She opened the bedroom doors and jumped a half step back.

"Malress." At either side of the door, warriors snapped to attention. The one on the left offered a minute bow and kind smile.

Eryx was going overboard. She was at home for crying out loud. Surely this wouldn't be the norm going forward. She waved over her shoulder and headed for the stairs. "I'm headed down for a quick snack."

The warrior on her right looked waxen, the corners of his eyes strained. Probably wishing he was out in the field with the rest of the guys instead of wasting his time on house detail.

"Everything okay?"

"I'm fine, my malress." Even his voice sounded tight.

Men and their pride. She shrugged and started down the stairs. Didn't they have any female warriors?

A startled inhalation and a hard grunt sounded behind her. She spun toward the sound.

The warrior who'd bowed as she left her room stared back at her, eyes and mouth wide. He clutched at a dagger buried in his sternum.

An arm clamped around her neck and a hand smothered her mouth with a vile smelling cloth. She shoved the unrelenting hand. Her mind clouded. Strength melted from her muscles. Her knees crumpled and she thudded to the floor in a heap. Darkness replaced her vision.

ERYX FLEW to the castle with a speed he'd never before attempted. Ludan, Ramsay, and Jagger's energy resonated behind him, albeit a good distance back.

Lexi's link was still dead.

"She's still alive," Ramsay said. *"If she wasn't you'd have felt it. Your mark's still black, right? Remember that."*

Right. So, she was either incapacitated, or in zeolite. Praise The Great One, let it be the latter. His feet hit the pavement with a boom.

The warriors guarding the entrance wrenched the doors open and dropped their heads.

Ramsay landed behind Eryx, yelling orders as he flanked him. Ludan and Jagger landed a second later.

"Quarans!" Eryx's bellow ricocheted off every surface and shook the glass windowpanes.

Four of the five quarans raced to his side, and stood at attention, their expressions tight.

"Where is my baineann?"

All of the quarans, save one, paled. The last, the one who'd volunteered his son for duty, stepped forward, eyes burning black with anger. "We locked down the castle as the strategos commanded and combed the interior immediately. We found one of her guards dead. The other guard and the malress were missing."

Wait a minute. There were only four quarans. There should be five. The one who'd suggested using Lexi as bait was missing. "Where is Quaran Stend?"

The brave one spoke up. "He is also unaccounted for, my malran."

Eryx's stomach clenched. "Which of the guards is missing?"

"The one recommend by Quaran Stend." The man's voice cracked. He lifted his chin another notch and motioned with his head toward the top of the stairs. "The fallen warrior is my son."

Eryx found himself at the top of the landing, the short distance a blur of shouts and muted colors. The young warrior lay in an awkward sprawl, his gaze empty, a dagger lodged in his chest.

Dropping to one knee, Eryx slid the blade free. Blood oozed from the wound and coated the weapon. He squeezed the hilt and slowed his breath. Lexi needed him. Sane and focused.

He faced the man's father and offered him the bloody dagger. "Your son will be afforded the honor of a warrior who died in battle. The honor of an elite. When we find the man guilty for this treachery, retribution will be yours."

The quaran bowed, the knife white-knuckled in one hand.

"Ramsay," Eryx said.

His brother strode forward.

"No one leaves the grounds until their minds have been scoured by someone loyal." Eryx glared at the remaining quarans. "Start with them."

He spun for his chambers. "Ludan, pull the staff together and start questioning. Jagger, scout the grounds. I'll check up here."

The small crowd behind him jumped to life with jumbled, low voices. Eryx strode to his suite. Everything sat in its proper place, no detail out of order but for the dead warrior being hefted away. The room's emotional residue reeked of fear and pain, a mix of fetid swamp and copper. Impossible to pull any clues beyond such thick taints.

Their suite proved no better. A rumpled indentation to one side of the bed where he'd left her only hours before. Her rosemary and mint scent still on the pillow. No trail. No clue.

Ludan had been right. He'd been too lax. Too confident. He should have taken out the Rebellion when the rumblings started, but he'd pushed it off.

And now his mate was gone.

"Eryx," Galena shrieked from the foyer.

He vaulted over the stairwell, landed on the first floor, and gripped her shoulders. No blood. No tears or bruises. "What's wrong?"

She shoved his hands away and motioned toward the open doors. "The guards outside just told me. Did you find anything?"

He shook his head and nudged Galena forward. Beyond the open doorway, Ludan and Jagger questioned staff in the yard. "Nothing yet. We'll keep digging. Maybe you can pick out something we can't."

They strode across the raised veranda, toward the garden where Ludan had the staff in neat little lines. Strewn across the path to one side was a mess of dark, rich soil and a jumble of krocious flowers.

"What's that?" Eryx pulled Galena to his side at pointed at the chaos. "They were for Phybe, she didn't show at my house today, so I brought them here." Galena jerked her elbow from his grasp and waved it off with a scowl. "I dropped them when I heard. I'll clean it up later."

Eryx let her go and followed. Then stopped.

Flowers. Bruised but colorful petals. The same kind the warrior's widow had clutched in her palm. *I think my friend was wrong about you,* she'd said.

"Galena."

Galena hurried to his side. "Eryx you're wasting time. Let's work with the staff and see what they know."

Ramsay, Ludan, and Jagger closed in as he pulled Galena to the pile of dirt and blooms. "These were for Phybe?"

She nodded.

"And she was supposed to be at your house today?" Another nod. "What does that have to do with Lexi?"

"She didn't show?"

"No. I went by her house to see if she was all right, but she wasn't there either. The woman who lives across from her said she's been gone since yesterday." Brow wrinkled, she glanced at Ramsay, now beside her, then to Ludan. "Am I missing something?"

Eryx crouched, picked up a dislocated bloom, and twirled it in his fingers. The same as the day he'd met Phybe. Its petals quivered in the wind—a perfect match to the tremors firing through his muscles. "It's a long shot, but I think she may know how to find Maxis."

He locked gazes with Ramsay. "Find me the widow."

CHAPTER 27

$\mathcal{L}$exi sputtered back to consciousness. Pain shot down the back of her head and a nasty paint thinner taste coated her tongue.

"Ah, there's our new malress."

Maxis Steysis. No way she'd mistake that voice. More to the tenor side than baritone with a healthy slathering of maniac.

She kept her eyes closed, pretending to sleep, but her sluggish heart kicked in an erratic rhythm.

"It's obvious you're awake. May as well face your foes head on."

A smooth, steady cloud of rage formed in her belly. She opened her eyes and a flicker of candlelight pierced her vision, the pain radiating down her neck and along her spine.

The dank, sparse cell reeked of mold and earth. With her hands bound behind her back, the burlap cot scraped her knuckles. No feeling in her fingers. Hard to tell how long she'd been out.

A long, skinny table sat flush against the far wall, the only furniture besides her cot and the ladder chair Maxis straddled. His face was shrouded on one side, the dancing candle barely illuminating the other. Long black hair with tight waves reached his shoulders. "The Chloroform packs quite a punch, doesn't it?" He gestured casually, indicating a slight female standing rigid in the shadows. "I'm sure you remember Serena."

Serena slipped into the soft light, the shadows slanting against the elegant angles of her face to create a sinister mask. "Your refined air's not so bold anymore."

She reached for Eryx with her mind. The link lay empty, a resounding dead end.

"Reaching for your fireann?" Serena's voice resonated against the gray marble walls. Snide as ever.

"Easy." Maxis placated his companion with a gentle tap on her forearm and a low chuckle. God, but his eyes were creepy. Green, but so light it looked unnatural. "You're in zeolite containment," he said to Lexi. "The room is surrounded with it."

Serena caressed Maxis' shoulder. "She probably doesn't even know what zeolite is."

"I know what it is." A complete lie, but no way in hell was she giving either of these sickos the satisfaction of knowing different. "Where's Ian?"

Maxis *tsked* with a wicked grin. "Let's not rush things." He crooked his head and the shadows sharpened the severe line of his jaw. "I thought we'd take some time to get acquainted. Me. You. Your fireann's lover."

"Former lover." Lexi spat the reminder with enough venom to take down an elephant.

Serena's lips flattened to a harsh line as she sashayed close, her blue eyes hollow pits of hate. "Perhaps we'll have the opportunity to reunite after you're gone."

"Funny." Lexi focused on the ceiling and wriggled her fingers to fight the stinging numbness in her hands. "I think you and Maxis make a better match. Your delusion to his insanity. Quite a combo."

Serena seized Lexi's hair and jerked her head off the cot.

Lexi snarled, unable to wrench free. "Figures you'd be the wimpy hair-pulling type. Care to take off the ropes and go at it for real?"

Serena snapped Lexi's head against the cot and retreated behind Maxis.

"Women," Maxis muttered and set the chair against the wall. "You'd do well to save your strength," he said to Lexi. "You'll have a long night of it once our friend gets here." Maxis ambled toward the door.

Serena stayed rooted in place. "You were out for a long time, Lexi." She drifted closer and peered down her nose. "Do you know how much information can be gleaned from an unguarded, unconscious mind?"

That nearly jolted Lexi from the cot.

Serena chuckled and joined Maxis at the door. "Have fun thinking on that while you wait."

ERYX STALKED toward yet another zeolite mine entrance, leaving his brother a safe distance behind. It was either that or choke him. Phybe was nowhere to be found, her link dead. Which meant she was in hiding, or Maxis had already tied off loose ends. Neither possibility did good things to his mood.

Ramsay's thin-and-diversify strategy only made it worse. "We need to spread our efforts, Eryx."

Eryx glanced at Ludan. "You want to shut him up before I kill him?"

"I don't do family interventions." Ludan kept pace, his boots crunching against the pebble and rock surface.

Ramsay stepped to his right. "Let's pull a few squads off the mines and get them scouting in Asshur, just in—"

"Don't say it." Eryx shot nose to nose with his brother, the pressure behind his eyes so brutal he thought they might pop. "Don't even breathe it."

Ludan gripped Eryx's shoulder. Nothing evasive, just enough to ward off sibling warfare. Still a ballsy move.

Eryx backed off, though not by much. "She's my mate. When it's your mate we can spread our men all over the damned globe, but until then it's my call." He whirled for the entrance, snatched two unlit torches, and tossed one to Ramsay.

Ludan grabbed a torch and backhanded a line of fire to light all three at once. Gold and red flecks reflected off the zeolite.

Brutal fucking crystal. Eryx sucked in a fortifying breath and stepped beneath the ledge. The zeolite's power ripped through his core. No mercy. No tenderness. Just nature's special blend of Myren disembowelment.

He shook his head and powered forward. "Same drill as before." He motioned to the first three tunnels. "Spread out and work them one at a time. Shout if you find something, otherwise retreat and wait at the top for the next section."

Faces resolute, Ludan and Ramsay disappeared down their assigned routes.

A steady *plip, plip, plip* filled the musty air. The torch hissed and crackled overhead, and the burnt pitch stung his nose. With each cautious step, rock crunched and the light from the outside grew dimmer.

He angled the light and scanned for signs of activity. The mines hadn't been worked in over a century, but that didn't keep boys and thrill seekers at bay. The tracks left behind were too recent for Eryx to gather much.

A sharp gasp echoed down the tunnel. Eryx stopped and listened.

Nothing.

He took another step.

Not a gasp. More like a hushed cry. "Phybe?"

A shaky whimper reverberated from the darkness, followed by a sniffle. "Phybe? It's Eryx."

Praise The Great One. Didn't he paint a picture, talking to what was probably his overactive imagination. Conjuring something from nothing.

"Please." A cracked voice whispered from no more than fifteen feet beyond. "Don't hurt me."

His heart lurched and then galloped. He lowered the torch, careful of every step. "I'm here to help you, Phybe. Not hurt you." His boot landed on an overlarge rock, and his foot slipped and crunched on the porous rock. He stifled an oath and tried to steady his tone. "Let me hear your voice, sweetheart. It'll be fine."

"Over here."

A dirty blue slipper came into view. Phybe flinched against the light, covering her face.

Eryx crouched and held the flame aloft. Urging her hands down and pushing wild blonde hair from her dirt-covered face, he let loose a shrill whistle.

Phybe jerked and covered her ears.

"Sorry." Beyond the dirt and rips in her pale blue gown she seemed more frightened than injured. "Can you tell me what happened?"

She shook on a fresh wave of sobs and hung her head so her hair covered her face. She pulled her knees in tight. "I didn't know," she whispered. "I was in such grief and he was so kind. I had no idea who he was." She couldn't get much more disjointed in her speech. Bits of data shot between gasping hiccups.

Just get her up and out of here and take the information you need.

He tamped down the thought. Barely. "Who?"

Her lower lip trembled. "He said his name was Wesley, but I overheard him in Cush. His name is Maxis."

The friend she'd mentioned. The one who'd given her the flower. "Maxis was the friend who found you?"

She nodded and hung her head again, shoulders shaking so hard he thought she might fall over.

Footsteps echoed down the path and Phybe scooted further away, eyes wide with fear.

Eryx gripped her shoulder and held her in place. "It's all right. It's my men. We'll get you out of here."

She shook her head in a frantic back and forth, her cheeks going fire engine red. "No. You can't. He'll find me."

Eryx gripped her tighter. "Maxis?"

She nodded and gulped a quick breath of air. "He'll kill me. The man who helped me said I had to stay here until it was safe."

"Who helped you?"

The darkness lightened by quick degrees as Ludan and Ramsay rounded the last corner. Phybe's gaze darted from one man to the next and she curled in tight.

Eryx carefully lifted her chin. "Who helped you, Phybe?"

"I-I don't know his name. But he brought me food. Said he needed time to figure out what to do."

"You linked with Maxis?"

She hung her head.

"I want to take you to the castle. We've got zeolite cells there, so Maxis won't find you. We'll go quickly, but you'll be exposed for a short time." He gave her a minute to let the plan sink in. "Are you willing to risk it?"

She batted a tear, but agreed with a tiny nod.

He handed off his torch and lifted her against his chest

before she could change her mind and headed toward the entrance.

"Maxis wants to hurt you." She lifted her grimy, tear-streaked face from his chest. "He offered Serena revenge against the malress. I heard them."

"They've already got her." He didn't mean for it to come out as harsh as it did.

Phybe ducked and gave into a fresh round of weeping. "I'm so sorry. Saul would be so ashamed."

He pulled Phybe closer. No matter what her transgressions, she didn't deserve to suffer like this. Not with the price she and her mate had already paid. "Your fireann knew your kind heart. Maxis saw it too and used it. It's what he does."

The tunnel went on for what felt like eons. By the time he reached the entrance, he thought sure he'd find the afternoon sun close to the horizon, but it had barely shaded the entrance. No more than forty, maybe fifty minutes since they'd gone in. As soon he cleared the rock's edge, the breath of his powers roared into place and he took the first decent lungful of air since he'd gone in. "Can you stand?"

She dipped her chin and he eased her to the ground.

"What will they do with her?" Phybe's nails bit into his forearm, whether for balance or from fear he wasn't sure.

He steadied her. "I was hoping you'd tell me how to find her before we get the chance to find out."

Phybe swayed, her knees nearly buckling. "My link."

"If you'll share your memories, we'll work from what you know and get you squared away where Maxis can't find you. We'll figure out the rest afterward."

"No." She released the grip on his arm and straightened. She trembled, but her lips hardened with resolve. "I failed once, but I won't fail again. Let me use my link. Let me atone for what I've done."

"Phybe, a battle isn't—"

"She's right." Ramsay stepped forward, eyes on Phybe. "Do you know anything about him besides where he lives?"

She shook her head. "I was only there one night, then he brought me home."

Ramsay looked to Eryx. "Maxis will be with Lexi. If he's got her anywhere but his home, we're screwed without her."

Ludan and Ramsay stared him down with hard, relentless faces. They viewed Phybe as an advantage. Even if with his baineann in danger, he saw her as a woman who'd already given her mate for their race.

"Please." Phybe gripped his hand. "Let me make right what I've done."

Almost twenty-four hours since they'd taken Lexi. Hands down, the longest day of his life.

Phybe waited for his answer, a determination he couldn't help but respect in her eyes.

"Ramsay, pull a squadron together. Only the most advanced warriors and only those you know intimately. I want four men guarding this woman along the way." He lifted Phybe into his arms. "Prepare the rest for full-scale combat."

CHAPTER 28

*L*exi leaned against the cool marble wall with its sparkling silver veins, exhausted. Wriggling off the cot had sapped a good chunk of her strength, and the aftereffects of the chloroform left her muscles muddled, but at least she'd go the next round with Maxis on her feet. Her fingertips burned, only a trickle of blood seeping past the tight binds at her wrists. She worked her hands in a circular motion and welcomed the fire.

As far as weapons went, the room coughed up a big zero. All she had were wits and time to plan. Backed against the furthest wall, she huddled in the shadows and prayed whoever came through the door next did so with complacent eyes. It was a long shot, but with Maxis and Serena's arrogance, she might get lucky.

Minutes ticked by. With every moment, she rehashed all she'd done and seen since coming to Eden. Made a list of the things she wanted to do when she was free. She'd get through this. She'd done it before. She'd do it again.

The candle flame near the cot barely stirred, the stalk

nearly a stub—four inches shorter than when she'd woken. Bound in a damped, locked cell, measuring the passage of time by the height of a candlestick. Kind of put a new spin on the concept of patience.

Footsteps sounded beyond the door.

Lexi sucked in a deep breath and held it tight. Her pulse thrummed in her ears, the volume growing louder with each rush of adrenaline.

The knob turned.

Lexi flattened tighter to the wall.

The door pushed wide and a man she didn't recognize shuffled past the threshold and stared at the cot.

He started to turn.

Lexi kicked the small of his back. Her bare foot connected enough to tumble him forward, and she spun for escape.

An arm snaked out and wedged into her gut, pulling her back into a solid chest. A sinister chuckle sounded at her ear and hot breath tickled her neck.

"Did you think I'd be that stupid?" Maxis said.

Anger detonated in her core and she struggled within his grasp. The man she'd knocked to the ground struggled to his feet.

Maxis drove her forward, the arm around her gut so tight it hurt to breathe. "Have to say, I'm glad you're a fighter. Makes the whole escapade more fun." He shoved her.

She toppled forward, ducked her head to keep from slamming it against the wall, and landed on one shoulder.

The cot's wooden legs scrunched against the rock floor. The man in the ivory robe inched forward.

Maxis crouched beside her head. His freakish pale green eyes glazed as he traced her lips. "I'd thought to save you for myself."

Lexi jerked her face away.

Undaunted, he stroked her cheek. "Then I realized how much more effective it would be if I passed you around. Let a few of your new countrymen have a chance to sample your wares—so to speak. I'll save my turn for last. I want to see defeat in your eyes when I take you. Know how broken your spirit truly is." He gripped her jaw between his thumb and fingers and forced her face to his. "You got away with your fate before. Tonight you won't be so lucky." He stood and tossed her face to the side so hard her neck snapped.

She gritted her teeth and tried to wiggle upright, only to be forced to her back by the stranger's hands on her shoulders.

"Cutter, you're such a leech." Maxis' sick laughter bounced off the walls. He pulled a gun from his pocket and waved it blithely in the air, eyes to her. "An irony your friend's weapon will be the thing that ends your life. But don't worry, you've got a long night of fun ahead of you first." He dropped it with a loud thud on the table.

"Where's Ian?" Lexi screamed and fought to get free. With sausage-like fingers, Cutter pinned her shoulders.

Maxis paused at the threshold. "You mean my insurance policy? He's tucked away someplace safe. The nice thing about humans is they don't require zeolite, which makes hiding them infinitely easier. Serena and I are off to check on him now, but I'll be sure to let him know you send your regards." He clasped the knob and his lips curled in an empty grin. "Enjoy yourself while I'm gone."

Lexi fought and leveraged her heels against the shaky cot.

The door clicked shut and Cutter's knee pressed into her thigh. He huffed out a laugh tainted with garlic and some other vile herb. "Go ahead and scream. I won't mind a bit."

~

COLD GRAY MASONRY and a black slate roof. Not the happiest looking place Eryx had ever seen, but it was sturdy. And big. Nowhere near the size of his castle, but more than one man needed.

Ramsay shifted to get a better angle through the treeline hiding them. "Ballsy move to build his house in the middle of a forest."

"Not ballsy. Egotistic." Eryx eased the springy branch back in place. "He thinks he's untouchable."

Kneeling beside Galena, Phybe stared at the sprawling home beyond the trees and worried her lip.

"You sure he's here?"

Phybe startled and rattled the leaves beneath her. Her tears had finally subsided, but her eyes were still puffy and red. "I'm too far away to isolate which room, but he's there."

His sister locked an arm around Phybe's waist. "You shouldn't be here," Eryx said to Galena.

Galena shot a mean glare behind Phybe's head. She'd followed his link as soon as she'd learned of their plans, armed with herbs and bandages for her own brand of battle. "It's not the first time I've been in the middle of a fight and Lexi might need me."

She had him there. He might be able to heal, but Galena could do it faster and better. Not a skill he wanted to do without if Lexi was injured.

Fuck, he was tired of waiting. "How much longer?"

"Men are in place," Ramsay said. "Jagger's finishing the perimeter sweep."

"Good, let's move in." Eryx started forward.

Ludan clamped onto his shoulder. "Not yet."

Something popped at the back of Eryx's jaw. Maybe a cracked molar.

"You rush this and we're screwed." Ludan's fingers tightened. "We're not armed for an ambush. Remember, she's a fighter. She's alive or you'd have felt it."

Eryx jerked away from Ludan and paced far enough away he could suck in a decent breath without the weight of everyone's focus. Adrenaline beat at him, greedy for a worthy outlet, and his muscles begged for use.

Fine. He'd wait and let the impatience build. Stoke his power. When the time came, he'd unleash every drop—and make Maxis pay.

~

MAXIS STEPPED out onto the rear veranda with Serena at his side. The air in Asshur usually ran colder than Havilah, but nowhere near the frigid temps of Brasia. Tonight was no exception. Clear skies stretched before them with random streaks of silver energy like fat falling stars.

Serena stepped lightly beside him. Her bare arm brushed his and her throaty chuckle floated out into the early night, her satisfaction at Lexi's impending troubles twisted in a way that mirrored the pains of his own past.

They stepped off the paved patio and a ripple of energy fluttered against his chest.

Maxis yanked Serena to a halt, covered her startled squeak with his hand, and masked their presence. Lifting their bodies from the ground, he edged them to their closest form of cover, an elaborate hedge overlooking the rear gardens. With a pointed glare for silence, Maxis touched down and dropped his hand from Serena's pouty mouth.

He cast his senses out across the property. The energy surrounding his home should be flat, untouched. The isolation from other homes and businesses ensured it unless he had visitors. Tonight, there was a subtle difference. Too subtle.

Serena pressed against him, her bottom sliding against his groin in a shameless display. "I sense nothing. I don't require the farce of impending danger to draw my attention."

"That's because your senses are nothing compared to mine." He cupped her breast through her silken top, and pressed his stirring cock into the cleft of her ass, the mix of danger and Serena's tempting body a heady cocktail. He tweaked her nipple.

Serena gasped.

"Now settle down." Lexi had been right in one thing. They were very well suited, and Maxis had every intention of showing Serena just how much. But that would happen on his timetable, not Serena's.

Satisfied he had Serena's cooperation, he felt for the strongest points of energy surrounding his lands. With each ping that filtered back to him, he drew a mental map. Surrounded. Not by a whole brigade of Myrens, but a lower, strategically placed number.

"We've got visitors. My guess is it's your ex and his warriors." Irritation mingled with excitement, and his cock hardened further against Serena's back.

"He's here?"

Her breathless voice slapped his pride. Perhaps those verbal jabs at Lexi had been more than mere provocation toward her nemesis. "Would you really go back to him?" He hissed more than whispered the words and gave another sharp pinch to the nipple still cradled in his hand. His other hand pressed hard between her legs, pushing her against his thick rod. "Think he'll give you what you need?"

Serena's head dropped against his chest and her eyelids closed on a moan. "He never did before."

Such an open, sultry capitulation. One that stroked a foreign place inside he couldn't quite comprehend. Something to contemplate. Later. After he'd handled his unwanted guests.

He reached out to Reese. *"Follow my link and bring your recruits. Do it quickly. Shantos has my home surrounded."*

Reese replied, cool and disaffected. *"You want me to mobilize a large number of troops with no notice and no knowledge of the terrain?"*

"You sound less than confident, strategos. I thought you'd relish the chance to demonstrate how well you've done with those you lead."

"I have no problem with my skills."

"Then you'll move them out and do it now." Maxis severed the connection. Reese's insolence was out of hand. No matter his unique place in Maxis' life and plans, he'd have to address the behavior soon.

Right after he found the betrayer who'd led the Shantos camp to his door.

KNUCKLES BLASTED across Lexi's cheek. Blood flooded her mouth, thick and metallic down her throat. She kept fighting, thrashing with everything she had to unload Cutter's weight.

His crazed laughter echoed from all sides. "Maxis said you'd be a feisty one. I can see where the malran would find you appealing." He inched his knees up and pressed her legs wide. "I wonder what kind of package we have underneath."

Lexi twisted, shifted and bucked every chance she got. All she needed was one weakness. One second to catch him off guard.

Veins strained at his temples. He shoved her loose tunic up and squeezed her breast. "The malran has nice taste."

Sweat fell from his forehead to her chest and her belly

lurched. She arched and yanked her tied wrists behind her back. "Get off me you nasty pig!" She slipped one of her silk-clad legs from beneath his meaty leg.

Cutter wrenched it back in place.

Her thighs shook, fatigue making the muscles almost useless. Cutter dove for her waistband and angled his back to the door. She tugged again. *Please, God. Not this. Not now.*

A slight figure stood silhouetted in the doorway. Cutter yanked her pants and the silk ripped.

Wild frustration bellowed from deep in her chest. She screamed, the sound a frantic boomerang to match her panic. She jerked her knees. One slipped from under Cutter. She braced her foot at his groin and shoved with everything she had.

A sound like cannon fire exploded. Cutter collapsed in a heavy mass across her, and the smell of gunpowder filled the small cell.

With trembling legs, Lexi shoved Cutter to his back and scooted away. He wasn't dead, but the gurgling groan didn't sound promising for survival. She damn sure wasn't sticking around to see if he made it. She shoved to a stand and the room turned a solid blur of gray. Her legs crumpled.

Metal clattered on stone and young, feminine arms gripped her just before her skull met pavement. Small, sandaled feet shifted beside her. Ian's pistol lay an arm's length away.

Lexi struggled to her knees.

A young woman with brown, tightly braided pigtails peered down with wide, frightful eyes. She shook so badly her sackcloth gown practically danced. Her voice trembled as badly as her body. "Are you all right?"

Cutter lay on his side, blood oozing from his open mouth. "Been better. Thank you." Woefully inadequate words considering what the woman had done to save her. Lexi tried to stand, but her quivering legs gave out.

The girl steadied her. "I couldn't let him…" The terror on her face finished saying what she couldn't. She might be young, but she'd seen worse than Lexi. God only knew how often.

"What's your name?"

The girl pulled her hands away and clenched them to her belly. "Brenna. Brenna Haven."

Okay.

Niceties done.

Time to move.

She stumbled to the chair against the wall and collapsed to the hard seat. Torn pants, bare feet, swelling cheek, numb fingers and shaky legs. Not bad all things considered. She shifted to show her still bound wrists, the sticky wetness promising a bloody mess. "Can you undo the knots?"

Brenna lurched forward and set to work, the harsh fiber scratching with each tug.

"Where's Ian?" Lexi said.

Brenna hesitated.

Lexi wiggled her bound hands, and Brenna ducked back to her task. "Who—Who's Ian?"

Lexi shook her head. "Never mind. We need to get out of here. I'll call Eryx and he'll help us."

The rope slid to the floor, and Brenna stumbled back. Her hands trembled against her mouth and stomach. "Is he…like him?"

"Like who?" Lexi glanced at Cutter. "Him?"

Cutter watched them, breaths shallow, skin pasty, but evil still glazing his eyes.

Brenna's head shuttled back and forth. "Like master."

Maxis.

That fucking bastard.

Lexi wobbled to a stand. "Eryx is nothing like him." Her thighs groaned under her weight, but she locked her knees. Brenna's arm wound around her waist, and Lexi trudged forward. With every step, her muscles perked up, motivated by the promise of escape.

"Won't…. make…it." Cutter's warning slithered across the room with a psychopathic edge.

Lexi spared the pathetic man a glance as they crossed the threshold. "We'll make it just fine."

MAXIS LASERED his energy toward the front of the house where his mole sat cozied up with Eryx and his precious warriors.

Phybe. Having so few links of his own, tracing the traitor had taken a matter of moments.

Letting Reese handle the little twit had been a mistake, an error he would rectify as soon as he and Serena were safe.

"The men are closing in," Reese snapped. *"Those approaching from the rear should go undetected, but those circling to the front will be at risk."*

"Unless there's a diversion to draw their attention away." Maxis had used his time wisely. Had plotted the perfect course. *"I have a distraction in place. Give me the word and I'll cover."* His fists and the muscles behind his shoulder blades clenched. He definitely had plans in place. Distraction now— revenge later.

"Whatever you're planning, do it now," Reese roared.

Maxis triggered his diversion. He'd wanted to throttle Phybe's brain the moment he'd located her so close to the man he loved to hate. Now he zeroed in on her mind and gave a strong, mental squeeze.

Her agonized cry pierced the night.

He pressed harder and sent shards of pain lancing through every cerebral path. Not too fast. He'd need to give Reese's men time to get into position.

But he could make her suffer for her betrayal—and leave behind a message for Reese of the retribution that waited.

CHAPTER 29

Eryx clamped his hand over Phybe's mouth.

The four guards around them drew their daggers and crouched for attack.

Phybe clawed her scalp, and arched into Galena's arms.

"What's wrong with her?" Ready for attack, Eryx scanned the open space around Maxis' home.

Galena jumped back and let the woman drop the short distance to the ground as though shocked. "He's in her mind. He's using his link to do this."

"He knows we're here." Son of a bitch. He should have stormed the place when he'd first landed. "You four, stay with the women. Ramsay, move in."

Ramsay took to the sky.

Eryx shot toward the estate, Ludan a familiar shadow behind him.

"*Eryx, incoming,*" Ramsay warned. Swarms of stoutly built young males attacked from all sides, outnumbering his crew nearly five to one. Worse if he and Ludan left them to the fight while they went for Lexi.

271

"Ludan, engage." Eryx changed course and threw his first shot.

"Go, all of you." Galena waved the guards toward the fight. Four men surrounding her and a dying woman was a waste Eryx couldn't afford.

Phybe writhed on the ground. She panted and pulled her hair while the grunts and groans of warfare erupted around them.

"He'll kill us if we leave you." Crouched and ready to attack, the guard kept his eyes trained on the sky.

"I'll kill you if you don't. Go."

The four exchanged quick glances. One laid his dagger on the ground beside her. "We'll be back." They took to the air as one and joined the fight, attacks raging both in the air and on the ground.

Galena tucked the dagger under her leg and stroked Phybe's brow. Maxis was still in the poor woman's mind, killing her slowly, and there was nothing she could do to stop it.

She'd be damned if she let him kill her family as well.

Lexi staggered up the wooden steps from her prison. With each step, energy surged faster into her trembling body. She ached for Eryx. For his arms around her, their strength and warmth. *"Eryx?"*

"Lexi," Eryx bellowed then grunted.

Lightning cracked and wind slammed the side of the house. Muffled shouts sounded from outside.

"Stay in the house. Do not come out. Do you hear me?"

Despite his hostile tone, she zinged with relief. She followed Brenna up the last stair and stepped into a medieval-looking kitchen. A cast iron pot hung from a monstrous hearth. A lone sconce burned against the far wall, but flame and lightning lit the room through a picture window. Men fought in the air and on the ground, their savage attacks rumbling against the home's stone walls.

Her stomach clenched into a hard knot.

"Lexi, answer me! Do you hear me?"

The bursts of light were too quick to make out the faces of those fighting. *"I heard. Where are you?"*

"Maxis has done some recruiting." Even in the midst of combat, his sarcastic confidence rang through. *"Stay in the house until we contain them. If they see you, they'll take you."*

He grunted.

The last thing he needed was more distraction, but something instinctive tugged at her. She needed to find him. If nothing else, just to lay eyes on him and see what he faced.

Gripping Brenna's hand, she stilled and concentrated on her link to Eryx. Nothing mattered but finding him. Knowing he was safe. A tiny spark in her brain registered a location she could feel but not see. She spun to face it. "What's in that direction?"

Brenna's hand hovered at her lips. "The main entrance."

Lexi snatched her twitchy savior by the elbow and tugged her close. "Then that's where we're headed."

MAXIS COULDN'T LOOK AWAY from the battle. His eyes burned from the flame and electricity flashing across the night sky. Shantos and his crew were outnumbered. Not by much, but enough to make the difference. Even if Eryx called in reinforcements, they'd never make it in time.

Four men shot from the ground and engaged.

Still good odds at three-to-one, so long as Eryx didn't have any others tucked away.

He cast his senses along the battles edge. More. At least one. Maybe two. He opened his link. *"Reese."*

"I'm a bit engaged at the moment," Reese said.

"And about to be more so." Patience. He'd make his traitorous strategos pay for his actions and attitude later. *"The four warriors who just joined the combat..."*

"What about them?"

"Scout the location they came from. Now. You've got at least one more lying in wait."

Reese grumbled then cut off communications.

The fool. He'd given Reese his heart's desire—a cause to fight for and an army to lead—and he'd chosen a pretty little female over one of his own.

Serena nestled against his chest. Battle fire sparkled in her eyes and her jaw hung slightly open.

"Tell me. How loyal are you to the Rebellion?" he asked. "Are you prepared to follow me?"

Serena turned in his arms and her expression shifted from fascination to smooth confidence. "Follow you? I think not. But, I will lead with you."

He jerked her closer and fisted one hand in her hair, his lips a breath from hers. "You think you can keep up with me, woman?"

Her wine-scented breath fluttered against his face. "And then some."

He tugged her head back another inch. "Then you'll be willing to link with me as a show of our partnership?"

Serena covered the hand digging into her lower back. The fiendish grin that played along her lips one he appreciated. "Only a link, Maxis? Nothing more?"

Maxis sneered at the suggestion. "I'll not mate with any woman, Serena. You'd do well to remember that."

Her eyelids lowered. A demure move that didn't fool him for a second. Her energy fluttered against his hand. "We'll see. For now, we'll keep with a friendly link."

Maxis snatched her offered bond and wrapped it in a mental vise. If she had any idea the gruesome death he'd handed Phybe not three hundred feet away, she likely would have reconsidered her actions.

He crushed his lips against hers and sent his wanton thoughts via link.

"It's time you learned what it means to be mastered."

She sucked in a ragged gasp and shoved his shoulders, but her chest rose and fell in a pattern of need. "No one masters me."

He tightened his arms around her waist, grazed her lips with his, and pressed his rigid cock into her soft belly. "I will." He shot to the ground before she could argue, masking them both from the chaos around them.

She jerked in his hold until she realized their height then stilled. "Where are we going? We can't leave the men behind."

"Reese will see to the troops." And he would see to Reese shortly after. "In the meantime, we'll go someplace private. Somewhere we can ensure you get exactly the attention you deserve."

Lexi followed her mental compass through candlelit hallways to a formal entertaining area. Brenna shivered beneath her arm as blast after blast of electricity and wind slammed into the sides of the house.

A trio of flames flashed through a huge window at the room's center. Lexi's heart sang and jolted at the same time.

Surrounded by rebels, Eryx and Ludan flew back-to-back punching and kicking those who came near and element-blasting those further away.

Her instincts screamed to move. To help. Or hide. Or something. But her feet stayed locked in place.

So fluid. Both of them. Mind bogglingly beautiful and seemingly at ease in the battle they waged. Eryx's braids swung with each move, his muscles slick with sweat, face smooth with calm judgment.

More aggressors approached. *"Eryx, three more. Behind you."*

Eryx swung around and fired.

Lexi kept her link open and scouted the skies. Through it their fatigue resonated, the burn of their muscles sinking into hers. There had to be some way to help. Something more than acting as a lookout from the shelter of darkness. She didn't dare question the men while they fought and knew they'd only tell her to stay hidden if she offered help. Graylin was a logical option for information, but she hadn't yet linked with him and wasn't technically family.

Galena.

She reached out with a tentative thought.

"Lexi. You're safe." Shock and fear mingled with Galena's relief.

"I'm safe, but Eryx and Ludan are fighting. They're surrounded."

"I know. I'm here with them." Galena's grave tone said more than Lexi wanted to acknowledge.

"They're running out of energy. Didn't you say there was a way to share?"

"You'd have to touch him, and if either one of us step into the fight he'll get distracted."

Lexi paced behind the glass, the oppressive stillness of the room pricking at her. She flinched with every burst of light aimed at Eryx and Ludan. When a nasty volt shot past Eryx's temple, she darted for the door and threw it wide. Eryx would likely kill her, but she'd rather feel his wrath than watch him fall and do nothing.

She centered herself as she had during practice and called the element of fire. The landscape came into mental view. She lifted her arms—and stopped.

The tiny tendrils she'd seen before wavered from every direction, each one connected to the fighters in the sky. She could even make out where Galena lay in the forest beyond, the translucent line pointing into the woods.

Thoughts shuttled back and forth. What if the connections weren't the norm for everyone else? What if this was another gift? The threads had boosted her practice attack. If she pulled from the rebels, could she funnel it through her links to Eryx and Ludan the same way?

Stretching her hands toward the melee, she pulled what she hoped was energy from the rebels and funneled it directly to Eryx and Ludan.

A twenty-five-foot wall of flame blasted from Ludan, and violent streaks of electricity pierced the chests of those attacking Eryx.

The stricken men careened to the ground with vicious thuds.

Eryx and Ludan kicked back into action as a fresh wave of rebels swooped in for attack, but they glanced her way.

"I don't know what you just did, but can you do it again?" There was no missing the fatigue in Eryx's voice this time.

"I think so." God she hoped so. She still wasn't sure what she'd done.

"Then stay where you are. Ludan and I will pull the rest in this direction."

"Who are those people?" Brenna crept up behind her.

"That's my husband." Lexi couldn't contain the pride in

her voice. And maybe she was a little proud of herself as well. "The men they're fighting are loyal to Maxis."

"I thought you said there weren't more like him." Brenna backed away from the doorway, poised to bolt.

Lexi wrenched Brenna to her side. "No one's going to hurt you anymore. No one. Understand?"

Eryx, Ramsay, and Ludan swooshed beyond the front door. The rest of their men whisked along the same path, following tightly behind. Jesus, were they leaving?

A wave of rebel men gave chase.

As one, Eryx's men turned and reengaged, circling around the rebels to cage them in.

"Eryx, I'm not linked to the rest of your men. I can't feed them the energy."

"Focus on me, Ludan and Ramsay. The rest will keep the others busy." Easy for him to say. The tiny threads of energy were more like a knot now. How the hell was she supposed to pick which ones tied to the bad guys? She focused on the rebels closest to Eryx, pulled a chunk of energy, and thrust it down her links.

Booming elemental missiles hurled men into lifeless heaps on the ground.

"Shit that's good." Ramsay grumbled.

"Focus." Eryx was past bark and well into bite. *"I want Lexi safe."*

Ramsay plunged toward the next batch of insurgents.

"One more time, Lexi." Eryx shifted into her line of sight. *"Ramsay, Ludan, let's finish this."*

Feeling more confident, Lexi pulled the energy of the remaining rebels with everything she had and shoved the energy back through their links. The current flew from her hands and she stumbled.

The three of them fired. Bodies battered the ground and crumpled in awkward poses.

The night turned eerily quiet, and the skies melted to velvety darkness. Even the peaceful swirls of energy that usually dotted the skies were absent.

"They did it." Breathy wonder filled Brenna's voice.

The landscape spun and Lexi gripped the door jam for balance. Her knees wobbled and her sight went fuzzy. Cutter—the fight—it was too much. Her body wanted the rest of the night off and it wanted it now.

She wanted her man more and was done with waiting.

Unwilling to leave Brenna, Lexi grasped her hand and tugged her forward. Flying was out of the question. Hell, she could barely walk, but she could get closer and save Eryx time once he was sure the coast was clear.

Ten feet from the door, Eryx's gaze found hers and he smiled from above. With one last scan of the sky, he angled for descent. The tired relief in Eryx's eyes morphed to abject terror. "Lexi!" He darted toward her.

Lexi spun.

Cutter stood unsteady in the doorway, propped against its edge. Pointed directly at her, Ian's gun shook in his hand. His lips formed words she couldn't hear, but his deranged smile said plenty.

Her vision sharpened on the minuscule action of his finger squeezing the trigger. Her muscles pushed her to move, but no one could move faster than a bullet, least of all her.

CHAPTER 30

Galena sat in her hidden spot, too stunned to move. It had to have been Lexi. She'd seen her brothers and Ludan fight since she'd been old enough to walk and never had she seen such a massive display of power. Somehow Lexi had upped their powers—regenerated their energy stores.

She'd find out how soon enough. As soon as the men finished checking the area for other threats and someone was available to cart Phybe home. She wasn't about to leave her new friend's body unattended—not after what she'd sacrificed.

Whatever Maxis had done to Phybe, it hadn't been quick. Or simple. Galena had tried to help the moment she'd sensed Maxis' presence slip away, but the mess he'd left behind was irreparable. Any attempt to intervene would have been suicide.

Phybe's empty gaze stared at the soft night sky, her skin already cooling.

Anger scorched through Galena. A decent person wasted. Phybe may have been misguided, but Galena had sensed her goodness, her almost childlike innocence. All she'd needed was someone to guide her.

A rich masculine voice, filled with sadness, sounded at her right. "If she'd stayed where I hid her she'd be alive now."

She gripped the dagger beneath her leg.

A man with loose, tawny hair hanging in waves to his shoulders shimmered into view.

"Who are you?"

The stranger stared at Phybe's lifeless body. Full-sleeved, black drast—a rebellion man. "Now I'm as dead as she is." He looked so sad. Almost tragic. "A cause that fights without honor isn't worth fighting, is it?"

His emerald gaze slid to Galena and something stirred in her gut. He seemed familiar, though that wasn't what prodded her. The feeling swirling behind her chest was foreign. Deeply relevant. She stuffed the response and straightened. "I'd have a hard time counting on honor for any man who fights with Maxis."

"You're right." Not a drop of flippancy in his response. Merely a confirmation. "I relinquished that the moment I agreed to his schemes." He inched forward and crouched next to Phybe's body. Placing his palm on her forehead, he bowed his head. His lips moved on what she assumed was a silent prayer. "I tried to do what was right in the end."

He stood and stepped back. Praise the Great One, he was tall. Tall like her brothers and Ludan.

"You're Galena Shantos." A statement, not a question.

She nodded anyway. Her brain refused to cooperate, the space beneath her skull on idle. She gripped the dagger tighter.

"You don't remember me do you?"

Galena shook her head, scrambling to connect his face to a name. "My name is Reese Theron." His face softened a touch, the hint of a sad smile at his lips. "It's rumored you've become quite the healer."

She warmed under his gaze. He knew about her? What she did for their people?

"Can you mend souls as well as the body?" The agony laced in his words would have yanked her to her knees were she not already sitting.

But she couldn't show such a response. Not to the enemy. "Souls are best healed from within."

"But there are those who can aid in the journey." His gaze traveled to the hilt of the dagger she gripped before returning to her face. "A woman as beautiful as you should never be touched by death."

What was it about this man? "I deal with death too often. I watched it take its toll on an innocent today."

He nodded sagely, mournfully. "Call your guards. Make sure they know you're in danger."

The green of his eyes deepened, bordering on ebony, and lines of unhappy weariness dug deep at his temples. He wasn't bulky like many of their warriors, but lithe and firm. Such long, strong fingers, relaxed at his sides. What would his touch feel like?

Gunshot rattled the night and a blood-curdling scream ripped across the densely landscaped yard strewn with bodies.

She needed to be with her brothers. To help.

She looked back to the man, his unhappy eyes refocused on her.

A heartbreaking, rueful smile played against his lips "Your face is a good one to remember. Go with The Great One, Galena."

He shot into the air, high enough Eryx' men would see him, and drew back his hand. A ball of electricity blossomed in his palm, directed at her.

Galena shot to the sky.

Jagger drew back for a defensive strike and two other warriors darted toward Reese.

Reese's ball of energy fizzled. He was no threat to her. Couldn't her brother's men see that?

On a dazzling burst, she darted forward.

A violent stream of lightning sizzled past her cheek and nailed Reese in the shoulder.

He jerked and spasmed, locked in the air by the force of the energy. The strike faded and Reese toppled toward the ground.

"Brenna!" Lexi dropped to the young woman's side and tried to stem the blossoming red stain just above her heart. Her skin was sickly white, pulse faint, pale lips parted and still.

"Eryx, get Galena." With tentative fingers, she prodded the wound. It was high enough it shouldn't have damaged her heart, but damned if it wasn't bleeding like crazy. She pressed down hard to staunch the flow.

Another scream echoed in the distance, but Lexi stayed focused on her task. Shouts and orders rang out.

Eryx crouched opposite her, peeled her hands away, and resumed the pressure with his own. "Lexi."

"We have to do something. She saved me." So much blood. Too much.

"Lexi, look at me."

She wrenched her head up.

Eryx filled her vision, blurred by tears. "Galena can't help us. This woman's human. I can try to help her, but I could kill her just as easily."

No! A silent wail inside Lexi's head, Brenna's innocent

face plastered front and center in her mind. Not fair. Not right. She'd saved Lexi. Not once, but twice, despite her fear.

"It's your call."

She opened her eyes, hope clamoring for purchase. "Will she make it? If we stop the bleeding, will she make it? Maybe we could take her to Evad?"

Eryx shook his head. "I'll never get her there in time. She's losing too much blood."

She'd promised Brenna she'd be safe. Damn it to hell, this night wasn't ending this way. "Do it."

Eryx swallowed, his eyes heavy with gravity she couldn't comprehend. "Clear the men," he said to Ludan over his shoulder. As he had the night of their mating with the gash along his arm, he focused on Brenna's blood-soaked wound.

Brenna convulsed and her tiny frame rippled at the invasion of Eryx's energy.

"*D*amn it, Ramsay. If you don't get out of my way I'll make sure your bowels work overtime for the next year." Galena crossed her arms.

Fear swept across her brother's face, not much, but enough to know he took her threat seriously.

Two guards hovering in front of Reese's holding cell gave her odd looks. The overbearing crap her brothers and their cronies had dished out since returning home was getting out of hand.

To heck with them. And everyone else. "So, what's it going to be? Let me in to help him or use your troops as food tasters?"

Hmph. Let the two little bastards behind him know they'd suffer too.

Ramsay jerked her to one side and lowered his voice. "Lena, what the hell's gotten into you? He's a prisoner. He fought with the Rebellion. Worse, he tried to kill you. Who in their right mind would want to go in there and try to save him?"

The Great One save her from shortsighted men. "For

starters, Reese didn't try to kill me. He only did it hoping someone would kill him. And Jagger would have if I hadn't diverted him."

At least that's what she thought Reese had intended. Why else would he have let the strike fade to nothing?

"And you damned near got yourself killed in the process." He was up close and personal now, nostrils flared. "What if Jag hadn't adjusted in time? Do you think he could've lived with that?"

Galena snorted. Ramsay and his theatrics could go to histus. "Jagger? Not be precise? Please. Could any of your elite team not be precise?" She stepped back and flecked a non-existent piece of lint from her gown. It matched her eyes perfectly. Picking her favorite gown this morning had nothing to do with healing a traitor. She just wanted to protect whatever information he could provide. Nothing more.

"Has it crossed your testosterone-laden mind he might be willing to give us information about Maxis? Something that might actually help us?" She backed off and cupped her cheek in mock surprise. "Oh, wait. Not if he's dead."

Ramsay's lips flatlined, a storm of anger brewing behind his steel gray eyes. "You have no idea who this man is or what he's capable of."

Galena's confidence stumbled. Ramsay was the easygoing twin. The one who cracked inappropriate jokes at even more inappropriate times. If he was this uptight, she needed to pay attention—no matter what her own instincts might insist.

She held her breath, and stood her ground. One heartbeat. Two. Three.

"But you're right," Ramsay finally said. "If he has information, we're wise to use it." He stepped back to let her pass. "I'll keep my distance, but I'm going in with you."

Galena nodded, more shaken by the interlude with her

brother than she cared to admit. "Fine, but hurry up. The way you warriors process injuries, there's no telling what kind of infection he could have by now."

Gathering her bag of herbs, Galena braced for the zeolite's impact. The dark, energy-zapping caves gave her the creepy-crawlies. The whole thing was downright depressing. How she was going to heal the man with only herbs in such a dismal environment escaped her, but she knew better than to ask Ramsay for more than she'd already won.

She ducked into the cell and the crystal's power-stealing impact ripped through her chest.

Silence.

Prickles danced along her scalp. Had he already passed? "Reese?" A whisper and still her query battered at her ears.

Two meager candles burned in the corner, the only light allowed for fear the imprisoned would find a way to stream energy through the usual light tubes. The candlelight danced over him where he lay stretched out along a crude cot.

"Reese? It's Galena." She took a few steps forward and sensed more than saw Ramsay's hesitation at the door. "I'd like to check your wounds." She crept closer and set her bundle on the bedside table. When he still didn't respond, she reached out for his undamaged shoulder. The warmth beneath her hand filled her with hope and alarm. He wasn't dead, but raging with fever.

Pulling scented candles from her bag, Galena quickly lit them using those already burning on the table. Healing scents and brightness flooded the room. "Ramsay, I need water."

Ramsay snapped to attention and issued orders to the guards beyond.

Charred and jagged, the wound was on the shoulder closest to her. She traced the edges and the scent of forest and sandalwood wafted from his skin. The combination messed with her insides in a not altogether unpleasant way. Brown-gold strands clung to his temples, tethered by sweat. Shallow breaths pushed and pulled between his full, dry lips.

"I have to heal you with herbs since we can't let you out." Could he hear her? Would he even want to? "It'll draw the fever out, but will take longer. It will hurt and I'm sorry for that, but I want you to live."

Other words trailed in her mind. Awkward words. Words that left her feeling traitorous. But she owned and accepted them nonetheless. She lowered her voice further so Ramsay wouldn't hear.

"Reese. I *need* you to live."

ERYX LAY IN BED, his fingers buried in his baineann's hair and his legs tangled with hers. In the short time they'd been together, they'd always woken this way, two bodies gravitating toward their perfect fit.

Midday sun poured through the windows, well over fifteen hours since they'd fallen asleep. He didn't think he'd ever been so close to losing consciousness, his energy nearly depleted by the time they'd finally made it home.

Lexi had been a different story. Between the bit with Cutter, two deaths, and Ian's disappearance, she'd been wound extra tight. Ludan had talked her into resting, promising he and Jagger would search for Ian if she'd sleep.

The whole homecoming scene replayed in his head and Eryx choked back a chuckle. Grown men fighting to fuss over one woman. Even Ludan. In the end he'd had to kick them out. Everyone else might have grown to accept and adore her, but Eryx needed her. To feel her curled next to him. Feel her breath against his chest. If Brenna hadn't intervened...

Lexi rubbed her cheek against his chest, a contented purr rumbling from her chest. She wriggled inside his arms. "Worried I'll run away?"

"Sorry, hellcat." He loosened his grip and stroked her back.

She breathed in deep. A slow, sultry sound that got his dick very on board with an intimate wake up call. "Don't be." She caressed his chest and met his eyes. "As long as I wake up next to you, I don't care what wakes me."

Her eyelids were heavy with sleep. Lena's easy touch had wiped the vulgar bruise Cutter had left on her cheek away like chalk. The callous burns at her wrists were gone as well, but he doubted her memories would ever heal. His certainly wouldn't.

His heartbeat raced at the thought. It was too bad Ludan had snapped Cutter's neck. Eryx would have healed him just for the gratification of drawn out torture.

Lexi pushed back. "Something wrong?"

"Nothing."

Lexi snapped to attention. "Ludan and Jagger. Have you heard from them?"

He shook his head. "Nothing yet."

She sat up, pulled her knees in tight and wrapped her arms around them. Gone was the peace of moments before, her rekindled anxiety streaming from every pore.

They'd barely talked of what had happened. His most immediate concerns had been with seeing to his men and tying up loose ends from the battle. They'd lost no warriors, but a few had sustained serious injuries. Those from Maxis' camp hadn't been so lucky.

"You can't ignore what happened." Eryx fought the urge to squirm. Deep down, he wasn't sure he wanted the details. The idea of what Lexi had endured made him more rabid animal than man. But her soul couldn't afford to bury it.

She shook her head. "I know what you're thinking, but Brenna got there before..." A shiver rocked her.

"It wouldn't change anything with me."

Lexi grew silent and her face turned a waxen gray. "I was in this position before."

For a second, he thought she wouldn't say anything more. No way was he moving. He barely dared to breathe for fear he'd startle whatever confession waited.

"I was fourteen and in a new foster home. The father..." She scraped a nail against the silk sheets and locked her gaze on the path she'd drawn. "Well, he liked young girls. The authorities learned I wasn't the first he'd tried anything with." She stretched out beside him, rolled to her side and laid a fist on his chest. "He never had the satisfaction of getting anything from me. And I was the last one he'll ever hurt." She swallowed and lifted her gaze. "Because I killed him."

His lungs burned and screamed for air, but he wasn't about to move. One wrong action and he'd shatter the moment.

She stared at his collarbone. "I didn't mean to. It was just reaction. The wrong place for him, the right place for me and a knife. The police investigated, found a trail of other girls, and they moved me. That was it." She looked up, her lips shaking no matter how hard she pressed them together between her words. "The first time for me was when I chose for it to happen. Brenna wasn't that lucky. Maxis raped her. She didn't say as much, but her face said it plain enough."

He pulled her close and offered a silent thanks to his Creator. For her trust. For her beating heart next to his. "Brenna's safe, and Maxis isn't stupid enough to go for you twice. Not that any of our men will leave you alone now."

Lexi pushed against his chest and tried to wriggle free.

"Did Ramsay ever find anything about the guard who took me?"

Eryx let her sit up. Barely. He doubted he'd let her have much distance for the next century or two. "We only know that a quaran and the guard who took you are missing. Whether they're in league together or the quaran is missing for some other reason, we don't know. It was a hell of an inside job, even for Maxis. It's not easy to get past Ramsay when taking the warrior's oath. If one or both of them flipped allegiance, it would have had to happen afterward."

Lexi smoothed the silk covering Eryx's stomach. "How can we know if others are part of his scheme?"

The space behind his eyes throbbed with determination. "Everyone will be scanned thoroughly from here out. On a regular basis. If there are dissenters in the ranks, they'll flee before they can be checked. A traitor wouldn't exactly be treated well if uncovered while surrounded by loyal warriors."

"You awake, sunshine?"

Ludan. His somo had exceptionally rotten timing.

Eryx pushed from the bed, snatched Lexi's robe, and held it open. "What?" Despite her question, she crawled from their bed and stuffed her arms in the black silk.

He wrapped the sides around her and cinched the belt tight. "Company," he murmured and kissed her temple. "Your errand boys are back." He snatched a pair of pants and a tank from the closet.

Lexi was hot on his heels, her curiosity suffering zero damage from the prior day's events. "Did they say anything?"

He stepped into ivory linen pants. "They wouldn't do that. Not without you there. Not on this topic." He pulled on the tank and snatched her hand. "Come on, we'll meet them and Ramsay downstairs. I've had enough of people filing in and out of our bedroom."

Lexi dug in her heels. "I can't go down there in a robe!"

He curved his arm around her back and pulled her close, nestling his nose alongside hers. "You can do anything you damn well please. You're a malress." He kissed her before she could argue, fusing their lips in a slick, heated tangle. Maybe business could wait an hour. Or two.

She pulled away, the first smile he'd seen in hours stretched across her face. "You're insatiable."

"I'm only getting started." Eryx tapped her nose and reclaimed her hand, threading their fingers together. "Come."

He guided her through the foyer, reining in his strides to match her shorter ones, until they reached a large wall tucked beneath the curving staircase. He pushed the two oversized engraved panels open with his mind.

Lexi gasped. "You've never shown me this before."

Books of varying ages and colors lined deep chocolate shelves, and brilliant sunlight streamed through four large arched windows at the rear of the room. The soft gray stone floors were covered with thick burgundy rugs inlaid with depictions of the Shantos emblem in platinum and black.

Lexi caressed the top of a black wingback chair, one of many arranged for conversation along the room. She honed in on the two regal chairs centered between the arched windows at the front. At either side, two elaborate desks sat angled so they nestled into the corners.

"I refused to use this room after my father died. It didn't feel right without my mate." Eryx cupped her nape. "It feels right now."

She smiled and his heart warmed. The same slow, steady heat as the sun through the window on the stone floors.

"Man, this is odd." Ramsay's voice cut through the quiet moment, and footsteps bounced off the ornate, gold ceilings. "I haven't been in here for ages."

Eryx faced the new arrivals, spinning Lexi with him.

Ludan and Jagger sauntered in behind Ramsay, dressed in human attire from their trip to Evad.

"Ah, man." Lexi moaned. "The next time you guys go over, stop by my place and grab more of my clothes. The dresses are great, but sometimes a pair of old jeans is just what a girl needs."

Ludan lifted one eyebrow. "I'll go get you every pair you own right now if you promise to wear some to the next council meeting."

"You stir the pot enough," Eryx said. "Now, tell me what you found."

Ludan cast a glance at his comrades then turned his attention to Eryx. "We hit Ian's house first. Figured Serena got the badge there and hoped they'd left behind clues."

"And?"

Ludan's gaze slid to Lexi. "Mild signs of struggle. Nothing to go on." He ended on an up note, a hint of something left unspoken.

"What's the rest of it?" Eryx asked.

Ludan pulled out a billfold-sized photograph from his back pocket. He dragged his index finger up and down the edge of the picture. "Things are getting interesting." He held the picture out toward Eryx.

Son of a bitch. He took the photo. "Jillian."

Lexi leaned closer. "That's Ian's wife. She disappeared about eighteen years ago. Devastated the hell out of him. But I don't think her name was Jillian. I think it was Madeline." She looked at each man in turn. "What? That's all I know. Except she was pregnant at the time. They never did settle the case, but Ian never stopped looking."

Eryx angled the photo so Lexi could see it better. "Look at it again. Didn't you meet Jillian the other day?"

Lexi's jaw dropped, and she snatched the picture from

Eryx. "Holy shit." She angled her head, eyebrows dipped down in a V. "You think his wife was Jillian's mother?"

"And Ian's her father," Jagger added.

Lexi shook her head. "That's crazy."

"Is it?" Eryx asked gently. "Put yourself in his wife's place, Lexi. She was about to bring a child into the world. If she was Myren, she couldn't tell Ian where she was from. He'd either think she was nuts, or she'd be punished if her revelation was ever discovered. Think about her deciding her daughter's future. A daughter who would most likely be born with gifts that would want out once she hit a certain age. Remember the signs you felt?"

Lexi backed into one of the thrones and plunked to a sit. She looked good there. Damned good. He would have said as much if the moment had been a little less intense.

"But she left him. It almost killed him." Her voice was thick with disbelief, filled with pain for her friend.

"How do you know it didn't kill her?" Ludan, always so blunt. "Jillian was barely one when we found her. They lived in a rundown shack on the edges of Asshur. Her mom was dead and Jillian was starving. The death was from natural causes from what we could tell, but we never found a father."

Eryx smoothed his hand along Lexi's shoulder, but her eyes stayed fixated on the face in the picture. "What matters is he very likely has a daughter. All the more reason to find him."

"We don't have any clues to go on." She looked up, her tension palpable. "The men Jagger noticed in Asshur tells us almost nothing. You've said combing the places we know will take significant time. What's to keep Maxis from killing him?"

Eryx sprawled in the chair beside hers. He pulled her hand into his lap and caressed her knuckles. "He told you himself. Ian's his insurance policy. A tool for negotiation if he needs it. He's not going to kill him. Not unless he's backed into a corner. That will give us time to find him."

"Galena thinks Reese might roll over." Ramsay scowled, not at all his twin's usual demeanor. "I don't like how she's acting around him, but we shouldn't discount the possibility."

Not a bad idea. One he should have thought of sooner. "How is he?"

"He's got an infection, but Lena's giving him herbs. She wants to take him out of zeolite for a full healing." From the snide tone, Ramsay didn't sound too happy with the approach.

Eryx was more inclined to heed his sister's instincts. "Knock him out and let her do it. If he has information, I want it. One way or another."

Lexi sat on the hillside peak many hours later, gazing on her new home as the sun dipped behind horizon. She rested her chin on her knees and absorbed the colors—plum, blue and mango—all framing the castle with streaming sparks of energy. She'd loved this spot the first time she'd viewed the castle. Fifty years from now she probably still would. Or five hundred years from now, seeing as her life span now stretched a bit further.

It was the quietest moment she'd had in a very long time. If the last week and a half had taught her nothing else, she'd make the most of it.

Eryx and Ramsay were still at the main training hall, barking orders and digging for leads to follow up on Ian and the missing guard and quaran. Ludan, no doubt, was glued to Eryx's side with his silent brooding.

She wasn't alone, though. Glancing over one shoulder at her new somo, she smiled at Jagger. She wouldn't be truly alone for a very long time. Not if Eryx had anything to say about it. The formal ceremony where Jagger accepted his new role wouldn't occur until preparations were completed, but she liked the idea of him as her protector.

The wind tossed her hair in a wild mass around her face. She chuckled. One of those dastardly feminine laughs every man feared. Eryx would be pissed if he saw it unbound, especially with Jagger so close.

It didn't matter here, though. She'd re-braid it before she headed back, and Jagger was smart enough to hold his tongue. Right now, she wanted to enjoy the air and relax, free to consider the many challenges she and Eryx had ahead of them.

The sky blended to a deep blue velvet and the torches along the garden walk blazed to life as workers departed for their homes. When a thick, velvet cloak was laid across her shoulders, she wasn't surprised. Eryx settled in behind her without a word. His legs framed her hips and he wrapped the full, warm garment around her bare arms.

"Anything?" she asked him quietly.

"Reese is still out, but recovering. Galena's resting."

Lexi hadn't realized how chilled she'd become until his hands settled on top of the fabric.

"Do we tell Jillian?" No matter how long she'd chewed on the question, she still hadn't found an answer.

"Not yet. Let's see how things go with Reese first. She needs to be told, but it can wait a few days."

Lexi nodded, accepting Eryx's opinion as she did few others. "I figured out what I want to do. What I want my role to be."

Eryx stopped moving.

"When this is over, I want to help other people like me," she said.

Eryx nuzzled closer and his mystic scent wrapped around her. "You don't have to wait. You can start now."

She shook her head. Damn, but her new home was beautiful. Magical. "Not yet. Not until we find Ian. After that I'll figure out a way to find them."

She leaned back and rested her head on Eryx's shoulder so she could see his eyes. "Are you worried about the ellan? About the prophecy?"

Eryx crooked an arrogant eyebrow. "Do I look worried?"

Lexi batted his shoulder. "Maybe you should be. I've come along and stirred everything up. It's going to make people nervous."

Eryx slipped one arm beneath her knees and lifted her so she lay across his lap. "The fates led me to you, Alexis. You're the destiny I dreamed of and searched for. No opinion matters to me save yours."

The Fates.

Perhaps this *was* their destiny. To come together in this unexpected Eden and forever change the future of their race.

BOOKS BY RHENNA MORGAN

The Eden Series
Unexpected Eden
Healing Eden
Waking Eden
Eden's Deliverance

Men of Haven Series
Rough & Tumble
Wild & Sweet
Claim & Protect
Tempted & Taken
Stand & Deliver
Down & Dirty

Ancient Ink
Guardian's Bond
Healer's Need

NOLA Knights
His To Defend
Hers To Tame
Mine To Have

Standalone
What Janie Wants

MEET THE AUTHOR

Rhenna Morgan is a happily-ever-after addict—hot men, smart women, and scorching chemistry required. A triple-A personality with a thing for lists, Rhenna's a mom to two beautiful daughters who constantly keep her dancing, laughing and simply happy to be alive.

When she's not neck deep in writing, she's probably driving with the windows down and the music up loud, plotting her next hero and heroine's adventure. (Though trolling online for man-candy inspiration on Pinterest comes in a close second.)

She'd love to share her antics and bizarre since of humor with you and get to know you a little better in the process. You can sign up for her newsletter and gain access to exclusive snippets, upcoming releases, fun giveaways, and social media outlets at www.rhennamorgan.com.

Ready to see what happens in the next installment of The Eden Series? Here's a sneak peek from

HEALING EDEN

In a world divided by war, falling in love is the ultimate betrayal.

Galena Shantos has never questioned her loyalty to Eden. As sister to the Myren king, she serves as a healer, one of the best in the army fighting to suppress the brutal Lomos Rebellion. She's never doubted the importance of stopping the rebels bent on enslaving humans, until she spots a warrior across enemy lines—and knows instinctively that their destinies are entwined.

Rebellion warrior Reese Theron has nothing left to lose. He's been forced to fight on the wrong side of a war he abhors in order to protect his family secret. His honor lost, as well as the trust of his own people, Reese has thrown himself into a battle he cannot possibly hope to survive. But after being rescued by a beautiful woman whose exquisite eyes seem to see him for more than the traitor he's become—he may have just found a new reason to live.

CHAPTER 1 - HEALING EDEN

A lightning bolt sheared past Reese into the smoke-filled night sky and left an acrid stench in its wake. Streaks of fire and blue-white fingers of electricity flared so bright he could barely focus. He wasn't getting out of this. Not this battle, or this life, with any modicum of honor.

Darting through the air, he dodged another electrical strike.

An elite flashed into view and swung wide, his bloodied dagger aimed at Reese's gut.

Reese barrel-rolled up and over his attacker, wrapped him in a chokehold, and masked their presence from the rest of the fighters. Praise the Great One, he should be fighting beside this warrior, not against him.

The warrior flailed and tried to break free, the lack of footing giving him zero leverage. He slumped, unconscious, into Reese's ready hold seconds later.

He lowered them both to the tree line at the battle's edge, out of site from the rebels. The man couldn't be more than twenty years outside his awakening. Probably barely into his elite torc and cuffs. Beneath Reese's fingers, the man's pulse thrummed slow, but steady. At least this innocent's death wouldn't be on his conscience.

A twenty-five-foot wall of flame exploded across the open field and rattled the air and earth around them. The bright flare faded under heavy night, and more rebellion warriors thunked to the mottled field.

The sharp rustle of leaves against the forest floor sounded down the tree line, one quick shift and then silence.

Reese backed deeper into the foliage and strengthened the mask that kept him hidden. It couldn't be a rebellion man. All those were engaged against the malran's warriors. Focusing his thoughts, he sought the soulless black thread that represented the link he'd grudgingly created with Maxis Steysis, and traced his location.

No, not the rebellion leader either. His energy showed more than ten miles to the east, well away from the fight. Reese levitated off the forest floor and floated through the trees. Gnarled and leafless branches scraped his cheek and shoulders. Darkness enveloped him, broken only by the bright attacks where the forest opened to the battle beyond.

There. Not five feet from the tree line, a figure knelt facing the battle. He drifted closer. The sweet, damp scent of soil and decomposing leaves overpowered the metallic residue of electrical strikes floating on the wind. Grunts, shouts, and the too-frequent thuds of perished men sounded in a haphazard pattern.

A flash spotlighted long, auburn hair. A woman. Bowed over a body, she cradled a fallen companion's head in her lap.

Reese angled to better see her and nearly faltered in holding his mask. His heart kicked in an awkward rhythm and reality faded to nothingness. Galena Shantos, sister to the malran. The last person he wanted to witness his disgrace.

Seventy years since he'd seen her this close. Her elegant features were still as staggering as the days when he'd trained to serve the malran, but there was more to her now. A confidence in the way she protected her charge and watched the battle. Knowledge behind her tropical blue-green eyes that spoke of experience and age.

And he fought alongside the men who battled her brother.

Galena flinched at another blast and hugged the limp body she cradled tight. As the light dimmed, she uncurled from her burden.

Another woman, her long blond hair stark against Galena's black tunic and leggings, and her sightless eyes aimed at the heavens.

No. Surely not. Reese crept closer, pressure building at his temples. The zings and thunder of battle rumbled louder, and his gut clenched.

Phybe. She'd been alive when Reese left her, tucked away in a zeolite mine where Maxis couldn't trace her link. He touched down in the thick carpet of leaves at Galena's right and dropped his mask. "I failed her."

Galena jerked and reached for something beneath one leg. "Who are you?"

Smudges marked Phybe's ashen face, her blue gown torn and satin slippers stained. Somehow Maxis had found her and finished the job he'd sent Reese to do. "He'll kill me for trying to save her."

More strikes burst through the thick residual smoke, the malran's fighters airborne and casting one attack after another. Fewer than twenty rebellion men still lived, half retreating north.

"A cause that fights without honor isn't worth fighting, is it?" he said.

Galena straightened and squared her shoulders. "I'd have

a hard time counting on honor from any man who fights with Maxis."

"You're right. I gave that up the moment I agreed to his schemes." He crouched beside them.

Galena tensed and tightened her grip on whatever she hid beneath her leg.

Reese palmed Phybe's forehead, cool and lifeless. *May your journey be swift and your spirit find peace with The Great One.* The same Myren prayer he'd offered his mother when she'd drawn her last breath. He stepped back. Maybe it was time to find his own peace. On his own terms. "You don't remember me do you?"

She shook her head. A terse, barely-there jerk as she eased from beneath her dead charge, crouched on the balls of her feet and coiled for escape.

"My name is Reese Theron."

She froze, flashes of light from the battle winking off the edge of her blade. She assessed him head to toe, no spark of recognition.

Maybe if he'd been braver all those years ago, he'd have had a chance with her. Or broken his vow and killed Maxis himself when he'd had the chance. He shook the memories off. He'd taken the wrong path and now it was time to pay. "Call your guards. Make sure they know you're in danger."

A gunshot rattled the skies and a woman's blood-curdling scream sounded across the battlefield.

Galena lurched to a stand and then stopped, zigzagging her attention between the shouts along the battlefield and Phybe's body.

Now was his chance. Either he took the brave farewell, or he'd die by Maxis' hands. "Your face is a good one to remember. Go with The Great One, Galena." He shot to the sky and built a violent ball of energy in his palm, sharp tendrils darting from its center. Drawing back, he aimed the bogus attack at Galena. Surely The Great One would understand.

An elite guard spun from across the skies and drew back for counter- attack.

Reese braced for impact.

A streak of auburn flashed below him. Galena, spearing through the air, her trajectory centered between the elite and Reese.

The energy in his palm fizzled. Not her. Not Galena.

Lightning fired from the elite's palm, sheered past Galena's cheek, and pierced his shoulder. He jerked and spasmed, locked in place by the force of the strike. Blue-black spots dotted his vision and his lungs seized.

A woman's scream ripped through the air. Wind whipped around him, dead weight as he fell, and darkness took over.

Galena twisted midair and shot toward Reese, wind blurring her eyesight.

His arms and legs flailed boneless as he hurtled to the earth.

She'd never make it before impact. Even if he survived the fall, Jagger's strike had been a killing shot, off by inches at most.

Reese crashed against the unforgiving ground, his head and limbs thunking against the trampled turf.

She landed seconds behind him. The sticky iron scent of blood, dirt, and sweat surrounded her. So many men strewn across the grass, their bodies contorted in unnatural shapes.

Less than ten feet away one of her brother's men struggled for breath, unconscious with a trail of blood at his temple. A loyal fighter who'd battled against an indecent and cruel rebellion.

But it was Reese her palms burned to touch. To feel the beat of his heart. She dropped to her knees and rolled Reese to his back, muscles surging with wells of strength she'd never felt.

His pulse fluttered beneath her fingertips, faint and irregular.

A thud sounded behind her. Her name registered, a voice she recognized. She ignored the call. Shedding her mortal form, she dove into Reese's unconscious body and let her spirit spread and assess. Gaping, charred flesh at least two fists wide, muscle and sinew around it lifeless from the electrical shock. She followed the damage, too much impairment radiating dangerously close to his heart. She couldn't lose him. Traitor or not, her instincts didn't care. Only knew this moment would shape the rest of her life in a way she didn't dare ignore.

Shouts rang out beside her. Short, brusque words delivered with a frustrated bite. Footsteps shuffled around her and the injured moaned. Detached in spirit but still connected to her physical senses, the muffled distractions rattled as she healed.

Five inches. That was the gift of her intervention. Had she not flown in the path of Jagger's bolt, he'd have pierced Reese's heart. Blood seeped from the violent gash and his heart trembled with the aftershocks of the delivering jolt.

Swift and sure, she spread her spirit, cauterizing and mending the most critical lesions. A touch here. A brush there.

Near his heart, a fine opaque mist appeared.

Her spirit vision faltered. The odd substance settled into every nook and cranny. It shimmered and sparkled, a mix between morning dew and midnight fog. Seventy years she'd been healing men and not once had she seen anything like it.

"Damn it, Lena, we need you." The admonition rang in her ear and a firm hand clamped on her shoulder.

Galena ripped her spirit from Reese's body and spun in a levitated twist to a defensive crouch, hands lifted to protect herself. Her vision wavered.

Ramsay came into focus, the whites around his gray eyes glowing in a way that promised dire loss of control and a vicious scowl aimed squarely at her. "What in histus is wrong with you?"

Her knees nearly buckled. Maybe she'd put too much into her healing. "He's wounded."

"He's a traitor. To me and to Eryx." Glaring at her, he swept his arm behind him. "What about them?"

There were dozens of them. Good men, battered, bloody, and fatigued. Most were upright and lumbering across the battlefield, checking for rebellion survivors. Six were laid out for triage close to Maxis' estate, Eryx and Ludan seeing to their care.

Her cheeks burned and her stomach pitched. There wasn't any logic to defend her actions. She'd acted on pure emotion and instinct, and put the lives of loyal men at risk, but she still wouldn't change what she'd done. Not a second. A truth she wasn't altogether sure how to process.

"Focus on the ones worthy of your gift. Not someone—"

"Enough." She straightened and met her brother's scowl. Every muscle shook with fatigue. "I watched an innocent woman die tonight. Held her in my arms while she screamed."

"Trust me." Ramsay glowered at the unconscious man behind her. "He's not innocent."

For years she'd trusted her brothers. Loved and followed them with unwavering loyalty wherever they asked her to go. Until this moment. She inched forward on trembling legs, hands fisted at her sides. "Innocent or not, I saw goodness in him. Watched him say a prayer over Phybe's body and felt his grief. Healing is my gift to use when and how The Great One guides me. Not to be commandeered and directed by a man swept up in the heat of battle. Life is life, no matter whose heart feeds it."

Ramsay sneered. "Even Maxis Steysis?"

Nearly six hundred years their families had been at war, since their grandfather left Maxis' grandmother pregnant at the altar in favor of a commoner.

"Everyone has a shred of goodness in them." Well, maybe not Maxis. But she'd be damned if she let Ramsay question her judgment. There was a reason she was drawn to Reese. She just needed a little time to figure out why. "If you'd stop and think for a minute you'd know saving him is a smart move. If he fought with Maxis, he knows things. Things you won't be able to learn anywhere else."

Reese's chest rose and fell, slow and steady. With a push from her senses, she registered the faint but solid rhythm of his heart. More than anything she ached to kneel beside him. To finish the job she'd begun and skim her fingers through his wild hair. Perhaps link her fingers with his long, tapered ones and rest alongside him while she waited for him to wake.

Praise The Great One, what was wrong with her? This protectiveness didn't make sense.

Eryx's best friend and somo, Ludan, shouted from the furthest edge of battle. "Ramsay."

Galena knew that tone. Had heard it after too many battles. Another warrior in need of care. With a last glance at Reese to placate herself, she headed in Ludan's direction. "I've got it."

Three steps in she stopped and glared at Ramsay. "You

may not care for him. May see him as the vilest of men. But do not disrespect my gift by hurting him."

She left her frowning brother behind, and prayed the promise of a traitor's information would stay Ramsay's hand until she returned.

GLOSSARY

- **Aron** - Mainstay livestock in Eden used for food and clothing. The hide is tanned to provide a soft, supple leather and is the predominant source of protective outerwear in the colder regions. The animal's fur is a cross between that found on a buffalo and a beaver in the human realm. The thickness and warmth of a buffalo, but shiny and soft as a beaver.
- **Asshur** - A region in Eden. Sun isn't unheard of, but tends to be more cloudy and rainy than the other regions. The population has dropped off in the last few centuries with inhabitants moving to more hospitable areas.
- **Awakening** - A Myren ceremony where people between the ages of eighteen and twenty-one are brought into their powers. The father (or paternal representative) is typically the trigger for the process, where the mother (or maternal influence) acts as an anchor for the awakened individual.
- **Baineann** - The female within a bonded union.

- **Briash** - The Myren equivalent of oatmeal, although its color is a deep brown and the flavor has a hint of chocolate and cinnamon.
- **Brasia** - A region in Eden. The terrain is covered in mountains, with heavy snow and difficult conditions prevalent in the higher elevations.
- **Briyo** - Brother-in-law
- **Cootya** - A type of cafe that sells common Myren beverages and snacks. Myren fruits and vegetables are the most common menu items, but some pastries can be found. Most feature an open-air area where customers can relax, while kitchen and serving areas remain indoor.
- **Cush** - The capital region of Eden. Densely populated with elaborate buildings.
- **Diabhal** - Devil.
- **Drast** - Field issue protective garment worn by warriors to protect the most vital organs in battle. Made of fine, metal threads, the garments fit their bodies closely. Day-to-day drasts are sleeveless, but the most formal version covers 3/4 of their arms. The necks are boat shaped to allow for greater comfort when fighting with the metal threads blocking most fire and electrical attacks.
- **Drishen** - A fruit found in Eden. Looks like a grape, tastes like lemonade.
- **Eden** - Another dimension, unknown to humans, within the fabric that surrounds Earth.
- **Ellan** - Elected officials that govern the Myren race alongside the Malran or Malress. Like most governing bodies, there are a mix of honest servants who seek prosperity and growth for the Myrens and corrupt, "lifers" who stand on antiquated ideas and ceremonies.

- **Evad** - The realm in which humans reside. Fireann - The male within a bonded union.
- **Fireann** - The male within a bonded union.
- **Havilah** - A more affluent and less populated region in Eden. Rain occurs, but mostly in the evenings with pleasant days full of sun and comfortable temperatures.
- **Histus** - The human equivalent of hell.
- **Kilo** - A fish the swims in many lakes in Eden, but is most prevalent in Brasia. A popular mainstay of protein in the Myren race, most often prepared by smoking in apple wood and basting with an apple and cinnamon glaze.
- **Larken** - A long-winged bird known for its singsong chirp. Colored primarily in cobalt blue, but the tips of their wings are lavender.
- **Lastas** - A favorite Myren breakfast pastry.
- **Lomos Rebellion** - A faction of Myrens that have long pursued the enslavement of humans and sought to overthrow the tenets of the Great One.
- **Lyrita Tree** - An exotic tree exclusive to the Havilah region. Trunks are dark brown. Leaves are long and slender, sage green in color. The blooms are exceptionally large and run from pearl to pale pink in color. Average height for a mature lyrita is thirty to forty feet.
- **Malran** - The male leader of the Myren people and the equivalent of a king in the human realm. Leadership has descended down through the Shantos family line since the birth of the Myren race, with the mantle of Malran (or Malress) falling to the first-born.
- **Malress** - The female leader of the Myren people and the equivalent of a queen in the human realm.

- **Myrens** - A gifted race in existence for over six thousand years that lives in another dimension called Eden. They are deeply in tune with the Earth and the elements that surround her. Their powerful minds and connection to the elements allow them to communicate silently with those they are linked to, levitate, and command certain elements. Their women typically have more healing or nurturing gifts, where men trend more toward protective and aggressive abilities.
- **Natxu** - A regular and expected practice of physical discipline for all Myren warriors. The moves and postures are grueling yet meditative in nature, resulting in peak physical performance and enhancing their tie to the elements.
- **Nirana** - The human equivalent of heaven.
- **Oanan** - Daughter-in-law.
- **Quaran** - The Myren equivalent of a general within the warrior ranks.
- **Runa** - Region in Eden, predominantly used for farming. The black soil is rich and sparkles with minerals. It's surrounded by "the blue ridge", a crescent-shaped formation of mountains that appear blue from ground level.
- **Shalla** - Sister-in-law.
- **Somo** - Sworn personal guard to the Malran or Malress.
- **Strasse** - A highly intoxicating Myren beverage made from berries found only in Eden.
- **Strategos** - Leader of the Myren warriors.
- **Torna** - An annoying Myren rodent. Larger than an armadillo, but similar in color with the skin surface of an eel. While not typically aggressive,

their teeth function similar to a shark and aren't afraid to come out fighting.

- **Underlands** - Not considered a region by most, but more of an uninhabited wasteland. The lack of rain makes agriculture nearly impossible.
- **Vicus** - A vegetable known for its extremely tart flavor, popular among the older generation.
- **Zurun** - A thick flaky pastry with a thin layer of icing in the middle, twisted in the shape of a bow. Rhenna never thought a weird dream, a bucket list, and an addiction to romance novels would lead her into publishing, but that's exactly how Unexpected Eden came to life. Okay, there might have been a jillion revisions in there somewhere, and a few points where her family thought she'd lost her ever-lovin' mind, but pretty much everyone's accepted that this author thing is chronic.